Threads of Fate: Convergence
Book 1

Holly Lawton

Cover design by Sarah Hanson

First published in 2024 by Blossom Spring Publishing
Threads of Fate: Convergence Book One Copyright © 2024 Holly Lawton
ISBN 978-1-0686195-4-0
E: admin@blossomspringpublishing.com
W: www.blossomspringpublishing.com

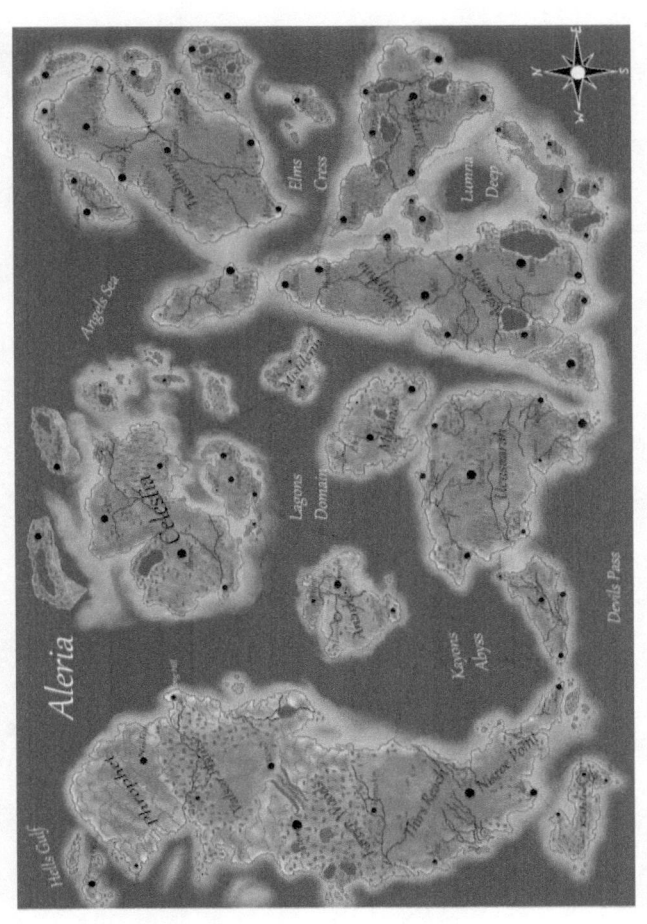

To my dad Chris and mum Steph.
Thank you for all your support in me throughout my life, for believing in me and my dream.
Your love and support have meant everything to me.
This book is for you.
Without you this book wouldn't exist.

Table of Contents

Prologue

"It is said long ago before we existed there was a race known as Elementals. They were divided into different magical clans, such as fire and ice...Chasen what are you doing?" Tagas chuckled softly at his little brother, gently setting the book to the side, watching as the boy was fascinated by the fireflies floating outside his window. Tagas rolled himself from the bed, dramatically scooping Chasen into his arms and blowing a raspberry on his rosy cheek. Squeals of laughter filled the walls of the room and the castle itself.

"S...stop!" Chasen gasped through his giggles, his face red from all the laughter, which made Tagas laugh even more and nuzzle his little cheek.

"Very well, little one, I shall stop my attack. Now come, the fireflies will be there at the end of my story." Tagas teased his brother who gave a sheepish look but snuggled right into his elder brother's side once they were back in his bed. With one hand Tagas opened the book back to its correct page while the other gently ran through Chasen's white locks, a sure-fire way to send the little ball of energy to sleep.

"Here." Chasen pointed to where his brother had left off in his story, making Tagas smile a little. So, he had been somewhat listening.

"Such as fire and ice. These people lived together in harmony using their magic to forge the world we see today. However, they could not keep their peace. Each Elemental clan started creating new species altogether, wanting to fill the land with beautiful life. It is said they started small with the fireflies and the birds, working until even the biggest animals were easy to create. But still they wanted more."

Chasen's eyes were glued to the book, admiring the beautiful pictures of swirling magic around different animals. It's what he loved most about this story and was why Tagas would always read it before bed, his parents being too busy for such things themselves.

"First the clan of earth created humans, dwarves, halflings, giants and even a type of elf. Then came the water clans. They created merfolk and the like, populating the oceans. Fire found a way to create great beasts of the sky – what we now call dragons. Each clan in its wake created a species of dragon in turn. The air clans created the mischievous fairies and rowdy imps but they also created pegasus and griffins to soar the skies. Plant elementals used their magic to create more woodland species such as treants and the mysterious wood elves. It is even said they graced some fairies with plant magic, creating a subspecies, as happened with elves." Tagas paused after turning the page to take a breath before continuing.

"The ice Elementals created snow fairies and the yeti; however, the yeti is stated to be mere myth as none have been seen. Finally, there were the light and darkness Elementals. Darkness created all manner of creatures, orc, goblins, trolls, and dark elves being just examples. While light created the sun and moon elves. But for these two, their accomplishments weren't enough. So, darkness with the help of fire created what humans call demons, while light created angels with the help of ice. Few of each were ever created for fear of their power coming on all too quickly. But once they were created these clans could not take back their mistakes, and so the demons and angels grew their numbers by mixing their blood with elves, birthing angel and demon-blooded children, forming the empires that still exist to this day. And... you are too young to hear the next part of the story." Tagas closed the book before the page could be turned to images of blood and war.

Normally there would have been protest from the little one, but there were only the small sounds of huffing air, making Tagas chuckle. "Your energy finally ran out, didn't it, little one." With a gentle kiss at Chasen's temple, Tagas moved him under the covers, tucking the youngest of their family into his bed.

"Sleep well, Chasen, may the angels watch over you." With this Tagas slipped from the room, closing the heavy carved doors behind him, a smile on his face as he nodded a greeting towards the guards stationed outside his brother's room. "He is asleep. Please inform me if anything happens or he wakes."

With the nods of conformation Tagas left his brother for the night. Come morning this would be his biggest regret.

Tagas walked through the intricately decorated hallways towards his own room. Sure, it may have been early in the evening, but he always found himself to be exhausted after a day running after his little brother. Not that he would change days like this, not for the world, not ever.

A yawn racked through his body as he brushed his hair from his face, opening the golden door to his room, giving a quick nod to his own guards before pushing the door closed behind him. It took the eldest prince mere moments to make his way to his bed, flopping down in a very unregal way, arms sprawled in front of him, legs still hanging off the bed. He still wore his clothes from the day, but that did not matter, for Tagas fell asleep the second his head graced the pillow. This was the same for all members of the Royal Family; the king, queen, Tagas, Sofiel, Anael and Chasen. Each and every one succumbed to sleep before the moon even reached its peak.

Rolling through the castle like an invisible fog, a strange magic was at work. The air thickened, creating confusion and illusions in the guard's mind. A shadowed man skulked through the castle unseen by the hundreds of knights stationed within its walls. No one could see this figure, let alone stop him on his quest. He reached his goal with practised ease. A pale hand reached out and clasped around the initial-adorned handle, twisting it slowly as if not to alert the occupant within. The pale hand retracted into the confines of his cloak after the door clicked open, the guards beside the doors not even noticing anything was amiss. It gave the man a sickening sense of satisfaction, knowing that these high-ranked guards were unaware that their charge was being stolen right under their noses.

After a moment of taking in this rush he slipped into the moonlit room, a snarled smirk crossing his features as his eyes landed on the prize he had come to take. He stalked across the room towards the double bed, blankets acting as a shield around the small child. Tufts of white hair were all he could see, for he knew this to be the child he wanted. The prodigy, with magical energy far greater than any in recorded history. Which meant one thing: the angel-blooded couldn't have him. This child would bolster this arrogant race's power, and they couldn't have that now, could they, even if it was at the cost of a child's life. Better this than letting him be the angel-blooded's weapon. They had done enough damage to this world. The shadowed man leaned down and manoeuvred the sleeping child into his arms. He had no need to worry about the boy waking, not with the magic taking hold of the castle. He was just dead weight in his arms and would be for hours yet. He could throw the little prince down the stairs and he would still stay asleep.

"I'm sorry, kid, but you are just too much of a danger to live." There was no regret in his voice, however. The man was glad to be doing this. He didn't care about this kid or what happened to him, that much was clear. With the child secure in his arms, he took long quick strides out the room and made his way back through the maze of halls, not once losing his way. The man knew exactly where he was going, as if he had lived inside the castle walls all his life.

He turned down the dank stairs that led towards the river, which allowed access into the castle for trade from the river nations. There bobbing was a small boat, nothing fancy and nothing that hadn't been in the castle thousands of times before. The only difference this time were two shadowy figures standing waiting. One eagerly accepted the child and stowed him away while the other started the boat.

"You know what to do with him. Go now before my magic loses its effect. Go!" he snapped. He watched the gates open and the boat, propelled by a current of wind magic, started to soar through the sky into the night.

It was done. By daybreak they would be too late to ever find the child.

~

Daybreak eventually came, and with it Tagas sluggishly pushed himself from the bed. Feeling confused and heavy, he raised his hand to his head with a groan. Blinking sleepily, frowning as he realised he was still in fact in his robes from the previous day. *Had he really been that tired?* Running a hand over his face Tagas moved to his closet, finding himself new robes to change into, shaking his head every time a yawn escaped his mouth.

He couldn't understand why he still felt so sluggish; it was an unrelenting tiredness that seemed to have a hold over him. After all he had slept from dusk to dawn. This feeling made no sense – he could go days without even a nap! But he couldn't dwell on it. He had duties to attend to after all. The first being rouse the little grouch known as Chasen. Tagas chuckled to himself as he left his quarters.

"Morning." He greeted his guards as he passed them, making his way through the halls, a smile on his face, thinking about how he should wake the little gremlin.

From the corner of his eye, something caught his attention. All thoughts ceased in a moment. He backtracked several steps, turning to face the family tree wall. Each name, painted in curved gold lettering, with a gem that shone iridescent and bright, but turned black when the person it had linked to had passed. Tagas stared at it, eyes focusing on the last name.

"Chasen… *CHASEN?*" Tagas took off down the halls, guards startled into action, following after their eldest prince. Several raced to alert their king and queen after noticing what Tagas must have. Chasen's gem had turned black.

Tagas couldn't get air into his lungs as he raced through the halls; every step felt so much longer than it should have. The few feet seemed like miles to the brother. He crashed through the door to Chasen's room, hoping that he would startle the boy awake, that he was there laughing and happy. But no, as he entered the room he felt his heart catch in his throat at the sight of the empty bed. He moved immediately to search every inch of the room.

"Chasen! Come out! This isn't funny, Chasen!" Tagas fell to his knees, hopelessness filling his eyes as his parents came crashing into the room, his father screaming at guards to search every inch of the castle, to find his son.

~

Nothing was the same after that day. The light and laughter that once filled the castle was replaced with a haunted silence. The nation mourned the loss of its youngest prince. Their light. Their hope. Their future.

Chapter 1

A Perfect Weapon, I Will Not Be

Clanging metal against cobbled stairs instantly filled the underground chamber as a broad-shouldered man descended into the chilly dungeon. It was hidden far from any others, guarded day and night by the best of the best, housing a single occupant.

This man wore polished black iron armour, its intricate design suggesting he was high ranking, helmet tucked under his arm, a displeased snarl gracing his tanned face. Saffron-coloured eyes narrowed as they fell on the room's inhabitant.

"Pretending to sleep will not save you from me," the captain, known as Caru, snarled. "Time to give in. The king needs his weapon functioning." He kicked the boy in front of him, colliding with his already bruised tissue and damaged ribs. The force of the kick was enough to shatter a normal man's rib cage, but all that emitted from the boy was a groan that echoed through the room. Caru let out a displeased growl as he threw scalding water over the bloodied and beaten weapon chained before him.

Coughs and splutters echoed within the empty room as the teen choked on the steaming water, teeth grinding together as his skin bubbled and blistered. Tired blue-and-gold-speckled eyes opened, strings of muddy brown hair falling in front of his face. Slowly his eyes moved from the ground up to look at the man above him. He made no other movement, he couldn't; his arms and legs were securely chained to the wall. The wall that he slept, ate, pissed, lived against - when he wasn't being trained, that was.

Caru gazed down at the teen in front of him with such malice in his eyes.

"After all these years you're still not trained enough, it seems. One is supposed to kneel to his masters, obey their orders. Looks to me like our little weapon is still in need of breaking in." A hiss left his lips. The snarled smirk came back when the teen dared to glare at him.

The weapon's eyes had hardened. He was not a thing to train. He was a person and he loathed being referred to solely as 'boy' or 'weapon'. He refused to be what they wanted when they subjected him to such horrors. He had been tortured, beaten, sliced open for various experiments. They had trained him day and night, for hundreds of years, with all manner of weapons and magic until he'd collapsed from exhaustion. Only to be kicked to his feet again, until he became proficient at them.

No. He wasn't going to be anything they wanted him to be. Not when he knew love was out there. He may not remember it, but he knew he'd had it before. He knew that he could have it again, if only he could leave this place and find where he came from. It wasn't his fate to be here.

As the boy continued to glare, Caru kept that sickening sadistic smirk on his face, reflecting elation at the weapon's remaining fight. It was going to make breaking him even sweeter. Slowly he crouched down until he was level with the weapon's eyes, his own eyes glinting with insanity. He took pleasure in his next words.

"Tonight, Prince Fayon will be assassinated, and our long-awaited war will begin. Which means the king expects his weapon to be functioning, listening to his orders and ready to annihilate all our enemies." Caru's words were deep, laced with darkness, not at all suited to the smile he matched with them. The boy pressed himself to the wall, unease filling the pit of his stomach.

"You're going to learn to fear me, Boy. Nothing those other bastards did will even compare to what I am about to subject you to. I will break you. You will be what my king wants. Trust me, little one, stop being so stubborn or you will lose the ability to even think for yourself. If it was up to me, we would have taken it from you the second you arrived here." Caru's face was so close to the teen's, breath warm against his cold skin, making him grimace at the rancid odour that accompanied it. But at his words, the teen felt as if he were ice himself. *Taking away his free will? What did that mean?*

Caru of course didn't believe for a second this weapon was ready to fight a war for them, but his king was impatient. They had waited eleven thousand years to take back what the angel-blooded had stolen from them. None were willing to wait any longer. The king was ready to kill his own son for this. He was going to make sure this weapon before him would perform as expected, even if it meant beating it into the pathetic child's head. Oh, how he had waited for his chance to be the one to break the child. If that didn't work then he could finally have the brat take the Draught of Zaro. With no free will, it would be perfect - a destroyer against its own kind.

The thought made him smile sickeningly, imagining the stinking carcasses left to rot in the open as his own family had. The brat's race had been the cause of his family's deaths. It was poetic to him that the boy would bring about the destruction of those people. He sneered at the mere thought of them, anger bubbling up again, eyes flashing with hate as he took in the teen. This boy would

3

feel the hatred he held now, he would suffer for what that race had done to their glorious demon-blooded nation.

"Not so brave now, are you, Boy. Don't worry, you won't feel a thing when it's stripped from you. My breaking you, however... oh you will feel that. Your kind doesn't deserve mercy."

The dirty, bloodied and bruised teen let out a low growl and spat on the captain's shoes upon hearing what was going to happen. Scared was something he had long since grown out of; this man would not break him. A pleased look crossed the boy's face when his new torturer looked enraged. It was the best insult he could give, after all; the teen never spoke.

That was the one thing they had neglected in teaching the boy. The teen knew only the words they had abused him with, nothing more. But this boy didn't need words to defy these men. No, he had a spirit they would never break. There was no fear on his tired features, his eyes burning with life and defiance.

He may not have known what his name was or how he came to be here. He did not know what life he had been taken from before this cold stone dungeon. They had taken all of that from him. What they could not take from him was who he was. He would not lose sight of his wishes or his morals. He was not theirs.

Caru rolled his shoulders and cracked his neck. Eyes filled with rage and bloodlust as he ran his tongue over his teeth.

"You will regret that, boy; the King has ever so graciously given me a day to break this pathetic defiance of yours. Though I won't need more than an hour before I have you begging for mercy!" He gave a horrifying cackle and his face lit up with sick pleasure. He really took great pride in this part of his job. He lifted his hand slowly up towards the teen, and it ignited in a burst of orange flames. The sickening smile grew as Caru brought the flames down to touch the boy's bare chest.

The teen's teeth gritted together but he made no sound as the naked flames touched bare skin. He would not make a sound, he refused to break. After all, he had been burned before by his own fire – the boy wasn't about to let the weak heat of his torturer's flames elicit a cry from him. Not when no one else had ever been able to make him cry. He'd locked that emotion away long ago.

The continued silence, however, just made Caru turn the heat on his flames up, increasing their intensity as his palm pressed firmly to the skin below. The captain continued until the flames were burning blue, his own fingers blackening from the intensity.

Caru had always taken pleasure in drawing screams from those he worked on. He always broke his victims, always. The longest had lasted a mere seven hours in his hands before he cracked, giving away the information they had wanted. This teen was foolish if he thought he could beat him, The Sadist of the Demon-Blooded. He had escaped his hands thus far, but finally, after six hundred years, it was his turn. If the boy had just given in, bended to his subordinates' tortures, he would not have to suffer as he was now.

The boy's dim-wittedness was Caru's gain. The teen made life harder on himself, the pain he experienced was of his own doing. He could have been treated better than even the king himself if he had only submitted. But alas he did not, which meant he was in charge of this boy now. In six hundred years the boy had been stubborn to a fault, remaining true to a self he couldn't remember. It

5

made Caru sick, although he knew well it would be both an asset and a curse to their control of him as their weapon. The determination would be a force to be reckoned with, yet a hindrance when the stupid boy was determined to fight against their control.

Caru knew this, which was why today he would break the teen in front of him. Make him obey in fear of this day repeating itself. Break him so bad their weapon would flinch at the mere thought of disobeying their order. Yes, he would break this teen with pleasure, and if he truly failed, he would simply destroy the teen's will. Making him a shell, a weapon through and through. The insane look filled his eyes again as he lifted his hand, admiring the bubbled, blistering skin beneath.

"Want to behave yet? No? Good." He cackled, his hand going straight for the boy's pale neck.

~

For thirteen long hours Caru took sick pleasure in inflicting pain on the young man. His fire had just been the beginning, of course. He had oh so much more he wanted to do. Caru used all manner of weaponry to inflict harm; mind-warping spells to torment the teen with his worst and most deep-seated fears, twisting them to form into reality around him, dark shapes, voices trapping the boy in his own mind.

Seemingly never-ending faces tormented him, some he could not even recognise. Some that drew a sense of longing. He saw flashes of white and gold, beautiful eyes - then they would be gone. The teen was left with pain in his heart, desperately calling out nonsense just to see those flashes again.

Of course, Caru drew immense pleasure on learning that this kind of magic drew some reaction – every time a single tear rolled down the teen's cheek. Along with the desperate garbled calls, it was music to his ears. Caru laughed away, taunting him. Thirteen hours was the longest anyone had lasted against him, and finally he was beginning to break.

The boy hung his head low at this, eyes squeezed shut trying to make the voices and images go away, but they were forever embedded into his mind. Voices of people he didn't know, words he didn't recognise... but at the same time he did. This magic left him disorientated. It was like he was being sucked into a hole, only to be spat back out at the worst moment, repeating on a loop, making his heart race painfully within his chest until he let that single tear fall.

Caru smirked gleefully at the bowed head, continuing for two more excruciating hours to crush what was left of the boy's defiance. Using whatever torture he could think of to continue to try to work open the wound he had created. To get the delicious screams he craved to hear, screams that would make him feel like finally he was getting some justice for his father, his mother, for his brothers. Excitement was coursing through Caru at that single tear – he was sure he could break the teen into nothing but a husk, willing to do anything to save himself from his own pain. He would be broken.

But as night fell and the time for the assassination drew nearer, he had still not been able to make the weapon utter another peep, not a tear, not a scream. Nothing. It had Caru grinding his teeth in frustration. He had just sat there taking whatever was thrown at him, blood running from his wounds, pooling under him, and yet he'd just sat there with tired eyes, staring at nothing.

Was that one measly tear all he had been able to get?

He had cut, slashed, burned, whipped and tormented the boy for more than fifteen hours, yet nothing! Caru let rip a scream of rage, punching a crater into the wall beside the stupid boy's face, growling when the kid didn't even flinch at that. He was The Sadist of his people, the man people fled from. No one had ever lasted in his torture, yet this brat had.

Caru's reputation was on the line now, and oh was he going to make this kid's life hell for that.

"Once I ensure my prince's death, I will be back. You will wish you screamed for me! Now you will be nothing but a soul locked in your own head. You will watch as you burn and slaughter thousands. Become the most hated monster ever to exist, and no one will know you are simply stuck, unable to control yourself. Let's see if that will break you!" he seethed, red faced, spit splattering across the boy's features.

Caru spun on his heel, fists clenched so tightly that if it wasn't for the leather of his gloves he would have cut through the skin of his palm. He stormed angrily up the stairs, armour clanking loudly as he did so, slamming the heavy metal door behind him with such force the ground rocked.

It was only when the teen could no longer hear the heavy footsteps of his tormentor did he sag in his chains, fingers flexing and unflexing. His eyes held anger in them, lips moving but no words leaving his mouth. He couldn't let anyone be killed; he had decided he hated the idea of death long ago. The concept of killing had been drilled into him all his life. He was supposed to kill for them after all. They wanted him to be their master weapon. A killer.

But he refused. He'd been refusing as long as he could

remember. He did not want to kill. Life was precious; even locked away he knew that he had to save his own life. He had to save this prince, no matter what kind of person he was. Being killed for the sinful desires of his father was not right. He had to save them both or their lives would end together before the sun rose. It seemed like fate had struck. Live or die, it was both their last chance.

With gritted teeth the teen clenched his fists and pulled himself up against his chains. Panting heavily, he pressed his forehead against the cuffs securing his wrists together.

"Powerful… weapon," he coughed, his voice barely audible from the lack of use over such an extreme amount of time. He chanted this to himself as he closed his eyes, focusing on the magic within him. He wasn't going to be their pawn – he refused. He focused on his chains. They were there to stop his flow of magic. He had learnt that long ago. If he was not training, they never removed them, so he could not escape. But they wouldn't stop him this time.

He didn't have time for this *not* to work. A life more than his was at stake, and he would rescue whoever this prince was. Today. Today he had to get past the suppressing magic within the chains.

The dirty, skinny, battered teen chanted over and over what they had told him all these years. He was a powerful weapon. He chanted endlessly as he tried to bring forth his magic, eyes and fists staying clenched shut, knuckles turning white at how tightly he squeezed his fists. He willed his magic to build up, to move anywhere that wasn't the inside of his body, to burst forth and destroy the chains. He opened his eyes after a moment to find nothing, his teeth gritted and he smacked his head back against the cold stone behind him.

What was the point of supposedly being this all-powerful weapon if he couldn't even get past these stupid chains that had held him captive for most of his life? He was useless. How could he hope to save anyone when he couldn't even save himself? He sagged in despair, looking at the cold floor below him, stained red long ago by his own blood. This was going to be his tomb, he knew it – he would die here just like that prince was going to.

The teen looked totally broken, all hope leaving him. He had been so determined to free himself, to save himself and the prince, to change his life... all that right now felt lost. He stayed sagged in those chains for no more than ten minutes, but to him it felt like an eternity. That was until a glint of blue caught his eye among the silvered burgundy of his blood. He lowered his head, eyes widening. What he had seen was a frozen teardrop lying perfectly on the icy stone. The single tear he had shed.

"Powerful..." he whispered, licking his cracked lips. His magic had worked to freeze the tear. He didn't understand – if he could freeze them then, why not now? What was different now? The teen sat staring at it trying to figure out what he was doing that could have affected his magic.

Suddenly his eyes widened a fraction – *was it emotions holding him back?* Had letting his single tear flow free been the key? If he no longer held in the emotions he had long been afraid to show, could he finally reach his freedom? Would he at last be able to see the light of day and experience the sun on his skin? Was it really as simple as letting himself *feel?*

He had spent so long holding everything in, everything back, that if this did not work he felt like he would be betraying all he had fought against. But this was the only chance he had left to escape. His last chance.

With gritted teeth he lowered his head, closed his eyes, inhaled a deep breath and screamed. He let everything they had ever done to him, the mental and physical pain, take over his whole being. Embracing the years of torture, all the pain, hate and sadness he had in his body, he screamed. Tears cascaded down his pale face, leaving tracks through the grime. Sorrow overflowed from his being, tears slowly becoming more and more solid until they formed perfect frozen teardrops yet again.

The room around him started to drop in temperature, the cobbled surface frosting over. His hiccupped breaths slowly became more obvious as their warmth met with the chilled air of the room, causing his breath to fog. Water droplets froze on his skin, clinging especially to his hair, eyelashes and eyebrows where sweat had caught. Intricate spirals of ice climbed across the metal chains that had held him in place his whole life, the cold biting at his torn and abused skin, causing his teeth to grit further and face contort into a pained frown.

The teen was so still as the frost continued to spread, until suddenly he pulled his arms apart fast, muscles that had been built from brutal training sessions bulging as the chains gave way, shattering as if they were made of nothing other than glass. He followed by doing the same to the chains around his ankles moving them apart violently until the metal gave way and shattered, allowing him to slump forward on the floor and crawl across the room, teeth chattering from his own magic.

The teen gave himself a moment, lying there on the cobbled floor, heaving in air, staring at the wall he used to be chained to in disbelief. He had really done it, he was free. He even let out a little laugh to himself.

Slowly he began pushing himself to his knees, using the wall as support. The young man got shakily to his feet, gaining strength the longer he stayed on them, determination filling his eyes as he looked up the stairs. He was going to go beyond this room, beyond what he knew, and he would save himself, save the prince these people planned to murder. Their new lives would begin today.

Their fates would be intertwined from this moment on.

Chapter 2

Operation Rescue

In another part of the castle, down in its depths, were the slave quarters. Here the king housed those he took as payment when taxes could not be paid, where the young and old alike were made to work within the castle. These slaves were the lucky ones, for most ended up in the lava mines, a place even immortals could meet a swift death.

Here a small girl awoke, orange eyes snapping open, almost glowing in the darkness. She bolted upright, ashen hair falling in front of her face, laboured breaths coming out in gasps as she tried to calm her racing heart. Little fingers curled up, fisting tiny pieces of loose straw from the bedding she sat upon. One hand soon moved to hold tightly to the front of her night dress. She bit her lip as she moved to ease herself from her straw mat towards the other a few steps across the tiny room. Reaching out, the small child shook the lumped form inhabiting the other mat.

"Myst, wake up… wake up, I saw the boy again, wake up!"

The lump grumbled and swatted at the hand at first before dramatically lifting her body with a groan, sleepily rubbing her eyes. This second girl, Myst, was the same age as the first, with matching orange eyes that were now grumpily looking towards her twin.

"Tis just a dream, go back to sleep, Nilee." Her words slurred almost like a drunkard as she lazily tilted her head against the wall, eyes drooping. It was late for these small ones. They were barely given the sleep needed for an adult demon-blooded, let alone a growing one.

"But My! I saw the door, the creepy door." Nilee emphasised with big arms as if saying that would clear everything up, which of course just ended up with her getting a dull confused look. Nilee grumbled, "The big big metal door! The one we found the other day, the one that was all scratched and dented in that deserted hallway. You know, when we had to hide before the mean man saw us exploring." Nilee was promptly shut up by a hand being slapped over her mouth by her now wide-awake sister.

Myst's eyes darted to the cracked door with fear. "Shhhhhhh! Do you want Rexa to hear you? She'll hand us over if she knows we went somewhere we ain't supposed to." Myst slowly removed her hand from her twin's mouth. She stayed leaning ready like a panther, ready to smack her hand back if Nilee decided to try to yell again. She was not affected at all by the big puffed-out cheeks and pout coming from her twin. No, Myst was looking at her with a bored gaze, just waiting for her hyper twin to get to the point. "Okay, so he's behind that door... so what? We can't do anyth... *no, Nilee,* we are *not* taking the key from the mean man!" Myst hissed seeing the look on her twin's face.

"Myst, we has to, we has to! A bad man hurt him really bad again. But I saw the boy! He got out, My! He ripped through his chains like *bam, pow!*" She punched the air to emphasise her point. She shook her own foot with its own metal shackle around it for emphasis. "We got to get the door open for him. He won't do it without us. My dreams showed me. Please, Myst, we have to do this." Nilee clutched at her twin's hand, holding it in both her own, orange eyes ablaze. She was going to do this with or without her twin's help.

Myst threw herself back with a groan before she rolled off her own bed, throwing her sister's clothes at her. They weren't walking around in nightdresses; they would freeze. At least with their ragged outer robes they would be a little warmer.

"And don't forget your cloak," Myst mumbled as Nilee smiled brightly and squashed the darker of the two in a massive hug, nuzzling their cheeks together before stumbling around to dress in the dark. She pulled her cloak snug around her, wobbling in excitement as she waited for her sister. She had to cover her mouth to stop herself from telling Myst to hurry.

Once the more hardened of the two little girls was ready, she grabbed her twin's hand, pulling her along gently but also keeping her behind at all times. She had taken on the role of mother for her twin, and nothing would ever hurt her, she would ensure that.

A little cloaked head poked out the doorway, the door only slightly open, enough for them to squeeze through.

Once Myst determined that the hallway was empty and that she couldn't hear any footsteps, she moved quickly down to the right, hand tight around Nilee's as they raced down to the dead end, avoiding the sleeping slaves that littered the floor all around them.

Myst ran her hand along the wall as soon as they reached the dead end, looking for the loose brick she knew was there, pushing it once she found it. A low scraping sound echoed down the silent halls as a hidden door was pushed open by the small child. The twins slipped inside as soon as the gap was large enough. Nilee hurriedly pressed the brick on the inside, making sure the hidden door shut firmly behind them.

Myst raised her hand, lighting it up with an orange flame, engulfing the pitch-black hall they now stood in a dull orange light. Dust particles were almost still, the air was so old and stagnant. No one used these passages anymore – in fact, Myst wasn't even sure anyone knew they existed. Well, anyone apart from them. They had found them on one of their many illegal explorations.

"This way, come on," she said, as she pulled her cloak tight around herself with her spare hand. She moved forward, lighting their way through the creepy passageways. Nilee stuck close to her twin, not wanting to lose her or the only source of light. They followed the markings they themselves had scratched into the walls, arrows and words pointing in all different directions, so they could remember what passageway led to which areas, and which they had yet to explore.

The pair walked in silence as they navigated through the maze of tunnels. The only sounds came from their echoed footsteps against the cobbles, and the occasional sniffs from Nilee as the dust-filled air tickled her nose. At one point she sneezed loudly, earning a glare from Myst, a finger to her lips and a, *"Shhhhhh!"*

Nilee responded by sticking her tongue out at her and muttering under her breath. "You shhhhh." A pout graced her face at being told off for *sneezing*, of all things. The little girl had been so busy muttering that she crashed right into her sister, sending them both tumbling to the ground. Myst fell face first into the wall housing their hidden exit. "Owey," Nilee whined, rubbing the red spot forming on her brow.

Myst, who now had the imprint of the wall grazed onto her face, remained silent, just moving to help her sister stand. The girl looked her younger twin over thoroughly for any scrapes or bruises – other than the red mark already on her face – and let out a relieved sigh when she found Nilee to be alright. She ignored the burning sensation of her own face.

"Watch where you're going, Nilee, you could have been hurt. Not to mention we could have been heard. We have to be quiet if you want to help that boy you dream of," Myst lectured with a worried look. Myst was quite clearly the role of protector for Nilee. A role she took on willingly when they were alone with no one else. No small child should ever have to take on the responsibility of a carer or have this look grace their face. Yet here Myst stood with no other choice.

Once Myst was sure Nilee got the message through that thick skull of hers, she slowly pushed open the exit, just a fraction, enough for her to peek through and see the hallway. There were four torches that lit the area. They barely created enough light to see one end from the other. It was dark, hazed in orange and grey, and as always deathly silent.

She took a deep breath, pushing it open more, cringing at the sound of stone scraping stone. This time she emerged halfway, enabling her to make out the door at the end of the hallway to the left, and to the right the bolted wooden doors sealing off stairs that led to the rest of the castle. Standing with his back pressed against the thick imposing wooden doors was the guard they needed.

Squinting, she could just about make out the keys against his hip. Myst gave a gulp, taking a deep breath as she shimmed her body out into the hall, pressing fingers to her lips and motioning to Nilee that the bad man was there. Then she held her hand up flat, signalling her to wait there as Myst started to slink through the shadows.

She took slow steps, making as little sound as possible, breath held at every little sound, waiting tense seconds to see if the bad man would turn and catch her. But he never did. Myst just kept creeping closer and closer until she was nearly right behind him.

Slowly the little girl extended her hand to try and snatch the keys off his belt. Her fingers had barely grazed them when he spun around and grabbed her wrist in a death grip. Growling down at her, hauling her into the air, grinning spitefully as he watched the child squirm and cry out in pain.

"What do we have ere, a little rat thinkin she can steal from me? You're gonna regret this, kid." His voice was hoarse and gravelly, sending shivers through an already terrified Myst, whose eyes were wide with terror as she stared at his scarred face.

She didn't know what to do – her breathing was rapid, her body squirming, legs kicking out at him. She tried desperately to make a fireball, aiming to hit him in the face. But he just grabbed her other hand, squeezing and squeezing her wrists together until she felt like they were going to be crushed into dust.

Nilee immediately started to panic. She spun around, looking for anything to help, a loose brick catching her eye. The smaller child gripped at it, pulled at it, not caring that it sliced into her fingers as it came free, and then she was running. Running fast, letting out a little scream as she threw the brick with all her might only for it to graze the man's foot. It clanked uselessly against the metal armour onto the cobbled floor.

Nilee backed away, instantly terrified when the evil man's gaze turned to her. He threw Myst against the wall and stalked forward, a demonic look on his face.

"Stupid brat, this was new!" he snarled, hand wildly gesturing to the small silver scratch in the black armour of his boot. Nilee was backing away as fast as she could but he kept closing the gap.

Myst was trying to get up again, ignoring the pain in her wrists, ignoring the trickle of blood from her head, horror in her eyes as he got closer to Nilee. Myst gritted her teeth, scrambled to her feet and was running, fire raging around her, orange flames lighting the halls, exploding as she watched a fist going down towards Nilee. Her flames weren't going to be there in time. Her sister was backed against a wall, hands thrown up in front of her. Then there was a flash of purple light.

Myst was blinded for a brief moment, her flames vanishing as she shielded her eyes. Eventually she blinked away the patterns of black and purple that clouded her vision. She saw Nilee, hands raised protectively in front of her, and the bad man on the ground, a smoking hole through his chest.

The twins stood there in shock. Myst stared in surprise at her younger twin, while Nilee looked in horror from her hand to the body in front of her. It wasn't more than a few seconds before the ashen-haired girl was on her hands and knees throwing up.

"He's dead... I killed him... I killed him." Her breathing was coming out quick as panicked tears rolled down her face. Myst was moving the second she heard her sister speak, pulling her tightly into her arms.

"You saved us, you saved us." Myst so badly wanted to ask how she had done that, what kind of power that had been. But that wasn't a question for right now, not when her sister was so distraught. She felt Nilee cling to her, while she herself stared at the man, just lying there, eyes open but unseeing. She had seen dead bodies before but she had never expected Nilee to be the cause of another's death. It made her feel sick, the dull eyes staring at her but not seeing. Dull eyes that would torment her sister for the rest of her life.

But she also could not find it in her to care that this man was dead. He had hurt her, tried to hurt Nilee, and she had known he was a cruel man. She knew his death was no great loss to this world. But his death also meant one thing: they definitely needed to escape now. They couldn't stay in this castle; that would be signing their execution order.

Myst carefully worked her sister's hands from her robes and moved forward, reaching over the man's corpse, snatching the keys right off his belt, moving like lightning just in case he decided to come back to life and grab her. There was a sigh of relief when he did no such a thing. It was time to see if there really was a boy in that room. For their sake she hoped so, or she had no idea how to escape this place alone. Their fate rested on this boy being real.

"Okay, time to free that boy... Nilee, come on, we need to go. Get up!" Myst grabbed her sister by the arm, dragging her to stand and not letting go until they reached the door. She didn't trust right now that Nilee would have walked on her own, not with the shock still on her face.

Myst gulped as she fumbled for the key, trying to find which one fit the lock, growing more desperate with each one that refused to turn. The heat coming off the door did not help. She couldn't tell whether the door was fighting her, like it knew she wasn't supposed to be there. Or whether it was her imagination. Whether it was enchantment or her mind's own doing, the heat was only making her heart race more.

Two keys left and she could hear her heartbeat in her ears. Myst was panicking now. They wouldn't be able to escape without help – she shouldn't have agreed to Nilee's wanting to free the boy. They were going to be caught and killed; she was going to break her promise to their mother. She couldn't keep Nilee safe. The spiralling thoughts that filled Myst's head seized when suddenly she felt the lock clunk as the key turned effortlessly, her eyes wide. They had done it! Then she screamed and dived backwards as the door came flying open, and a dirt, blood and grime-covered teen tumbled forward onto the floor.

Both girls hid behind the door, clinging to one another as they peered out at the teen boy before them.

"Is he alive?" Nilee whispered.

Chapter 3

Fate's Plans

Using the wall, the young teen pulled himself to a standing position, sweat rolling down his forehead, lanky brown hair falling in front of his face as he breathed heavily. After all, his body had taken a beating today. He wasn't well – he hadn't been well in a few hundred years but that was not going to stop him on his mission. He was going to save himself, yes, but he was also going to save this prince and hopefully stop a war in the process. He didn't want to play a part in anyone's death.

Slowly he started making his way forwards, ascending the staircase. It was funny; having heard people travel up and down these stairs all these years he had imagined them to be far longer than they were. But in reality, there was barely anything between where he had been captive and the steel door that faced him now.

The boy gingerly reached a hand out to test the door. It was a fool's wish to think it would be as easy as pulling the door open, but he still tried. He still had a child's hope after all. Soon his head came to rest against it, chewing on his lip. He hadn't thought this far ahead. He could barely hear through the metal so he knew it must be incredibly thick; it would take too long to shatter as he'd done to his chains. The only bright side to this was he couldn't hear anyone on the other side.

"Come… think," he whispered to himself. "Taught you things… how… destroy… you… need… destroy… think!" He frustratedly slammed his fist against the door, repeatedly, until he sank to his knees. Tears streamed down his face. Why was everything so hard? At every turn there was something else stopping him – *was fate just messing with him?* He escaped his chains only to make it up a staircase. *Why did fate toy with him so cruelly?* He had hope only for it to be snuffed out yet again.

"Come on... Think... useless weapon. Useless... so useless..." He let out a sob. His head pressed to the cold steel door, his tears having by now cleaned streaks of dirt from his face, showing the pale skin beneath the brown dirt. Once he let his emotions out, he just couldn't seem to hold them back anymore, the tears kept flowing.

The boy leaned against the door, sobbing for what felt like hours but in reality was little more than five minutes. He wallowed about how close he was to seeing something outside this dungeon, to being able to stop a death, to get out and live a life he wanted to, and not be what they were trying to make him. To find love, and find his place in this world.

The door stood in his way to all of those things. His gaze shifted down when one of his tears landed on the burnt skin of his arm. His head tilted to the side, feeling the sting of water on it. The teen just stared at the burn before his eyebrows furrowed. Slowly he moved his hand in front of his face, flexing his fingers, looking back at the blistering skin of his arm, then to the almost completely faded scars on his fingertips. Scars caused by himself, by his own use of fire magic.

The boy had been trained in all manners of weaponry as well as magic. His blood had been mutated and manipulated to enable him to use not just the magic of his own race but of many races, and this included fire magic. A magic known for destruction and devastation, a magic

23

that in the boy's case had burnt its user, resulting in the many scars. But also a magic that may just be his salvation.

Flexing his fingers again, he brought his hand over the lock of the door, his face filled with uncertainty. Would this even work? But it was the only plan he had. Steadying his breath and flattening his palm, he channelled energy in the form of heat into his palm, gritting his teeth harder the higher he made the temperature soar, until the steel under his palm was starting to glow, red, yellow, even white, keeping the heat inside his body rather than sparking it into flame.

He bit down on his lip hard when the pain started to be joined with the horrid stench of burnt flesh. But he did not stop. He clenched his teeth and scrunched his nose, breathing through his mouth to avoid vomiting at the smell. He felt relief when he saw molten metal starting to slide down the door onto the floor, his hand sliding further and further through the locking mechanism. It was looking like he was going to free himself.

Then suddenly he fell forward as the door swung open. He had been so thoroughly concentrated on his task that he had not been listening to what was occurring on the other side of the door.

So just as he had made it halfway through melting the lock, he suddenly found himself toppling forward, his face smashing into the dark stone ground. A crack resounded through the hall – the breaking of his nose as he failed to catch himself.

"Is he alive?" he heard a small voice from behind the door.

The teen slowly pushed himself up, blood rolling from his nose, when he heard the voice. Almost immediately he sprung up, staggering backwards away from the door, pressing himself against the small outcropping of the wall. This was a new voice he had never heard before. He had no idea who they were or what they intended to do to him. He took a defensive position instantly.

He used the wall to guard his back so that no one could attack him from behind. He refused to be taken back down there, to be shackled again. His thoughts raced a mile a minute until finally he looked to see who the speaker was. Frowning when no one was standing in front of him, it was not until his gaze lowered that he saw two small poorly-dressed little girls, one whose hand was resting on the handle of the door that had just swung open. The other held a little rag towards the older boy. It was all the two slaves had to call a handkerchief.

"For your nose," Nilee said quietly, eyes wide as she gazed at him. The boy in her dreams was real.

The boy dared not move as he analysed the pair. They were young – no more than six in the terms of human ageing. One had dark black hair and orange eyes, while the other had grey ashy hair with black speckles through it, but with the same orange eyes. Next, he took in their clothes. Their robes were old and incredibly faded, patchworked where tears had happened, and obviously too short for them.

What was even clearer were the little metal cuffs on each of their ankles. These two were clearly of demon blood, yet they were just as much slaves as he was. He did not understand these people. How could they be so horrid to their own kind?

What kind of king was the man that reigned here? And what type of man was the prince? He could be just as cruel for all he knew, but he had to save this prince to prevent the war Caru had been so excited about. All he could do was hope this prince might be a kind soul, however a distant hope that seemed to be right now.

The teen stared at the two girls a moment. Neither had moved except to hold the rag out to him. The boy slowly inhaled, relaxing his tense muscles as he lowered his guard. They did not seem to be like any of the others he had met before. For now he decided to trust these two small girls.

Tentatively he reached out and took the handkerchief from the ashen-haired girl, pressing it to his nose. All three just stood watching one another, wondering what the other's next move would be.

"Who are you?" A shy voice came from the ashen-haired girl, who by now had retreated the moment he took the rag from her hand. Only her orange eyes could be seen peeking out from behind the iron door.

The boy looked honestly confused on how to answer that question. He had no idea who he was. All he knew was what they called him. That was the only answer he could give.

"I... am... Weapon," he said slowly, being careful to think of the words he needed, his voice barely a whisper from lack of use, speaking almost like a child just beginning to form sentences. A frown never left his face, especially when the black-haired girl frowned as she shook her head, telling him clearly that was not the correct answer to the question.

"Weapon ain't a name; names are what your mama gave you." She sounded all exasperated as the boy just looked even more confused, as if he had no idea what a mother was in the first place. Myst just shook her head dramatically before pointing her thumb towards herself.

"I am Myst and this is Nilee. Those are names, see what I mean? Weapons are things, not names." She jammed her thumb towards her sister when introducing her, hands going to her hips, looking expectantly towards the boy now, orange eyes showing she was expecting something from him. In the form of a *real* name.

He opened and closed his mouth a few times. It was clear by his face he didn't know how to respond. All his life he had only been called Weapon, from what he could remember at least. But apparently that did not class as a name.

"I... I... do not think... I have... name... Always Weapon... or useless." His words all chewed up and mangled, taking a long time to get what he wanted to say out. Definitely not talking like any other teen Myst had ever met.

Myst looked towards her sister and pulled a face, as if to ask what was up with this guy. She was starting to think that maybe they shouldn't have let him out. She had never met anyone who looked so beat up or sounded so odd. He had a weird accent and spoke as if he didn't know how to form sentences. Maybe that's why this guy said he was often called useless; he didn't seem like much of a weapon, or like he would be much help at all really.

But he was their only hope of getting out of this castle. There had to be a reason her sister had dreamed about him. He was actually real, so he had to be able to help them, because if he didn't, she was certain they were all going to be dead before sunrise.

Looking up at a boy who had called himself a weapon, she was officially thinking her sister's senses were on the fritz. Why dream of this boy? He seemed completely

27

helpless; how could he help them get away? Usually, her sister's senses helped them, not put them in danger.

Myst scrutinised every inch of him. She really didn't see why Nilee had been so determined to help this weirdo. But they had now, so no turning back. It was clear as day though that she did not like him one bit.

"Uhhh how can you not have a name? Everyone has a name, even slaves have names, so you gotta have one," Myst said aggressively.

The boy just looked down. The weapon was what he was called, what everyone called him. If that didn't count, then what was his name? *Did he have one before he came to this place?* Maybe he couldn't remember a time before that cell, but he was sure he had one. Someone out there had to miss him, he had to have whatever a mama was out there who had loved him enough to name him once. He just... he just couldn't remember what that was. Myst just gave a dramatic huff at his pathetic-looking face and crossed her arms.

"Fine then, Mr no name, listen here! We helped you get out so now you're gonna help me and Nilee get outta here too, you got it?" She pointed her finger accusingly at the boy as if he were about to bolt and leave them or something.

However, unexpectedly the boy just gave a slight nod of his head. He wanted to get away himself; he had no reason to not help the two little girls. They seemed to be no danger to him, although there was a guard on the floor seemingly smoking, so he felt it would be unwise to make them angry. His stomach churned a little, hoping that the man was not dead, but he didn't check, he couldn't bring himself to. Instead, he knelt down to the floor and slowly reached for the cuff on Myst's ankle, causing her to jump back.

"Hey! What do you think you're doing?"

"Get off." The boy stared at her, pointing to the metal. Myst watched him with suspicious eyes as she slowly shuffled forward, letting out a hiss when the cuff became cold upon his touch. It shattered seconds later, causing her eyes to widen.

"How... you ain't one of us... what kinda magic was that?" she asked with a look of amazement on her face. She watched intently as he moved to Nilee and again shattered the cuff as if it was nothing. Both girls were so amazed because this kind of magic was like nothing they had ever seen. They didn't snap out of it until the boy spoke as he stood straight again.

"Will help, but must... save prince... needs... saving... ple-please?" He struggled to find the words he needed. Speaking was completely foreign to him – he was having to think back throughout all his years of captivity, trying to piece together the words he needed. Trying to remember meanings, how sentences were supposed to go. He really was trying hard and doing incredible considering it was a complete gap in his knowledge. "Leave... with him... not... without. No kill."

Myst was just staring at this boy as if he had grown two heads, her face going slightly red.

"*Save him?* Why does he need saving! He's the son of the king – I bet he's just as cold hearted! Why should we..." She trailed off when Nilee grabbed her sleeve and gave it a gentle tug and nodded her head. Myst stared at her twin blankly. She wanted to go into the heart of this castle, with guards everywhere, further away from freedom than they had ever been, all because of this boy from her dreams.

She knew Prince Fayon was supposedly a good man. He helped where he could, and the people all loved him for it. But that didn't mean she should risk her neck for him. Myst just looked at the pair, before clenching her fists and stamping her foot, letting out a growl of frustration because she was outnumbered.

"Fine! But if we die… I… I… ughhhh, come on!" She pivoted on her foot and stormed back off towards the secret tunnel entrance, with Nilee skipping happily behind her. The boy hurried after them when he realised they had agreed, doubling back when he passed the guard and picking up the silver sword from his side.

For a moment he stopped, head bowed for the dead man before he moved again. Giving the sword several swings to test its weight as he followed after the two small girls, he seemed satisfied with it. As he moved, he left a small, splattered trail of silvery burgundy blood. He was still very much wounded from Caru's torture, but that did not slow him anymore. He was determined this was his chance of freedom, everything seemed to point towards it. Fate had decided today was the day. He climbed through the door in the wall and Nilee made sure it sealed behind them.

With the door closed, the hallway was deserted again except for the dead body of the guard. The only evidence left of what had transpired was the dead man, the iron door, partially melted on the inside, keys still in the lock on the outside and a trail of silvery burgundy blood, which stopped at a solid wall.

It wouldn't be shift change until first light; their escape route was safe for a few hours yet. They had to move fast or the passageways would be given away, flooded with guards as soon as an alarm was raised. Myst knew this, and she wouldn't let them stop even for a moment. They would get to the prince and get out fast, there was no other option.

Chapter 4

Rescue the Prince

Barely audible footfalls of two people were all that could be heard within the winding tunnels. The boy's seemed to dissolve before they even reached the ears of the girls. It was as if he were weightless like a feather. The three travelled in utter silence; no one spoke a word as Myst led them through the tunnels. She barely even stopped to check the scratchings on the walls telling them the direction.

She knew exactly where she was going, and she knew she had to get there in as little time as possible. She could only hope the prince was in his chambers – it was late enough that he should be, but there was no guarantee. If he was not, Myst wasn't sure what they were supposed to do.

Myst had them walking with great pace. It was even hard for the fully-grown teen to keep up with her, she was not wasting a moment. Myst rather abruptly stopped at a dead end, staring or rather glaring at it. Luckily, she had been far enough ahead that this time no one crashed into her.

"This is His Highness's Chambers," Myst grumbled as she reached out to press the stone to release the door.

"If he ain't here I got no idea where to find him, so don't go thinking about trying to find him, alright?" Her hand trembled a little as it hovered over the stone. She was terrified the prince really was inside the room, and the thickness of the stone made it hard to tell if he was or not. But if he was, she was certain he would kill them all for trespassing. After all, why would a prince need saving?

The boy hadn't said why, and she hadn't tried to ask. This was feeling like an awful idea now. Nilee seemed convinced, but Myst felt like this was a trap. It just didn't feel right. She was scared, she didn't know what the teen knew, she didn't know what Nilee had seen or heard in her dream. She was in the dark, and she hated it.

As Myst finally moved to press her hand down on the stone mechanism, the boy's head cocked to the side. He gently stopped her hand, eyes closed, his head tilting more. He was listening. After a few seconds he released her bruised wrist, allowing her hand to slam down onto the stone.

The second she released the lock on the door, the boy moved in the blink of an eye. Both girls were thrown behind him as he propelled himself into the room. His sword moved like lightning, sparks flying as blade met blade, blocking the attack that had been aimed at the prince's back. The prince had already locked swords with another assassin, making him unable to save himself from the incoming blow.

Fayon had been expecting this attempt on his life. His father had been more distant than usual, harder on him, and not so secretive about his plan. So, Fayon had been in the midst of waiting for the guards' shifts to change before he made his move towards the stables to meet with Lulen. However, that had not happened. The second he had opened the door to his chambers, two assassins had descended upon him, one from the door, one from the window behind him.

Fayon had barely had time to draw his sword to block the frontal attack, his crimson eyes widening as he saw

33

the second charging him, while the first had locked their swords together. He had gritted his teeth, ready to try to force his body backwards fast to avoid the blow when suddenly his vision was full of muddy brown, followed by metallic red and sparks of white.

The second assassin skidded backwards as the new male pushed forward with all his strength, sword held in front of him, energy coursing through it in waves of blue, making it a deadly sight to behold. Fayon did not have a second to debate who this new male was or whether he meant to harm him. For now, he had saved him, and that was enough to trust him.

The pair engaged the two assassins, Fayon moving with brute strength. His moves had great force behind them, beating back his assailant's attacks with incredible strength and trained military movements. The younger teen moved as if gravity held no meaning to him. Despite his wounded body and the blood that dripped from his injuries, he moved with the grace of a bird, lightning speed and with astonishing accuracy. Watching him was like watching a beautiful dance; at times his feet would move in the most intricate ways, avoiding every attack that came his way. At others he was a blur delivering a deluge of blows upon his adversary.

The prince and Weapon moved in sync, blocking attacks for the other while avoiding their own, beating back the assassins.

"No!" the teen cried as Fayon sliced the throat of one assassin, creating a fountain of blood that splattered up to the ceiling, staining everything. The boy rendered his opponent unable to move, leaving him unconscious, slumped against the wall. He didn't take that killing blow; he was not a killer, not the weapon he was supposed to be.

Upon seeing the crumpled body of the second assassin, his eyes widened. He moved fast, bending down beside the fallen, hand shaking as he tried to take the pulse of the other assassin. That sick feeling returned when his hand soaked with blood instantly, no pulse to be found. The boy started to tremble; he was supposed to get here before anyone died. He couldn't stop the death, he couldn't stop it.

The teen crouched there shaking, lost in his own sorrow when he felt the cold point of a blade to his throat. Slowly he lifted his gaze from the body to meet the eyes of Fayon for the first time.

Blue and gold met with crimson, staring, neither speaking nor moving, as if sizing each other up. Fayon looked rather unkempt for once in his life. The ribbon that held his black ebony hair in place had long since disappeared and strands stuck in all manner of directions, while the younger teen looked just as wrecked as he had his entire life, still creating a puddle of blood under himself, but neither seemed affected by or acknowledged it.

Neither teen moved, the older keeping his blade to the younger's neck.

"Who are you?" Fayon asked, his voice deep and smooth. There was no hint of wavering, he was strong and steady as if this situation had not affected him in the least. He pressed the blade deeper into the boy's skin when he was met with silence, drawing a prick of blood as he did so.

"I asked who you were. Speak before I end your life as well." Fayon's eyes narrowed as his saviour and now prisoner remained there in silence, fingers pressed to the pulse point of a dead assassin. Fayon's distrust in this person was clear.

All of a sudden Nilee came rushing out from the hidden tunnels and grabbed onto Fayon's leg, clinging on to the base of his rustic black robes.

"Don't hurt him! Please don't hurt him! He can't answer – he doesn't have a name so you can't hurt him! You can't."

"Nilee!" Myst yelled at the second girl as she darted out after her twin, desperately trying to pull her from the now thoroughly confused-looking prince's leg. "Let go, Nilee! You gotta let go of him!"

"No! Not till he lets him go! He wanted to save you, so you can't kill him, you can't!" Nilee kept crying as she was shaken off the prince's robes onto the floor. She was about to try and cling to the leather boots when the teen on the floor finally spoke. All eyes in the room focused on him the second a word left his lips.

"This one heard... wanted to... have you... killed, so... escaped to come... and save prince. This one also... po... pom... pr... prom...ised to get... girls out." He sounded as if he was scared, causing a stutter to occur. He missed words, making the prince's brow furrow. The boy did not seem stupid; he had clearly received training. But he was in a horrible state. Fayon watched as the boy then proceeded to bow his head respectfully, pushing the blade further into his own skin without flinching.

"This one... begs... prince... let him... keep that pro...mise."

Fayon removed his sword in an instant as the teen before him nearly drove his blade deeper. The sword went straight to his side. Fayon just stared at the torn up bloody mess in front of him. Looking into his eyes when his head lifted again, he saw nothing but light, hope, no pain, a frown forming on Fayon's face, making his sharp handsome features scrunch in a way that did not suit him.

He couldn't understand it. *Who was this boy? How had he heard they had planned to kill him? Who were these girls and how did they all know about a passage even he did not know of? Did this boy really have no name? Was that why he spoke in the third person? Did he know how to speak or was he truly unable to form cohesive sentences?* Hundreds of thoughts ran through the young prince's head until finally he sheathed his sword.

"You have no name?" Fayon asked slowly, keeping a wary eye on the people he had decided to trust for the moment. His guard, however, was very much on high alert. Seeing the shake of the younger's head, Fayon formed a picture in his mind. The boy was definitely tortured, the state of his body made that obvious. This gave him two options as to the younger's past. One being they had cleared his memories as a form of torture. Or, he had been imprisoned so long he didn't know who he was anymore.

The slight point to the teen's ears suggested he could possibly be of elven descent. He was definitely not demon-blooded, but still could be of an immortal race. This meant his life span was greater than that of humans or other races. He would also age slower. Fayon himself had just turned nine hundred and fifty, which was the age at which an immortal was considered an adult. Fayon was sure this boy had not reached that age as of yet.

This led Fayon to believe it was unlikely he had lost his memories naturally. He could see no reason for a child like this to have been held so long he would forget.

Despite his admittedly incredible swordsmanship skills, there was nothing extraordinary about him. A form of torture likely as a punishment for having stolen was a more likely conclusion to come to. That was the conclusion Fayon settled on, that the boy was simply a thief who'd got caught and punished. Fayon took a deep breath, hand still tight on his blade.

"No name... and you came to save me, after promising these two girls freedom. Have I got that correct?" With another nod of confirmation, he turned to the two girls who now clung to one another, terrified. "And you two. I assume you have names, correct? You know these passages? Do they lead anywhere in the castle? Could we use them to gain access to the stables?" He stared intensely at the pair's orange eyes, almost seeming alive as they rippled with movement.

"Y... yes, Your Highness. I... I am Nilee and... and that's Myst... we can take you there," Nilee whispered, daring to meet his gaze.

"Then I request that you lead us all there, and in return I will aid you all in escaping my father's domain as compensation for saving my life."

The two girls' eyes widened when they heard the prince promise to help them leave, while the boy on the floor seemed not shocked in the slightest. There was almost a warmth in his eyes that suggested this had played out exactly as expected.

"O...okay! Yes, Your Highness! I can get us to the stables no problem, you just follow Myst and everything will be a okay!" The girl jumped into the air, sticking her thumb towards herself, suddenly bolstered with all her usual confidence.

Fayon's lips twitched a little at the corners at what she

said – he was almost showing a smile, which had Nilee dreamily staring at him while Myst pivoted on her foot, hair spinning around so fast the braid on the right side of her head whipped her nose. The girl ignored the fact she'd just whacked herself in the face and marched back into the tunnels. Nilee scrambled after her, only to both pause when they realised the older males were not in fact following them yet.

Fayon was staring down at the younger teen, hand held out for him. It took a moment before the boy reached out and grasped it. With that, Fayon gently pulled him to stand, noting the strength behind the teen's grasp. He had more than just formal military training, of that Fayon was certain. The prince made sure to be careful of the injuries that plagued the younger's body as he pulled him to stand, a light frown on his face as he looked the boy up and down.

Not only was he in poor condition to look at, just covered in fresh and dried blood, but all he had to cover himself was a pair of under trousers that were torn at the bottoms. His feet were bare, he had no inner or outer robe covering his chest. They may have been located in a volcanic plain, but within the walls of this castle the night air was dangerously cold. This kid would freeze to death if he did nothing. Fayon let out a sigh as he dropped the boy's hand and glanced over to the girls.

"Wait just one moment, then I shall follow," he informed the girls behind him, before bringing his eyes back to the shorter boy. His gaze lingered on the teen in front of him before he moved to scoop the satchels from the ground. However, he did not stop there. He moved back to his own storage chests and fished out a few things into the bags, glancing back at the boy every few seconds before sealing them up and throwing a cloak at the boy.

"Put it on or you will freeze before we even make it out of the city, let alone the realm. Now let us go. I hazard a guess it won't be long before someone follows your trail of blood." With that Fayon was signalling the girls to move, taking long strides across the room to follow them.

The boy had caught the cloak and was now holding it delicately in his hands, fingers trembling slightly, almost as if he was afraid to break it. After all, it was the first gift anyone had ever given to him. He ran his fingers over the cloth, feeling the coarse texture of the fabric, the weight telling him it was thick and warm. It was clearly expensive; the fabric may have been coarse but it was beautifully detailed with black trim. And it was the warmest thing he could ever remember. To a boy who had nothing, it quickly became something cherished. Suddenly he jumped when Fayon's hand came firmly around his bicep, pulling him along.

"You're supposed to wear it, not cradle it like a baby and stand there daydreaming." Fayon's voice was harsh but it did not feel like a scolding; there was a sad undertone to it, like he was pained by what he saw.

The boy stumbled a little to catch his feet as he was pulled along by the taller teen, almost crashing to the ground when Fayon stopped and took the cloak from his hands. The boy looked startled at the loss and opened his mouth before suddenly warmth enveloped him. Fayon had swung it around his shoulders, and the boy instantly wrapped it tighter around himself, a happy little smile on his face. *Was this what it felt like to have someone care for you?* he wondered.

"T... thank you..." The boy sounded so unsure that

they were even the right words to say, and the sidelong look Fayon gave him did not help reassure him that he was correct.

"Don't thank me, it's just a cloak… it's not even that great a one," Fayon huffed, turning on his heel and continuing after the silently whispering girls in front.

The boy just shuffled along behind him, holding the edges of his cloak tightly. He thought it was great, at least. Maybe this wasn't what being cared for felt like after all. It was just confusing – he would try to ask the twins later. They seemed to know a lot.

The twins kept looking back, whispering and giggling a little to themselves, which was making Fayon's eyebrow twitch in all honesty. He was a patient man, well known for talking, listening and helping where he could. But when you are trying to escape a castle after an attempt was just made on your life, he felt rather irritable. Silence was key in getting away.

"Please keep sound to a minimum unless you wish to be caught." His voice came out a little harsh, causing Myst to huff but go quiet. Fayon felt a little guilty when he saw Nilee's startled face but said nothing, instead he remained silent, gaze fixed ahead of them, for the moment at least.

The stables being the other side of the castle meant it wasn't a fast process winding through the hidden halls, the result being Fayon found himself looking more and more at the boy, finding himself wondering about him. Adding question upon unanswered question to his mind, until he couldn't hold back anymore and turned to him, walking backwards, his hands clasped behind his back in a regal manner.

The boy instantly furrowed his brow, looking up

towards the taller one, not understanding why he would walk this way. It seemed inconvenient as well as a hazardous way to move around.

"Fen." The name slipped from Fayon's lips without thought. The smaller teen paused his steps, staring at the elder with wide blue and gold-flecked eyes. Fayon nodded and repeated the name again. "Fen."

Suddenly a smile erupted on the young man's dirtied, abused face, a smile so blinding that Fayon had to spin around on his heels to look away, heart thundering uncomfortably within his chest.

Fayon lightly gripped his tunic, frowning to himself. A smile had made him feel so uncomfortable – what was wrong with him? Suddenly Fayon nearly crashed into the young man as he moved to get in front of him. How in hell had he moved so fast? Fayon hadn't even heard him let alone seen the movement.

Fen grabbed at Fayon's hands, eyes brimming with emotion, making the uncomfortable feeling within Fayon grow. He didn't do well with emotions; he wasn't used to whatever this feeling was. It was hard to tell whether he liked it or not, but when he heard that voice, filled with such life and excitement, Fayon decided it wasn't such a bad feeling.

"Fen!" The battered boy grinned, eyes sparkling. He had a name, someone had named him, given him an identity. He'd never had that. The excitement was evident in his voice. "Thank you... I like... Fen. I am Fen." Fen was still holding Fayon's hands within his own.

Fayon just stared at the boy, wincing at the roughness of his voice, the disjointed speech. Just how long had he been isolated? Just who was this boy? Who had neglected to teach their child the basics of the common tongue?

Perhaps if they escaped, he would find the time to change that. Suddenly, Fayon felt incredibly awkward for planning that. He cleared his throat and rolled his shoulders a fraction, realising he hadn't responded to Fen, who still stared at him.

"Good... Fen suits you." It may have sounded like a random name, the first name that came into Fayon's head, but he had very much considered his options before the name just came blurting out of his lips. The name was one from a tale he'd once heard.

The character from within the tale had saved a prince from being poisoned, by drinking the poisoned wine himself when the prince had not believed his warning. The Fen from the story had died a hero. He'd stopped an assassination that would have led to armistice breaking and war erupting across the lands again.

The teen in front of him had saved his life, even though he'd clearly suffered great abuse at the hands of Fayon's race. Saved him to put a stop to what his father had planned. Fayon was certain it was a similar goal to the assassin in the story. His father wanted war.

Fen seemed like the perfect name for him.

Fayon realised that he had stopped walking. Three sets of eyes were staring at him, one annoyed, one curious and one set that looked worried. Worry did not suit those stunning eyes of his, Fayon decided at that moment. He did not wish to see Fen worry ever again.

"My apologies, I didn't mean to delay us. Come on, Fen." Fayon gave a smile as he stepped around Fen, releasing his hands to continue after the ever-huffy Myst.

"You said *shh*, but *you* talk a lot! And no fair, *we* found him, why did you get to name him?" Myst grumbled from the front of the group, her arms crossed over her chest, all mopey. It was like she was arguing over naming a pet, not a humanoid being, which caused Fayon to actually let a chuckle loose.

Fen tilted his head at the sound. He liked it; it was happy. Then he looked at the pouty Myst.

"Myst not like... my name?" Fen asked curiously catching up to walk stride for stride with Fayon. He seemed to be growing confident in speaking.

"No! I wanted to name you!" Myst stomped her foot down with a scowl on her face, before she saw Fen looking downtrodden at her response, earning a jab from her sister. Myst grumbled again but relented. "I suppose the princey did think of a good name," Myst begrudgingly admitted. She was still mad that she didn't get to name him: she'd wanted something cool, like Blaze or Slasher, or, you know, something bad ass. 'Fen' was so normal.

Fen just started smiling as he watched them all. Fayon was chuckling, Nilee was beaming, while Myst was stubbornly pouting. The long-imprisoned teen wondered if just maybe this was what being around friends was like. He happily walked behind the group, following Myst's lead, all the while thinking he wouldn't mind if these three could be his friends.

Chapter 5

Surrounded

The sun was starting to emerge when the group of four reached the exit to the stables, a stone slab just like all those before opening with a slight grinding sound echoing in the silence.

Nilee poked her head out, eyes narrowed as she looked left and right for any guards, trying to be all sneaky about it. All she saw were unconscious ones slumped and tied inside one of the stalls. Two horses were saddled by the slightly-ajar barn doors, each with packed saddle bags.

Beside the horses a young man paced. Nilee's eyes widened and she gasped dramatically, causing the tall man to spin, drawing a dagger. She stared at him and he stared at her. In front of her was a man with pointy ears and blond hair! She was mesmerised; she'd only heard about elves, never having seen one before.

She had always thought they had long hair, but this one's hair was cut rough and short, his pointed ears pierced in multiple places. What was most amazing to her was his blond hair! Sure, she herself had ash hair, but that was about as light as it came in the demon realm. No blondes or whites, or anything so fair. Green eyes were also a no in the demon realm. This was so much fun for her. Until Myst pushed her over and she fell flat on her face.

"Don't just stand there, we gotta gooooo," Myst grumbled as she jumped out the wall. Fen crouched down to pick up the fallen girl as the elf pulled a second dagger upon seeing the three. Myst moved to squish Nilee's cheeks, checking for marks the second Fen had her up. Luckily Nilee only had a red forehead with no scratches. She would not have forgiven herself if there were.

The elf's breathing picked up as more people filed through the wall. This wasn't part of the plan – who the hell were these people? And where was Fayon? They were supposed to leave before daybreak, yet daybreak was happening *right now*, and instead of Fayon he had two children and a rather roughed-up teen.

"Who are you all? What have you done with His Highness?" The elf's voice was as stern as his face as he inched towards the seemingly-unarmed group, daggers now in both hands.

"Lulen, stand down, they are with me," came Fayon's deep voice as he stepped out from the wall, looking towards his visibly confused friend. "It's a long story, and we don't have time for now. Get a third horse saddled for Fen. We have to leave before my father realises his plans have failed."

Lulen looked very concerned. Plans had failed? What had happened in his absence? He had left his friend for no more than five hours. Somehow in that time their escape now included two children and what looked like a beaten homeless boy. The king's plan had failed? They had not expected the king to even attempt anything yet, that's why the escape had been planned for now. It was supposed to be safe from detection at this stage. That had clearly gone out the window.

Every kind of scenario ran through the elf's mind as he quickly threw a saddle over a brown splotched pinto horse, fastening the satchels his prince had thrown to the sides. He pulled the buckles tight, glancing constantly to those barricaded doors that attached the stables to the castle, his heart pounding in his chest with every extra second they were wasting.

"Mount up," Lulen commanded as he finished the last strap. His voice, although as stern as before, did not hold the tone of hostility any longer. Instead it sounded so musical to the ears of the girls and Fen. It was something none of them had experienced before. The melody of an elven voice. It was so beautiful Fen could not help but stare.

"Don't stare; get on the damn horses before we are all killed!" Lulen snapped, hostility coming right back in the form of irritation.

Fayon placed a hand on his shoulder, a frown gracing his handsome features. The gesture was to tell him to calm down. Lulen took a deep breath after catching Fayon's gaze, before he himself mounted his own horse without another word. The grey stallion moved with unease, sensing his master's.

"Pass me one of the girls," Lulen said, glancing at Fen, who the girls seemed to cling to.

Fen moved without another word. He scooped Myst up under her arms and lifted her up onto the horse, setting her in front of Lulen. He didn't react to the stretch and ripping of his wounds or the sounds that came with them. The elf's eyes darted over the boy's body, as did Fayon's as well.

"Is Myst... Don't lose... her," Fen said. They did not know each other; there was no time to tell him any more than that. Fen was simply giving trust to someone Fayon had full confidence in, to protect the little girl. Myst looked rather excited at the prospect of riding with the elf now she was on the horse. She had a cheeky grin as she leaned back into him, staring up to see his annoyed scowl. Oh, she would like messing with this hardass.

Fayon himself had already mounted his horse.

Fen lifted Nilee onto the pinto and then pulled himself up with ease after, looking as if he'd spent his whole life around horses with his posture and confidence.

"Give me your reins, I will lead your horse," Fayon said, holding his hand out to take the reins from Fen who simply shook his head no.

"She will follow... group... no aid... move faster... without... leading her." Fen gently stroked the mare's neck, who bowed her head as if to confirm what Fen had said with disjointed words. Lulen stared with blazing intensity at the interaction. Not at the fact his words were so childlike, but at the horse's response to her rider.

What was this boy? To have bonded and understood a horse he had not so much as seen before today... Lulen's distrust in the teen was growing by the minute. He was not normal. But right now, they needed to get out. He snapped his reins, glancing at Fayon, watching as he lowered his hand. With a nod from his prince and friend, Lulen was off, his stallion bolting out the stables with instant speed, the two other horses joining. The sound of hooves pounding against cobbled ground instantly occupied the still morning air.

"Stick close," Fayon called as he looked back at Fen and Nilee. "We have a practised route. If you see guards, don't stop, keep moving, do not get separated from us. We won't be able to come back for you."

Fen gave a sharp nod. He had no plans of going back. He would not be put back into that hell and used against his will to destroy innocent people. This was as much his stand as it was everyone else's in this group. They all wanted freedom from this realm. They would all get their freedom today, no matter what.

The horses and their riders weaved between buildings, keeping any line of sight that the king's guards might have of them fragmented at best. They moved at great speed before the ever-rising sun. In mere minutes the great walls of Nisha started to loom into view. Thick black stone, hundreds of metres high, an impenetrable wall designed to keep those inside in, and an omen for others to stay out.

Fayon gripped the reins in his hands tighter when the wall came into view. This was the hard part, not getting out of the castle but getting past the walls. They encircled his father's whole capital. No one could leave. Those of their race that resided outside the walls, they were kept in the realm by treaty rules, forbidding them from leaving Prophet's lands.

These walls had very few exits, which were small, only opened for supplies or troop movements, and heavily guarded.

It had taken Lulen several weeks to figure out which exits had the least guards, and which one they should make their stand and their escape.

"Get ready!" Lulen called from the front of the group.

It was barely a minute after he said those words that haunting alarms blared all around them. The king had finally learned of his weapon's escape, his son's survival, and the passageways found and stormed. He had every on-duty as well as off-duty knight called to action immediately to get them both back.

Lulen could hear them gearing up, and he was sure the three demon-bloods could as well, because soon after those alarms sounded angry shouts and the roaring of hooves against cobbled stone surrounded them. From every direction the king had his troops charged through the streets. This did not change the plan, even if they were being surrounded. He had planned this out.

Lulen kept on his course. He was certain that no one knew where they were headed. They were prepared, they had been careful, no one was going to get to the gates before them. Lulen's gaze was locked ahead, determination on his face. He had no intention to stop their pursuit. Nor would he if his horse hadn't suddenly reared up with a startled cry as Fen and his mare cut them off.

Fen had placed himself between the other horses and the gate, hand held up to say stop. He shook and tilted his head, seemingly listening.

Nilee was squeezing onto Fen's hand, eyes darting around, something Myst had seen her doing countless times before. She was definitely looking for something. Then she threw her hand out with a pointed finger seconds later, a confident look in her eyes.

"What are you doing!?" Fayon panicked, as his friend was almost sent flying off his horse along with Myst, who laughed out of all things.

"Are you trying to get us killed? What are you doing? Crazy bastard!" Lulen yelled, anger ripe in his voice. He knew he shouldn't have trusted this freak.

"Not... that way." Fen spoke to the other members of the group, not indicating he had heard any of what they had said, or that it hurt his feelings. What he did pay attention to, however, was the questioning look on Fayon's face.

"Death... that way... go... this way... Fen... will lead." He looked slightly frustrated with himself, his communication skills making it hard to get what he wanted to say out fast, when they already had so little time to waste anyway.

So, Fen did not waste time in waiting for their replies before taking off in the direction Nilee pointed. His direction changed the second she would shift her finger. He didn't even glance back, he somehow knew they would follow him. Fate had led them to be together, it wouldn't separate them now. Fayon gritted his teeth and looked to Lulen, before he went after Fen.

"You're not seriously following him!?" Lulen cried out as he raced after Fayon, trying to get him to turn around. Then his head snapped to the side, eyes widening. He had direct sight to the gate he had been leading them to from this angle. It was not only sealed tight, unlike the schedule, but it also had a massive military presence building there.

Lulen looked back ahead, heart beating wildly. *How had they known their plans? The troops had got there too fast for them not to have known. How had this boy sensed what even he as an elf couldn't? They were dead now.*

Lulen knew there was no way he or Fayon could find another way out before the king's men caught up to them. They would all be executed on the spot.

"Fen, it's just a wall up ahead! You're going to hit a dead end!" Fayon's voice suddenly rang out. Fen was leading them directly towards a solid wall. Lulen's heart pounded, every alley or street they passed he could see guards, horse archers, mages. He could see their deaths and they were literally headed into a dead end with nowhere else to go. They were quite literally running towards death.

Fen's eyes were locked onto one point ahead of them, before he suddenly swung his mare around, galloping towards Lulen, snatching his bow from where it was tied to the saddle and an arrow from the quiver. Nilee held on for dear life at the sudden movement as again Fen spun around, galloping straight back towards the wall, bow drawn, arrow nocked in perfect form.

Magic channelled through his body, blue eyes growing brighter than ever as he channelled light magic into the tip of the arrow. It shone a dazzling, almost blinding white. The heat emitting from the arrow was making Nilee lean back into Fen, trying to get as far away from it as she could, until suddenly the heat was gone.

The two children, the prince and the elf watched as the arrow fired in a beautiful arch, leaving a trail of white light as it flew. Then when it connected with the great black wall it sparked. A giant cracking sound echoed, drowning out all other noise as creases in the wall formed, white light splitting it apart like a sword would cut through flesh, until the wall could no longer take the force of its push and with a loud explosion was launched apart. Chunks of wall soared through the air, crushing anything in their path, demolishing buildings with ease.

Everyone stared in shock at the giant hole in a once-thought impenetrable wall, and then at the boy who broke through it with a single arrow. Lulen was the first to snap awake as arrows started to rain down around them.

"Ride! Don't stop!" he cried out as he kicked his horse's sides, spurring him into a gallop. Fayon followed his lead soon after, and they raced after Fen, who was already galloping through the rubble to get to the outside. The king's men thundered after them on blackened steeds. It was a race against time. The group never stopped, riding until they knew they were in a land the demon-blooded army couldn't step foot in. Riding until those black walls would only be a memory. Riding until the dead burnt land turned into lush green. Not until their horses were exhausted did the three men and two girls stop.

Tension high among them, they could no longer see those who had been chasing them, and they had long since crossed over the borders of Prophet, where the demon-blooded were meant to remain. But still, they couldn't relax. Fayon knew that if his father was willing to murder his own son to ignite a war, then he probably wouldn't think twice about having his armies cross the long-standing border that detained their race to that desolate land.

If his father needed to, he knew that they could run to the other side of the world, hide within the angel-blooded's walls and he would still send assassins after them. His weary gaze cast back one more time, eyes scanning through the trees to see not another soul, at least for now. Only then did Fayon's shoulders relax a fraction before he turned to examine his group. Lulen looked tense and angry, Myst was sitting in front of him, squirming in discomfort on the horse. Poor girl, thought Fayon, she must not have ever ridden, let alone for so long at such a distance. They really had to take a break, for the children in their group as well as their horses. Dead steeds were not useful for running away.

"Alright, we take a break here for now. Take the time to rest, find water, but do not light fires. Just because we have left Prophet's borders does not mean we are safe. We have to be prepared that my father may break the treaty. As soon as the horses are rested, we leave." Fayon spoke with all the authority expected of a crown prince and none of the arrogance one might assume a demon-blooded to have.

Lulen was first to dismount, lifting Myst to the ground, saddles and saddle bags following soon after, glancing over his shoulder at the dirt-covered teen still sat atop his horse. The elf raised an eyebrow when he saw the teen was just staring up with wide eyes at the leaves above his head.

Fen had a true look of amazement on his face. He had heard about trees when they drilled their tactical advantage for stealth, and disadvantage for defending into his brain. What they had never told him was how beautiful they were.

He reached his hand up to run his fingers on the smooth waxen surfaces. It was like nothing he'd even touched before. The smell was making a smile grace his face, and he could have sat there for the rest of time and still found something new and equally as beautiful to look at. His eyes followed the way the wind made the branches move, and the blossom petals that gracefully fell to the earth. He held his finger up when a white butterfly flew in front of his vision.

"What… are you?" he whispered, still reaching out as the delicate creature flew out of sight.

Fayon was watching Fen the entire time. He paused even unbuckling the saddle to witness the awe on the teen's face, making Fayon wonder just what kind of life this boy had experienced before today. He had never seen someone look at the world this way. Even he, who had been around barren fire-filled land his whole life, did not see the life, the green around them, in such a way.

If it were up to Fayon or Fen, neither would have moved, but Lulen was not having any of this. They had to be on alert, not staring into the distance. So, he cleared his throat loudly, snapping the two younger men out of their trances.

"Dismount, give your horse a break," Lulen said in a slight growl, gaze harsh towards the beaten boy.

Chapter 6

Shocking Discovery

Lulen slammed Fen against the nearest tree the second they had all dismounted. Fen's eyes widened as he was held there by the elf. Lulen's fists tightly entwined in the boy's cloak, eyes blazing with anger. The pair stared at each other, one in fear the other in unbridled anger.

"What the hell are you? How did you know where to go? What kind of magic was that?! Answer me!" Lulen roughly shook the terrified youngster, until Fayon gripped Lulen's shoulders, pulling him back with a rough jerk, planting himself between the angered elf and frightened Fen.

"You need to calm down, you're frightening Fen and the girls." Fayon's voice was calm but held a stern note within, sending shivers down not only Lulen's spine but Fen's as well as he stayed hidden from view behind the taller teen.

"Calm down? Did you not see what that thing just did?! Nothing he did should have been possible. *I* couldn't even hear those soldiers so how could he? How could he blow up a wall with one arrow? Fayon, he is dangerous, he could be part of your father's plans! We cannot trust him. It is all too much of a coincidence."

Fayon of course had informed Lulen of the attempt on his life at this point. The fact that it would have been his father's excuse for starting a war was confirmed by none other than Fen. They had managed the conversation only after they had left Prophet's borders. Fen's knowledge just added fuel to the fire, that was Lulen's suspicions.

A long frown began forming on Fayon's face as he took a slow glance back at the younger boy behind him. *Would a spy from his father really help him escape the realm?* But now that Lulen was pointing things out, Fayon couldn't help but form doubts about Fen. He did not know the teen. Fen had come out of the blue and saved his life, and then had been the reason they'd all evaded execution. He was the only reason they'd avoided detection and escaped as far as they had. It all seemed far too good to be a coincidence.

Could it be that this was his father's true plan? That Fen was executing this escape, getting him across the border as a way to start war instead of his murder? Fayon couldn't imagine his father choosing a plan that involved less blood but here he was, considering Fen to be a spy. Had their meeting been planned all along by the same man Fayon had tried to escape for so long? The longer he thought this, the more he became just as much on edge as Lulen seemed to be. *Could he really have been so stupid to have fallen for this teen's plans?*

Fen just stared at the two with wide confused eyes. He hadn't done anything to help that man, that unspeakably cruel king. He had just wanted to take back his life, and to stop Fayon from losing his own. The boy could not understand how they could think he was suspicious, but he did not know how to defend himself. Luckily for Fen, he did not need to.

"But Fen only did what I said to do," a tiny voice called from behind the three males, each of which turned their gaze to the ashen-haired Nilee, looks of surprise gracing their faces. Fen still just looked terribly confused as to what was happening. Fayon moved to kneel before Nilee.

"What do you mean, he did what you told him?" A wary look in his eyes as he waited for the answer.

"I *saw* it! If we went there everyone would be covered in blood on the floor, with the scary man laughing over you," Nilee said, eyes all wide and scared. "Then he dragged Fen away again. Then I saw a different way out; there was a crack in a bit of wall, so Fen followed where I told him to go." Nilee squeaked it all out at rapid speed. Honestly, it was a little hard to follow, even for Fen, who actually knew this already.

Complete silence followed what Nilee had said, as everyone tried to wrap their heads around exactly what the little girl had just blurted out to them.

Lulen eventually spoke up, a light frown indenting on his features. "You have the gift of foresight."

Nilee gave a firm nod. "I saw Fen and found him. He was real, so..." She was interrupted by Fayon, who finished her thoughts.

"So you knew our deaths would be real if we did not follow what your visions told. Fen believed you simply because he had no reason not to. Correct?" Fayon turned his gaze to Fen, who was slowly nodding his head in agreement.

"Should... I not... have?" Fen asked quietly. He was so unsure in himself at this point. He had believed her without thought – was that not something he should have done? Was he not supposed to break the wall? He was now realising he didn't know how to act or what to do outside his cell walls. Everything was a decision he needed to think through now. He shouldn't just do what he was told – that would be no different than having stayed confined in his cell. Everyone could see the spiral happening within Fen's head about the choice he made, so Fayon stood himself back up and gripped his shoulders. Fen jolted, eyes flashing up to meet his.

"You did the correct thing. You saved us all by choosing to believe Nilee. Thank you. Lulen, stop with your fears. He has given no reason for us to distrust him. He saved our lives. That should be enough." Fayon's gaze locked with Lulen's, making sure his friend knew that he was not happy with his actions. Lulen growled lowly but moved away with a stunted nod to say he would do his best to heed his prince's words.

"Her powers still do not explain to us just how he managed to blow up a wall with one arrow. It also most definitely does not explain the magic he used. It was not a demon-blooded element. Whatever trust you seem to have for him, Your Highness, you should be careful. We truly have no idea what he is or what he is capable of." Lulen laid out all his suspicions for everyone to hear. He may have agreed to try trust, but he was not going to drop his guard until he had all the answers.

Even Fen himself honestly didn't know how to answer those questions. He had no idea who he was or what he was capable of. He hadn't thought the powers he had used were anything special, but they apparently were not an element demon-blooded could even use. *Did that mean he wasn't even demon-blooded in race?* He had always assumed he must have been, now he really felt like he knew nothing.

Fayon frowned a little seeing that Fen looked lost. It truly looked to him like Fen had not only never had a name but didn't even know his identity. That was something Fayon couldn't imagine, not knowing where you came from or how you came to be. He wondered if there was anyone out there looking for and missing Fen, or whether he was an orphan. Not knowing, Fayon could only think how that might make Fen feel, and yet he always tried to smile. Fen really was brave.

"Right now, it doesn't matter. Fen has given us no reason to mistrust him, and who is to say that the power he used is not of our race? Nilee here has a rare power that isn't attached to any race, maybe what Fen used is a similar skill."

Fen raised his gaze to Fayon, a small smile lighting up his grubby face. That same smile made Fayon feel so uncomfortable, but so alive.

"For now, we need to focus on staying alive. That starts with getting food, water and cleaning Fen's wounds before they become infected." Fayon spoke after a moment of just staring at Fen's smiling face, before he moved to look through the saddle bags, finding clean robes for the younger. They would likely be big on him but they would do for now.

He set to the side white under robes as well a grey outer robe. He worked through his other bags until he found Lulen's spare boots and the matching sash to put around Fen's waist. Next, he found alcohol, their herb bag and some bandage rolls. Fayon bundled all of this into his arms, but before he could move, Lulen came forward and snatched them from his prince.

"Stay with the girls. You have no medical training. *You* come with me," Lulen muttered as he grabbed Fen by the arm, pulling him along. The younger nearly fell as he was twisted around, stumbling a little to keep up with the elf's brisk pace. Lulen followed the sound of running water until they reached a little river. It was not fast flowing, but it was at least deep enough for them to wash from. It would do.

Lulen released the boy, pulling a rag from the pile as well as a bar of scented wax that should be of help removing the dirt and other encrusted fluids from his skin. The elf threw the two at Fen once he found them. Fen caught the rag and wax block as it was thrown at his face, looking towards Lulen with wide eyes.

"Get in, wash all that grime off so I can see what I am working with. Wash your hair while you're there, it looks like straw." He truly hated being around people who didn't bathe. The teen stank of sweat, dirt and the metallic scent of blood. Honestly, it was so bad he wasn't sure if the kid had ever had a bath.

What kind of parents couldn't even teach a child to wash? Lulen thought to himself. Or let him get so beat up in the first place. He did not understand the cruelty that seemed to be the nature of most within the demon-blooded realm. Especially within its capital. It was a culture so unlike his own.

Once Lulen had thrown the rag and said his piece he moved to sit himself on a moss-covered rock, placing the supplies down, the clothes behind him so Fen could at least be semi-covered when he worked on his wounds. After that Lulen crossed his legs, pulling his dagger out of its strap on his thigh, slowly sharpening its edge. He watched as the sparks flew off in front of him, listening to everything going on around him, even what was happening back with his prince. Lulen was the one who would hear danger coming first; even the demon-blood's hearing was inferior to his. So, he had to be on alert at all times. There were no exceptions, not even while waiting for Fen to wash in the river.

Fen looked at the water for a long time before he slowly peeled the rags from his body, the crusted fabric pulling at the skin it had become attached to, ripping old wounds open as the scabs came away with a sickening sound. But Fen reacted little to the pain it should have caused, there was no hesitation in his movements. He pulled the clothes away in one swift motion. The only item he was careful with was the cloak Fayon had given him just a few hours ago, its fabric already stained with the silvery-hued blood.

Once disrobed Fen stepped into the ice-cold water, moving until it came above his waist, slowly lifting his hands up until water dripped between his fingers, watching mesmerised. This was the first time he'd had a bath. Usually, water was just thrown over him. Although the river was ice cold, it wasn't unpleasant to Fen. It was almost a perfect temperature. He'd always found it so: the colder water used to torture him had always been far more bearable then the hotter. His body did not react to the cold as it had the heated water.

Fen slowly washed the years of grime from his body until gradually pale white skin surfaced, rubbed slightly red in areas from the scrubbing of the rag. He found himself constantly dipping his full body under the water to wash his face, back, chest, hair, every part of him. The feeling of being clean was something he had no words for. He simply closed his eyes, lying back in the water, feeling the sun on his skin, and the eased movement of his joints as nothing pulled his skin tight anymore. If he could he would have soaked there for hours, just feeling like a person and not a thing to be used, but he knew Lulen was waiting for him, and the elf already disliked him. Fen did not want to give him more reason to distrust him.

So, slowly Fen climbed back out the water, feeling the

chill of the wind against his skin as the water dried, putting on the trousers that would eventually be covered under his robes. He carefully settled himself on the ground in front of Lulen when he was done.

"About time," Lulen huffed, putting the dagger down and looking up at Fen. His whole world seemed to freeze. Staring back at him could not possibly be the same person. Gone was the grime-covered prisoner. Instead, in front of him sat a jewel.

The mudded brown hair had not in fact been that colour at all. No, now it was washed, Fen's hair was beautiful white, with loose waves in it as the waist-length hair gently swayed in the wind. The white of his skin made the blue and gold of his eyes stand out more. The black of his eyelashes made them look even bigger. Then there was the glowing gold mark on his forehead. It swirled beautifully. The same gold could be seen running in beautiful lines throughout his body, gold light that had been hidden beneath the grime before now.

Although Fen had looked beaten before, now clean with his wounds revealed, this boy's body looked like it had been put through a shredder. There were gashes upon gashes littering his skin, large, singed areas of blackened skin, which had clearly been burnt. Lulen could see the tell-tale signs of lashing marks on the teen's shoulders, giving him a good idea of what Fen's back must look like. Silvery blood sluggishly oozed from some of the wounds. Most of his upper body was covered in heavy bruising. He'd been used as a punching bag in all likelihood, Lulen thought.

But then there was the fact that Fen had no sign of infection, and there were no scars to be seen on what intact skin there was. Lulen didn't need to question what was sitting in front of him right now, not with that level of immunity and healing he possessed, especially not with the gold markings and white hair. Only one race had those features.

"Oh, seven hells," Lulen breathed out. "That crazy bastard. Oh, orcshit." Lulen moved forward with the alcohol and bandages to get Fen patched up. "It was light magic. It makes sense now. You're not of the demon realm at all. How the hell did he manage to get an angel-blooded out of Celestia?" Lulen muttered as he worked.

"Angel-blooded? Celestia?" Fen asked softly, confused by Lulen's muttering. He was slightly concerned the elf had lost his mind.

"You... you really don't know what you are?" Lulen said softly. Just how long had that deranged man had this child for? "You're what is known as an angel-blooded. Celestia is the home of all angel-blooded. They are rarely seen, they do not leave or allow others into their realm. Or, I should say that they haven't in hundreds of years. Which begs the question: how did you come to be in the realm of your kind's mortal enemy?"

Fen just stared at Lulen with such a lost look in his eyes. "Have... always been... in... cell." His words were said with confidence, the pause between words becoming shorter, although still strung together poorly.

But no matter how Lulen looked at it he knew he had to be nearing a thousand years of age. If he had been taught as a normal child would have been, his words should be perfect, not disjointed, like he was constantly trying to think of the words he needed. Meaning maybe, *just maybe*, this boy had been telling the truth. Maybe he *had* always been in that cell... or at least so long that anything before was lost to time.

"I wonder why..." Lulen muttered softly, moving around to Fen's back to finish up tending to the injuries. The frown on his fair face ever deepened as he counted the extent of his wounds. Monsters.

Were you simply a means for Aphir to vent his frustrations of your race upon, or did you commit a crime? What possibly could that mad excuse of a king have wanted with a child? Lulen thought to himself. The long silence made Fen fidget and Lulen snap out of his thoughts.

"Get dressed, your wounds are wrapped for now, I will change the bandages tomorrow." With that Lulen walked away to stand in the tree line, allowing for Fen to dress in private, as well as time for him to think. It wasn't more than five minutes before the elf and angel-blooded were walking silently one in front of the other back to the group.

While the two had been gone Fayon had been hard at work. He had organised their supplies – if it had been just the two of them as planned, the dried food they had would have lasted a week. But now with three more mouths to feed they barely had enough for two or three days. So, after setting the twins up with brushing down the horses to help them cool, Fayon had scavenged around for wild fruits and the like.

When the pair finally returned more than two hours later, Fayon, Myst and Nilee were all sitting on the grass, the twins making drawings in the dirt while snacking on some blackberries Fayon had scavenged, thoroughly enjoying the new taste. Fayon sat with his arms crossed, sword held in a firm grasp, keeping his gaze flickering around their surroundings. Crimson eyes snapped to his left when he heard a light rustle of leaves, slowly moving into a crouching position, sword sliding from his sheath a fraction, whole body tense, the muscles in his jaw taut as he waited. The twins moved fast to hide behind the older, clutching at each other tightly, clearly terrified they had been found already. Then Fayon's sword slipped from his fingers and clattered heavily to the ground.

His eyes grew wide, and he slowly rose to stand at his full height as Lulen entered their small clearing. And behind him... Fayon had to rub his eyes and shake his head. There was no way the teen that had been covered in dirt, an unremarkable face with dank brown hair, which had been nothing extraordinary to look at, was the same one standing before them now.

Fen now looked as if he had been carved from pure marble. His features were exquisite, sharp jawline, fair skin that was smooth and unblemished... well, where no current injuries resided, anyway. The white hair acted like a halo, the dark eyelashes so long and perfect around those eyes.

Fayon stood there awestruck, eyes eventually landing on the golden swirl mark on his forehead. One that he also possessed in red on his own forehead. A symbol of blood. Red demon, gold angel.

"So pretty," Nilee squealed as she popped out from behind Fayon, running to Fen with such bright eyes. Fen flushed a little rosy when she called him pretty.

"Can I touch it?" she proceeded to ask, lifting her hand to his hair, making small grabbing motions. She had been in such awe seeing blond hair, but to see pure white hair like snow, she was star struck. Fen smiled, instantly sitting so Nilee could run her fingers through it, Nilee's mouth forming an o shape. It was the softest thing she had ever felt.

Fen looked surprised when it was Fayon who came and sat behind him next. He moved to look back towards him when he felt his callous fingers run against his scalp, through his hair. Lulen watched the scene unfold with a frown on his face. His prince should have been putting as much distance as he could from an angel-blooded. Instead he sat in the damp grass and combed the knots free from Fen's hair.

Sitting silently, working until the wavy hair was beautifully smooth, Fayon carefully bunched up two front portions of Fen's hair into a bun on top of his head, pulling the grey ribbon from his own ponytail, letting his ebony hair cascade down his shoulders, tying Fen's hair into place.

"It's perfect," Nilee giggled, pulling two bits loose so they dangled down.

"He looks like an angel," Myst mumbled, before realising she was being looked at. She crossed her arms, making a *hmph* noise and sticking her nose in the air, denying all knowledge those lame words ever came from her mouth.

Fen actually had a dark blush over his cheeks and nose at all the attention on him. He'd never had such compliments or felt so relaxed as he had in the moment Fayon's hands were running through his hair. He smiled softly, looking back at Fayon when his hands finally fell away, golden blue meeting crimson red, the pair staring at each other.

"She's right, it's perfect," Fayon said. Fen's eyes widened a little, and the prince quickly cleared his throat and stood after realising what he'd said. "Right, uhh, I'm glad your wounds have been treated. There's berries to eat... I need to scout the perimeter. Lulen, let's go,"

Fayon rambled out, grabbing Lulen's tunic as he went past, the elf almost chuckling at his prince.

Fen was left watching their retreating backs with a bewildered look on his face.

"Come on, Fen! Come eat! They taste reallllyyy good!" Nilee gently took his hand in her tiny ones, tugging at him to get his attention. Myst held the bark they were using as a plate out to him.

"Here. Eat." Myst shoved it against his chest after a moment before sitting with a glare, until he popped a handful into his mouth, which seemed to satisfy her.

Chapter 7

Aphir's Anger

Aphir's fist split the mahogany desk as it connected, anger radiating his whole being, a menacing aura of red engulfing him, as splinters of wood, maps and plans went scattering through the air. Caru was bowed down on one knee before the man, shoulders tense as he dared not look up, teeth gritted as ink splattered across his face and armour, trying to keep a calm composure when in reality he was terrified.

"You let them get outside my domain?" Aphir's chest heaved, his voice low and dripping with malice, black eyes wide with rage. Aphir had been alerted shortly after Fen had escaped that his cell was empty. Moments later he learned of the failed assassination of his son. His chambers had been set ablaze in an instant, his anger unrivalled as he stormed through his castle walls, ordering everyone to start looking. He had made his way straight to his weapon's cell, following the bloody trail and blowing open the walls to the passageways. He himself had led the charge, following the bloody trail to no avail while he had Caru seal all the gates.

Aphir's anger at learning Caru's failure was to be compared to the legendary black dragon Zyrhou's. It had had the whole realm quaking in their boots.

"T...They blew open the walls, my Lord," Caru started with a stutter, barely hiding his flinch as Aphir snarled.

"Fayon escaped! With my weapon! You useless bastard! Not only have you failed to kill my son, but you lost my masterpiece!" He screamed, his fist connecting with Caru's jaw, sending the smaller male toppling down. A bruise bloomed on his cheek instantly, blood running from his nose as he scrambled back onto his knees and kowtowed in front of his king.

"I'm sorry, I'm sorry... this lowly one begs for his king's forgiveness... he will fix this. I will find the boy, I'll drag him back with my bare hands... this lord will have his weapon back, he will, he will..." Caru's forehead smacking against the ground constantly, the mighty soldier grovelling for his life, bowing, arms outstretched on the floor, face red from the force of his head connecting with the cold cobbled ground with every bow.

Aphir looked down at his captain in disgust, a sharp flash running through his eyes before black flames engulfed Caru. The smell of burning flesh instantly filled the room, along with the haunting screams of the once high-ranking man. Aphir's face twisted into a sadistic smile, as he raised his hand to increase the intensity of the flames, his hair wild, crown tilted to one side as he began to laugh.

The twisted laugh soon covered the screams, which slowly began to diminish until there were none. The black flames wiped Caru from existence in a matter of seconds, leaving nothing but ash and char on the floor he'd once grovelled upon.

Slowly the king's laughter fell into silence. He let out a long-drawn sigh, jewelled hands crossing behind his back as he walked through the ashes. He held no respect for Caru in life or death. Aphir just walked straight through, shaking the bottom of his robes free of the grey powder as he stopped at the door, straightening his sleeve with a small tug, correcting his royal appearance.

Aphir then threw open the heavy doors to the hallway,

standing there silently for a moment, observing the pale faces of his royal guards stationed outside, their faces tinted green with nausea.

"Captain Caru is no longer your commander. His incompetence was far too great this time. Fetch me Lord Culvat," Aphir drawled, a bored look on his face. He really should have drawn out his subordinate's death – he had nothing to take out his anger upon anymore.

Two plans, hundreds of years in the making, foiled just like that. It was very safe to assume he had never quite reached this level of anger, yet the calm exterior frightened the young guards more. One raced off at once to find the lord before their king found their lack of response deserving of the same fate as Captain Caru.

Aphir turned back to his study, glancing around at the mess he had created and moved a hand to rub his temple, eyebrow twitching in irritation.

"Someone get the maids to clean this up." There was another flurry of sound as another guard raced off to do as their king bid.

Aphir himself shook out his robes and walked to his chair, leaning to the side, one arm propping his head up, legs crossed and the other hand lightly tapping his fingers against the wood. He looked incredibly majestic. There was no doubting Aphir was extremely handsome, a sharply-angled jaw, piercing onyx black eyes, beautifully curved nose, long unruly black hair and defined muscles on his long limbs. He was every bit as regal as a king should be.

But what he lacked was personality. He was feared by all, a tyrant who happily enslaved his own people, not just other races. Those around him feared that to put even a toe out of line meant facing horrible punishments or

71

even death. Those who thought as he did rose high in society. The realm's capital Nisha was filled with those following Aphir's every whim, plotting to create war and chaos in the world, to bring back their mighty nation from the ashes their ancestors had left them with.

He was to the wealthy their saviour and lord, while he was the poor's captor and tormentor. Those with no power forced to conform to him, their voices otherwise silenced or their families enslaved. Aphir was the perfect tyrant, one who because of old treaties was ignored by the world, making his ambitions and aims all the more easy to attain. He'd take back what his father had given up, regain what they were owed and massacre all in his way, his enemies having little warning of the calamity about to descend upon them. He would ensure this world would burn for thinking they had pacified the demon-bloods to Prophet for all of time.

Aphir would make sure this world would know pain like no other and ensure the angel-bloods were blamed for the fate this world would fall to. Revenge would be his no matter what he had to sacrifice to get it.

He fell heavily back onto his chair, watching as maids scurried in, setting to work quickly removing all signs that such a brutal murder had been committed in that room just minutes ago. They were clearly well trained and talented in cleaning up after their king, having had to clean up such aftermaths of rage many times before.

The tapping of Aphir's fingers picked up speed the longer he waited for Culvat, a frown of irritation forming upon his brow. Scorch marks and smoke appeared in the wood from where he tapped. Making him wait was not a good idea. Clearly his men all had death wishes today.

His gaze immediately shifted to the door when in

swept a rather unremarkable-looking man. His greyed hair was tied in a neat ponytail, his jaw firm, but his crooked nose and dull eyes left anything to be desired. This man truly was graced with poor looks. His robes were black with silver stitching around the sleeve hems and neckline. The silk outer robes opened enough at the chest to see the plain grey under robes beneath the finery. It was obvious from his build he was a warrior, yet no armour adorned his body, as if he had been in too much of a hurry to don a warrior's garb and had instead chosen the simpler robes of a noble.

The man bowed down on one knee in front of his king, lifting his head for grey eyes to meet black.

"I have heeded my King's summons; how may this lowly lord be of aid to His Greatness?" The man known as Culvat spoke, his accent thick and well spoken. He was a demon-blood of high calibre and station with over eighteen thousand years in this world, yet still looking as a human would in their prime of life. In short, he was the elder to the king, the man Aphir sought counsel from when his plans needed a mind of great wisdom. There were very few demon-blooded alive today that held the knowledge this man had.

"I assume you already know what has happened?" Aphir slowly sat himself up, eyes lowered to meet his subordinate, waiting for the man's nod of conformation. "What does my adviser suggest we do? The boy is not dead, we have nothing to frame the angel-blooded with. If we leave Prophet without that, the world will hold no blame to those angel bastards! What's more, if they are not accused of a murder that starts a war, their pride remains undamaged and there is no way they will leave that land they have sealed themselves within. My vengeance, our *retribution*, will not be complete until anyone descended from an angel is lying dead at my feet! With the world spitting on their very existence! But not only this! What is even worse is my masterpiece, the weapon of prophecy. The thing to win all wars was taken by my good-for-nothing, powerless shit of a child and his whimpering elf servant!" Aphir's voice grew steadily louder and more snarled as he went, fist slamming against the chair's arm rests, fingers clenched so tightly that blackened blood slowly dripped from the creases of his skin.

"My King, please remain calm, there is no need for anger... all is still salvageable. If my King is willing to listen to what I have devised to fix our current issues, of course." Culvat spoke with no fear in his words. He clearly need not fear that Aphir would kill him; the man needed him after all.

Aphir leaned forward instantly, hands clasped together, head resting on them, a cruel smirk running across his lips.

"Enlighten me, Culvat. Just what has your brilliant mind concocted this time?"

Culvat's lips curled up nastily. "Come with me, my King. I think you will enjoy what I have created."

Chapter 8

Culvat and Velka

Aphir looked down at the mutilated body in front of him. It was laid out on a stone table, clothes in fine battle garbs, the face smashed in beyond all recognition. He circled around, mentally checking off things in his head. Correct height, hair colour accurate, the correct muscle tone for a trained fighter, one who had focused solely on weapons training rather than magic, likely as their magic was either feeble or non-existent. The body had been cut down with slashes across the legs, arms and chest, two through-and-through stab marks, one that pierced the heart and the other a lung. Then it looked like the attackers had kicked the deceased in the face as a message. A chuckle escaped his lips as he stopped circling the body and looked to Culvat.

"Impressive. If I were not already aware my son had escaped beyond my realm I would have been fooled. This is rather a perfect copy of Fayon. Where were you able to find such a specimen?" Aphir ran his fingers through the blooded ebony hair, enjoying the sticky feeling it left. Oh, how much more he would be enjoying this moment if it were actually that useless son of his. But that would come with time – he would have Fayon's head on display.

"I located him as a child, grooming him to be the perfect decoy if the need ever arose. In this instance he was needed to provide a body to offend the honour of our dear angel-blooded brethren. Of course, his face would have fooled the common subjects, but I felt they would be far more enraged had our prince's attackers mutilated his body. His face was the obvious choice. The attack and murder of our only prince was very vicious after all." Culvat spoke with great pride in his work. The youth had been more than willing to train to be his prince's decoy. Of course, his death had to look authentic as well. He had his best trained assassins jump the boy on his return to his chambers.

Culvat had stood in the shadows, watching with great fascination at the child's defence against his attackers. He truly had put up a magnificent fight, even slitting the throat of one of his favourite men. But in the end, he couldn't compete against far older and far more experienced assassins. He had fallen to the ground, drowning in his own blood as his face was kicked and kicked, breaking apart any distinguishing features. It wasn't until he'd been gasping and gurgling that the two long swords had been thrust through his chest, Culvat's creation ceasing to exist in that moment.

A perfect end to his life, the perfect body to offend those arrogant angels into leaving their domain to defend their honour. To prove they did not kill and break the treaty, to protect the innocents as those poofy bastards had always claimed to in the past.

"With the body and the weapon provided to us by our contact, no one will be able to dispute that an angel-blooded killed the prince. They will be forced to join the war; it will be called for by all those who allied themselves with them. The king will have no choice but to protect those who blame them while trying to clear their names of any wrongdoing, just as they always have. This time they will be the ones slaughtered under our blades." Culvat held up a beautiful white long sword, its hilt covered in intricate swirled silver and a jade handle.

The white blade was incredibly thin but the metal did not bend or crack, no matter what weapon or surface it clashed against.

The craftsmanship of the angel-blooded was unparalleled and uncopiable. This weapon was proof of a treaty breach, a treaty that stated demon-bloods would not leave their realm, and the angel-blooded would not breach their borders.

This sword could be used to show the angel-blooded had broken their oath and put the final nail in the coffin needed to start Aphir's long-awaited war.

"What about the preparations for finding my weapon?" Aphir asked as he began to leave the cool room, a wave of his hand signalling the morticians to deal with the body. The funeral after all needed to be fit for a prince.

"I have sent ravens to our allies outside of Prophet's domain," Culvat said. "The Tong Hill giant clans have been alerted to the situation, as well as the Valser Plains orc packs. They will further inform the Terret goblins. They have been told to form raiding parties and attack settlements to create panic and turmoil before we even declare war. They have all of course been informed of the true goal. To locate our weapon. The instructions are as follows. Fayon and anyone else travelling with the angel-blooded are to be killed on sight, but the boy himself is to be captured alive and unharmed. They will bring him back to you, my King. With that, many dark creatures are already looking. It will not be long before all our allies hear of the hunt. Your son will not be able to hide his group for long."

"Good, very good. You never disappoint, Culvat." Aphir chuckled darkly as the pair walked side-by-side,

Aphir towering over his counsellor.

"Of course, my King. My job is to make sure your ambitions are realised. I have used every resource at my disposal to ensure it."

Aphir's hand came to rest upon Culvat's shoulder, a pleased look gracing his handsome features. It almost made him look sane. Almost. Culvat of course looked most pleased at this gesture of praise. He had ensured that he still had his king's favour.

"Have a reward of crimson pearls set up for whoever brings my weapon back. Let's liven up the hunt a bit." The smile turned sadistic. Each of those pearls was worth at least five hundred gold pieces. A reward of twenty or so should ensure that those pathetic life forms stop at nothing to get his weapon back to him. Yes, that would do nicely.

Aphir was a very pleased man. His thwarted plans had in short been pieced back together, and he had a body for his people to mourn. A body which would have a grand funeral and spark the hatred in his people against the angel-blooded, leading to an unquestioned want for war.

His son, after all had been loved by those roaches, which had its merits when it came to his final plans. Within the span of two weeks his whole realm would be geared up and ready to march to war. Those who had settled on the lands around would have been killed, their homes razed to the ground by his underlings, and most importantly he would have his weapon. His perfect weapon. That boy would be back in his grasp and this time he wouldn't allow him any free will. That had been a mistake on his part.

In leaving the boy's free will intact he had hoped to cause more pain to the boy's family when they realised who was slaughtering their people. But no, the child had been too stubborn, much like anyone of his blood. So his free will would have to be stripped from him the second he got his hands back on him. No prophesised child was going to unite the world. No. He would have him destroy it.

"Tell me when the Draught of Zaro will be completed. I want it in the child the moment he returns."

"Velka has assured me she possesses all the ingredients to brew the draught. It should take no more than two moon's time to brew." Culvert had his arms crossed behind his back as he spoke, a light frown crossing his face at what he had to say next.

"Why do you frown?" Aphir said as he glanced at the shorter of the pair. Hearing his companion's audible sigh, he was already very aware he would not like what was about to be spoken.

"Velka has, however, requested she not brew it until the subject is captured and on his way back here. The danger levels of allowing it to ferment before consumption pose a risk to destroy the mind instead of simply locking it away. If that were to happen, she assures me that we would lose any chance of a weapon and be left with a lump of useless flesh." Culvat spoke very seriously. He had to make sure Aphir knew the risks and did not command anything that could completely destroy the child they had all worked so hard on creating all these years.

Aphir stood still for a long time, frown etched on his features. Waiting to brew it meant it could not be administered the second he was captured. However, he could not afford anything else setting his plans back, and a useless weapon would do just that. With an annoyed grunt he spoke.

"Very well. Inform her the moment he is within the realm she shall create the draught. Also have her burn any mentions of cures from our records." In the slim chance the angel-blooded beat them in battle, he did not want them to ever be able to set free his weapon from his control. The boy would forever cause them pain.

"All mentions of a cure, my King? But surely…" Culvat hesitated. It seemed too risky. What if they themselves required the cure to fix the weapon if things went wrong? He could not even propose such words before his king spoke again in a harsh tone.

"Did you not hear me, Culvat? *All* records. No one will free him this time, there will be no loose ends. Do you understand me?" His eyes flashed with a murderous look that instantly had Culvat bowing his head.

"Forgive me, of course His Highness is correct. I will see to it that the records are destroyed personally." Culvat quickly scurried backwards into the door, keeping himself bowed low until he heard a grunt and the swishing of a robe as his king stormed away, out the room and down the hall. It was only then that Culvat let out the breath he'd been holding. In the matter of one conversation, he had gone from being praised to nearly strangled. He knew better than to question Aphir yet had tried anyway. He was truly lucky to have walked away unscathed from that interaction. Others Aphir met on the way would not be so lucky. His temper truly had no rival.

Slowly, Culvat raised his head and straightened his posture, gently brushing off his robes, clearing his throat, making the guards behind him stand to attention.

"Prepare the body for procession, a black veil to cover his face. There is no need for the people to see such a sight – it is best left to their imaginations as to the state the angel-bloods left their prince in. Imagination is a far better tool." Culvat smirked to himself. Yes, let them imagine what had happened to his face. It would bring such uproar, and in turn more people flocking to join the army's ranks in revenge for their treasured prince.

"Yes, my Lord," came a chorus of young voices, a shuffle of movement occurring behind him as he slowly walked down the hall, arms clasped in front of him, nodding his head to all those who bowed as they passed him or he them. He made his way through the castle's maze-like mess of halls until he reached a dark spiral staircase at the southern end of the grounds. Ascending the steps, Culvat made his way up into what the common folk referred to as the tower of death.

In reality it was Velka's apothecary, a room filled with exotic herbs and animal parts. It was a haven for those in the brewing arts, and hell for those who were subjected to what came out of it.

Culvat pulled a handkerchief out of the sleeve of his robe, pressing it to his nose as he pushed the door open with his foot, not daring to touch anything with his hands. Especially after what had happened the last time he was here.

Inside the room there was a short, thin girl in faded purple robes, her brown hair screwed up in a messy bun with strands flying in every direction and needles stuffed through the bulk to keep it in place. Her yellow eyes were glowing as she held a jar in front of her eyes, watching the tongue inside wiggle and squirm, causing her to cackle away. In short, she truly looked mad. The room itself was covered in shelves, piled with books, potted plants as well as jars stuffed with curiosities and exotics.

The smell of decay was overwhelming. It truly deserved the moniker given by the commoners.

"Velka, if you're done watching the sprite's tongue wiggle we have matters to discuss," Culvat said. His pinched nose caused his voice to be slightly pitched, his face wrinkled in disgust at the state of the room. "Do you not know how to clean? Disgusting."

The woman spun to look at him, a pout on her dark lips.

"Oh Culvey, don't be such a killjoy. It's not every day I get a part that still moves after it's cut free from the body, now is it." Velka cackled away, jumping up and down as she hugged her jar. She looked no older than a fifteen-year-old human but her actions made her seem even younger. Yet in all reality this crazed lady hugging a jar of cut-out tongue was nearing five thousand years old.

Culvat of course gave a disapproving look to the younger demon-blooded, making her stick her lip out in a pout yet again and place the jar down with a dramatic huff. Velka then pulled herself up onto a table, leaning back with her arms behind her, legs crossed as she stared at him with those crazed eyes of hers.

"So, Culvey, what's brought you to my house of horrors? Did you bring me something fun? Oh, please tell me you brought me something fun," she purred out, cat-like eyes glowing in excitement.

"Stop with that ridiculous nickname, Velka," Culvat said in a hard tone before pulling a jar out of his sleeve and placing it down by her hand. The woman instantly sat up, gasping in utter excitement. A wicked grin spread across her face as she snatched the jar up to her eyes, inspecting it with great enthusiasm.

"Oh Culvey, however did you find me a dried

mermaid's heart? It's *magnificent,*" she cooed, holding the jar close, making the elder shake his head at her.

"You are incorrigible. The king has agreed to your request to delay the brewing until we have the child back in our grasp. He has, however, also requested you destroy any records you may have on a cure to your creation." Culvat forgot his idea to not touch anything in favour of wiping a finger across a shelf, rubbing the dust between his fingers with a frown. He thought briefly about sending maids up to clean Velka's orc-sty of a room when he was distracted by Velka gasping and spluttering. Culvat rubbed his temple as the woman waved her fist angrily, jumping down from where she had been sitting, storming forward and poking him hard in the chest with a dangerously pointed nail.

"How dare you! Those records are my babies! I won't do it! I won't hurt my babies!" she yelled out, shadows in the room darkening and creeping up around them as her anger bubbled.

"Simmer down, woman. Do you really dare go against our king's demands!? You will do as you have been commanded if you wish to live," Culvat snarled, glaring down at her, their eyes like daggers as the two had a battle of wills. The shadows around the room slowly receded as Velka's anger simmered down, her teeth still bared at the lord in front of her, however, letting him know she was still displeased. After the shadows went back to normal, she released a little hmph noise and crossed her arms, spinning around.

"You big meanies. Fine, I'll destroy my notes. I hope you're happy." She let out a little feral growl as she walked mournfully to her shelf of tattered leather-bound books, fingers gliding across the spines until she came to a black cover that was barely being held together with how worn through it had become over the years. Pulling out the volume, slamming it down on one of her many workstations, she carefully flicked through the aged yellow pages and ripped out a handful with practised ease.

"Here, that's everything there is." Velka pouted as she shook them out towards Culvat, covering her eyes with a hand when he snatched them from her grasp, only to look back in time to see the small remnants of charred paper falling to the ground.

"Such a waste of hard work," Velka wailed pathetically as she crouched to draw patterns into the ground with the black paper. She pouted as she did so, making Culvat grind his teeth in irritation.

"Just be prepared to make the draught, and clean up this damned room. Its filthy. Truly appalling, Velka."

"Oh, Culvey is always so moody. This room is perfect, purposeful chaos. If you don't like it don't come and see me." Velka smiled sweetly as she stood back up, slowly walking her fingers up his broad chest. Her moods switched in an instant. "Although you could never not visit; you would miss me far too much," she whispered in an almost purring manner, a frown on her face when Culvat snatched her wrist up, using it to shove her back violently.

"Crazy woman," he growled spinning on his heel and exiting the door, Velka's laughs echoing behind him as he went.

That woman truly was infuriating. A shameless flirt, a crazy woman. If it were not for her brewing skills he would have killed her years ago.

"One day, your uses will come to an end, Velka," he

growled to himself as he clenched his fists.

As he descended the staircase he slid his left hand into his sleeve, pulling out the real yellowed pages Velka had given him. Culvat was not stupid. To destroy the cure could cause all manner of problems. But he could not have the witch know that her work still existed. No, he had planned far head of even Velka's madness. He had simply stored a scrap of paper within his sleeves on his way to see her, switching it for Velka's notes in the seconds she had looked away. He would simply memorise the cure himself. Whether he would burn the papers or hide them after he had yet to decide, but to not have the cure at all?

That would put his life in danger but he could not have her know, as he had no doubt she would alert Aphir. But he was doing what was best for their goals. His king may not see it, but they had to be prepared. This child had escaped once when no one thought he could. He couldn't risk the boy becoming useless to them. He also needed to be prepared if the draught was somehow used on Aphir instead. Every possible outcome had to have a counter strategy. This cure was the Draught of Zaro's counter strategy.

"Forgive me, my King, but I must disobey your orders this time. For the games have begun, and we must be prepared for everything. Soon, my King, you will rule over all." Culvat spoke to no one, but his words were for the whole world.

Chapter 9

You Were Supposed To Be What?

Fayon looked up at the sky. The sun was already beginning to set and he'd watched more than a few ravens fly overhead in the past few hours. In all likelihood he knew that they were messenger ravens, which would mean his father's dark creatures, his allies, would be looking for him soon. They had rested here long enough. Who knew how close those vile creatures were to them to begin with? Fayon did not wish to find out. They would be quickly overwhelmed if they did encounter any of these orc packs and the like.

"Think much harder and that pretty head of yours may explode," Lulen teased as he dropped down beside the younger. He had been using the trees for vantage points after Fayon had dragged him away a few hours ago, while Fayon had been on the ground. Neither had gone back to their little camp as of yet.

"You have seen the ravens, haven't you. It's just as we suspected. Your father wouldn't let you go so easily," Lulen said, looking up at the sky as Fayon was doing.

"The danger keeps growing. We should find somewhere safe for you, Fen and the girls to hide. I should go on alone," Fayon said softly, his fists clenching at his side. He didn't want to lead anyone to their deaths by having them stay beside him.

Lulen just snorted at that, shaking his head at Fayon's look of surprise. "With all due respect to you, my Prince, hiding us somewhere will do no good. We are safer in a group, protecting each other. Besides, your father is not so unobservant as to not realise I aided in your escape by now. My life is no less dangerous being beside you or away from you. Given the choice I will stay beside my friend." Lulen smiled, his eyes crinkling in the corners as he gently punched the younger's shoulder. "There is also the fact that with the markings on all your foreheads, no person is going to willingly protect those two little ones. Therefore, they will be safer with us protecting them rather than trying to find someone else who would take in a demon-blood. Then of course there is Fen. I'm sure you've realised what he is by now. Even with your oddly calm behaviour around a race that typically demon-bloods have hated, and vice versa..."

"Before you continue that statement, Fen is not like that. He wouldn't have saved Nilee or Myst, he wouldn't have come to save me if he thought like that. Fen may be quite literally a race created by the angels to counter the demons' creation of us, but I do not fear him, nor will I change my first impressions of him. That he is a kind soul." Fayon glanced sideways at his friend, crimson eyes almost dancing with emotion as he spoke.

Lulen smiled softly. "Always so fast to judge me. I was commending you on not reacting as most of your race would have. Although..." He paused looking very seriously at his friend, as if he were about to say something grave. "What was with you so gallantly moving to do his hair hmm?" Lulen nudged his shoulder, bursting out into musical laughter when he caught the slight red to the tips of his ears.

"It was his eyes," Fayon muttered.

"Hmm what was that? His eyes? Were you mesmerised by them? Is that why you combed it out and used your own ribbon? So, you could look at his stunning eyes?" Lulen jumped back when he was swung at, laughing at the scowl he was receiving. "Ay ay, alright, I will stop my teasing. But in all seriousness, Fen's safety is even less guaranteed. I cannot think of a single good reason as to why there was a bruised and beaten angel-blooded within the castle walls. I suspect it is not just our names on the list your father has been sending out." Lulen sighed, hiding and travelling with a group of five was going to be rather tricky. He would have to rethink some choices, he had to take into account the two girls. They were not going to be able to scale a mountain, they could be carried but it made things too dangerous. "We will need to take a different route than I had planned to. It's riskier for being spotted but the girls cannot scale a mountain as we could."

Fayon rubbed his face but nodded in agreement. "You are sure we will be safe in the Fareen woodlands?"

"My people will not bring harm to you or our group. Nor will they disclose your being there, on that you have my word." Lulen put his hand on his chest.

Fayon let out a relieved sigh. Good. They would have somewhere to take refuge, somewhere that wouldn't be so easily infiltrated by his father's spies. He just hoped it would stay safe.

Lulen rolled his shoulders a little as he started walking again, pulling Fayon by the arm to avoid leaving him standing there alone in thought.

"We should set off soon – we need to pack and use the night as cover. We will be harder to spot, and the cooler air should allow the horses to run for longer. The further we can get before your father's allies begin to move the better." Lulen spoke softly as they walked across the leaf-covered ground. Their footsteps were silent, as if their feet didn't even make contact with the earth.

As the pair arrived back at the clearing, they found a rather sweet scene indeed, that even made Lulen smile softly. Nilee was curled up on Fen's lap fast asleep, while Fen and Myst were sitting using leaves to create pictures. It was such a sweet scene, one neither thought they would ever see. The image of an angel-blooded caring for demon-blooded children as if it were the most normal thing on this plain. Fen glanced up and smiled seeing them. He had not reacted at all to their arrival at that point, which had Lulen questioning whether he had known it was them, or if Fen wasn't as alert to danger as he needed to be. They would need to discuss that.

Fen saw that Lulen was about to speak and proceeded to gently put a finger to his lips, asking him to speak softly as he didn't want to wake Nilee.

Fayon just smiled back, moving to sit himself down beside Fen and look down at the picture the pair had been creating. There were a variety of colours; yellows, reds, greens, blues and pinks from nearby flowers that had clearly been picked. The little childish art was just a messed-up jumble. Fayon couldn't tell what they had been trying to create, but both looked proud and seemed to be waiting for him to say something.

"It's beautiful," he reassured them, looking at it for the first time. Myst reacted like a child, smiling away as she moved to grab some sticks to add to her work of art. Then there was Fen. He had to be about eight hundred years old at least, seventeen, an adult in terms of human ageing, and yet he had such a childlike happiness to his face at that moment. As if this was the first time he'd done something so simple. So carefree. Fayon felt an increasingly familiar ache in his heart.

89

"Fen... how long have you been in my father's realm? Why were you there? Prophet is not a place for creatures of light," Fayon asked softly. He had no idea what he was expecting the answer to be. He had honestly been dreading asking; finding out scared him. Finding out the depth of his father's insanity was a terrifying notion, but not knowing how Fen would react to being asked... he felt terror to his core about that.

Lulen who had been quietly repacking and resaddling the horses paused what he was doing, tilting his head to listen. He was beyond curious as to the answer to Fayon's questions.

Fen poked at the ground with a stick, watching the mud give way. For a moment it seemed like he wasn't going to say anything. But then he dropped the stick, sucking in a little breath, opening his mouth to speak.

"In realm... cell... all life... not... don't re...remember... before." Fen looked at Fayon, eyes questioning whether he understood him. Since he was sure there was a time before but whatever it was, he did not know... He wanted them to understand that. He must have memories of before that cell somewhere in his mind. He just... for now, all he had known was that cell.

Fayon's heart hurt even more hearing that. If Fen only had memories of that cell, he must have lived there even as a small child. His fists clenched tight. Why do such a thing to a child? The wounds, the torture, his disjointed speech...

Fen's speech pattern told him he was piecing together words he had heard to try and match with how they spoke around him. Even with the almost toddler-like speech, his voice was gentle, like waves washing against sand. Fayon promised himself then and there that he'd make sure he taught Fen as they travelled, to give him a proper voice. Something he was certain Fen had not had nearly ever in his life.

Fayon was sitting almost making an education plan when all his thoughts stopped in an instant, grinding almost everything to a deadly stop. All because of the next three words that came from Fen's lips.

"Was... his weapon."

"Weapon?" Fayon choked out, anger boiling within him, threatening to spill out as Fen simply nodded in response to his question.

"To kill... did not want... escaped... say... wanted Fay... dead. I wanted... you not... dead." Fen spoke softly, looking at him with a breathtakingly bright smile. Fayon's brow furrowed a little, before smiling and gently patting Fen's soft white hair.

"Thank you. For escaping him, saving me and saving yourself. And Fen? Don't... don't stop calling me Fay. I rather like it." His voice held so much emotion that Fen's eyes shimmered with worry for him. But the smile came right back when Fayon told him he liked his name. Fen almost wiggled in happiness at that.

Fayon felt like he'd swallowed a bitter pill. All this time he had hated his life, how his father treated him, plotted against him, and yet three floors down Fen had been tortured for hundreds of years. Yet his decision to escape only came when Fayon's life – someone Fen had never even met – became endangered. Tortured all those years yet still he was able to see the world for its beauty, able to smile and have a childlike wonder about everything he saw. He was able to care about people he'd never met before, trust without fear despite everything he'd endured. Fayon kept his hand resting on Fen's head, simply admiring the teen before him. If this was how all angel-blooded were, he could not find any reason for the hate towards them. *They were beautiful in every way... <u>he</u> was beautiful in every way.*

"Is Fay... alright?" Fen asked quietly, staring at him with wide blue-golden eyes, sitting perfectly still as Fayon's hand rested on his head. Fayon smiled softly, pulling his hand away and nodded.

"I am alright, Fen... I promise you won't ever be treated like that again. I... no, *we* all will keep you safe."

Fen moved as he said that and patted Fayon's head just like he had his a moment ago, tilting his head to the side with a big smile, eyes twinkling. It utterly lit up his face, making Fayon give a tiny, twitched smile right back. The awful feeling in his chest subsiding a fraction the second he saw the smile. *Fen truly is amazing*, he thought, *to smile like that after all he's endured.*

"Trust Fay."

Just like that he had Fen's trust, he had done nothing to earn it but a few simple gestures, but he would never betray the trust he was given. Fayon knew that the second Fen uttered those words to him.

Fen had saved his life, been tortured, escaped a horrid fate. He was battered and bruised yet smiled like he had lived a truly amazing life. Even if Fen became the best warrior, mage, healer, whatever he would become, Fayon swore to the heavens then and there that even on the day Fen no longer required protection, he would still be there right by his side. For the rest of time. They were fated to meet, fated to laugh, hurt, cry, run, fated to have converged at this point. He had no other way to describe it, but he was sure Lulen, the twins and Fen must all feel the same. They were fated to meet and travel together. He would protect them all with his life.

Fen watched thoughts running through Fayon's mind, staying quiet and not disrupting him. He glanced at the sleeping Nilee, then to the silent-as-a-mouse Myst, a small frown on his face, before he finally looked at Lulen.

Lulen had his head bowed. A kidnapped angel-blooded, no memory of his past and made to be a weapon. It made no sense – the demon-blooded had enough power and magic to combat against angel-bloods in a war, so why steal one of them to turn into his weapon? Fen had to be special in some way that they weren't seeing. It was the only logical thing that made sense.

To the eye, yes, admittedly he was truly beautiful, like a carved jade statue, but he was sure all angel-bloods had been described as so. The gold mark on his forehead symbolised his rank within the angel-blooded society, but Lulen had little idea of the different markings, so he couldn't just assume Fen was high born. He could already see the marking was completely different to the red Fayon and the twins possessed.

His power had been impressive, but light magic was one of the two powers all angel-blooded had the Elemental blessings to learn. Whether the magic was powerful by angel-blooded standards was again something he couldn't hazard a guess. There was a chance his Lord and Lady may know, but it would be weeks before he could even ask them. For now, those questions couldn't be answered. All he could do was think of scenarios that seemed diabolical enough for Aphir to have concocted.

So was it that Aphir had just wanted to wound the

pride of his enemy by having them slaughtered by their own kind? Or maybe make them hesitate when seeing what he could turn even an angel-blooded into? If it was that one, he had failed miserably. Fen seemed utterly unaffected by the torments of his past, at least on the outside anyway.

A prophecy maybe? Lulen could hazard a guess that like most races there were a mountain of foretold events and prophecies within Celestia. Maybe Fen fell into one of those.

His hand came up to pinch the bridge of his nose. So many questions with no answers. For now, one thing was clear, Fayon and Fen were both in danger and for the events of the last two days to have unfolded as they had, their fates were intertwined. If it were a prophecy, both had to be involved somehow. But then there was Myst and Nilee. Himself, even. All five of their fates were interwoven – that he was sure – but a prophecy to include so many people? It was just highly unheard of. He was sure, once he returned home, he would find some answers. There had to be some answers there.

Lulen let out a loud sigh, which made Fen frown even more, as both Lulen and Fayon seemed so lost in thought. He was beginning to question whether he should have said anything in the first place, given how they all reacted. He watched as Lulen shook his head and pulled the last saddle strap taut.

"While this was very enlightening, we really need to leave before Aphir's patrols start moving. If you have any more questions, ask them as we ride, Fayon. We have wasted enough on your foolish whims." Lulen sounded incredibly cold and unsympathetic towards Fen, as well as harsh towards his prince.

He ignored the glare of Fayon and the guilty look on Fen's face as he made long strides over to the group. Saying nothing more as scooped Myst off the ground in one swift motion, hauling her into his arms before moving back to his stallion, placing the small girl on before he mounted up behind her. Myst looking entirely put out being carried like a child.

"You big meany!" she huffed out. "And don't pick me up! I don't like you. Grumpy elf." Myst stuck her tongue out at him, although she was completely ignored by Lulen, only receiving a disapproving look from Fen.

"Stand up already, we do not have time to waste. You act as if you're not being hunted by an insane king. Get up!" Lulen snapped.

Fayon gave Lulen a little glare, before he carefully took the sleeping Nilee from Fen's lap and cradled her against his chest.

"Mount up, I'll pass her up to you," Fayon spoke in a whisper as the pair walked to the splattered mare. Fayon carefully helped situate Nilee safely against Fen once he had mounted up. The sleepy girl nuzzled as close as she could into Fen.

Fen himself had one hand on the reins and the other wrapped around Nilee to make sure she would not fall as they rode. With the pair situated, Fayon finally mounted his own steed, a midnight black stallion, one he had raised himself.

Lulen moved the second they were all ready, pulling sharply to the left, away from the looming mountains that they would have originally raced towards. Now Lulen was steering them instead westbound, towards the human settlements. They would reach those by the eve of two days' time. Then, sticking to the outskirts of these small villages and towns, they would start heading southwards again until they reached the Valyrine pass.

A chunk of the Valyin mountains had been carved out over time by dwarfs for trade access between the two sides of the mountain. If they were lucky, they would only take two weeks to reach this area. Although it was longer than heading directly for the mountains and scaling them, it was far less dangerous for the children of the group.

However, it wasn't safe by any means. The danger with using the passage was it was known for its ambushes and slaughters, making it one of the most feared regions this side of the Valyin mountains. Merchants, caravans... you name it. No one passed through without hired mercenaries and guards to protect them.

Their group of course couldn't afford to do that. It would take time they didn't have. They had to reach this pass before any of the region's orc or goblin clans descended down on them. In short, it was a race against time. They could afford little time to rest, or make the silver needed to afford protection. It was risky but the only course of action they could take at this point.

"Don't let your guards down. If anyone sees anything we change direction or hide instantly," Lulen said, finally looking back at the two younger men as he rode, receiving their confirming nods.

With that, on their journey through northern Aleria, Lulen and Myst brought up the front, while Fayon rode side-by-side with Fen and Nilee. The real challenges were still to come, but it seemed only Lulen was aware of that fact. The real danger was only just beginning. Escaping the black walls would soon look like child's play. Their lives were in far more danger now than they had ever been. Lulen had the responsibility of five lives on his shoulders. Tension consumed his posture as they rode into the unknown.

Chapter 10

Darkness Begins Its Descent

Two days passed in the blink of an eye. The eve of that second day was now looming, and Lulen was growing tenser by the second. There should have been sounds of humans by now, he was sure they were close to settlements. He had kept a constant eye on the stars as well as the rise of the sun, so they could not have got lost. Yet he heard none of the sounds he would expect.

There was no rowdy laughing of drunkards, or children giggling. He heard not the sound of dogs barking. It was like an all-encompassing silence. There was even an absence of birds chirping. His hands tightened against the reins as he slowed himself to a stop.

The last two days had seen Fayon riding beside Fen the entire time, Myst having moved to sit in front of him soon into their ride. The girl wanted to be able to talk to her sister after all. Fayon had kept to his thoughts and spent nearly the entire time teaching Fen words and their meanings. Myst and Nilee were all too happy to help Fayon in his endeavour. Of course, this teaching also included telling Fen every little thing about anything he showed an interest in. The two small girls and Fen's eyes had almost been glued to Fayon the entire ride, soaking in everything they were told. So much was new to even the little girls after all.

Fayon's lips were turned up at the corners almost the entire time, completely amazed by how much they could question and what they took in in such a short time.

What was even more impressive was that just the day

before Fen's speech had been disjointed at best. Yet today he had filled in his gaps. With just Fayon's small help, Fen spoke fluently, sounding nothing like someone who could not fathom such words hours ago. Fayon suspected he had the knowledge all along, it had just gone dormant from lack of use and contact for hundreds of years.

In short words, the twins and Fen were thriving. The new environment had had a positive effect on each of them, Nilee coming out her shell, Myst less defensive, still just as tough though, and Fen... he was just Fen, but with the ability to express himself properly for the first time. Even Lulen who had stayed silent and on edge the entire journey was impressed.

The four were completely engrossed in a conversation about frogs of all things when Lulen had stopped, the two horses rearing up a fraction when they found their path blocked by Lulen's now sideways grey stallion blocking their way forward.

"Lulen, what's wrong?" Fayon asked before the elf placed his finger to his lip and cocked his head to listen again. Fen copied the motion, eyes closing as he focused in on his other senses as he had been taught.

Lulen's frown deepened as he listened, turning his gaze back to Fayon in a questioning look. When he received a shake of the head his body grew more tense. Neither of them could hear anything. This was not a good sign.

"We carry on slow..." Lulen didn't even finish his words when Fen held up his hand in a motion of silence. Which surprised everyone; Fen had never interrupted anyone before.

Fen's eyes remained closed, his head tilting more in

the direction of the wind, focusing on what the wind was telling him. Burning, the charred scent of cremated wood, and intermixed he could make out the faint stench of charred flesh. His nose wrinkled in disgust before he lowered his head further, focusing on sound this time, the crackling and popping that cooling wood made after a fire, small chunks hitting dusty ground. Shuffled heavy steps moving away from them. He suspected they were around 700 paces south of where the charred wood was.

Fen began to piece together what had occurred. Large creatures moving away, silence, smoke and burnt flesh... His chest began to grow tight. There had been an attack, and he already knew from the smell it had been a massacre, such needless hate and death. This was exactly what he wished to stop. His jaw clenched and the four members of his group all looked confused at their angel-blooded companion, worry evident on some of their faces.

Nilee reached and gently held Fen's hand, making the angel-blooded's eyes snap open.

"Fen?" she whispered out, almost sounding scared.

"What did you hear?" Fayon asked, looking as curious as Lulen. Both males had far superior hearing to most races, so it was safe to assume Fen had as well. But for him to hear what they could not... it didn't seem like it was natural. As neither had heard of angel-bloods possessing hearing greater than those of elven bloodlines or demon bloodlines. Only full-blooded angels and demons had greater senses, and they were all buried in history now.

"There was a village a thousand or so paces in this direction," Fen said, "maybe consisting of 20 houses, possibly less. It's been burnt to the ground. The smell of blood indicates some were murdered, the burnt flesh suggests others were burnt, alive or dead I don't know. I cannot discern any heartbeats or breathing among the ashes... There are faint footsteps of a group moving southbound, maybe a party of fifty. They are heavy footed. It's difficult to say accurately – a larger race, definitely. Maybe about seven hundred paces from the village at this point. They were likely the ones who massacred and burnt it down." Fen spoke with confidence and full tactical knowledge, so much so to both elder men he sounded like an experienced general, tactician and tracker all in one.

To the little girls what he spoke of scared them endlessly, to think a whole village had just been wiped out. It was like something out of a horror story. Everyone just sat staring at Fen in utter silence as he continued speaking. He was definitely no longer a stuttering toddler. Fayon had taught him swift and well.

"I suggest we do not move until they are out of hearing range, then move forward to the village. If there are survivors we should aid them. If not, I believe that the funeral rites of humans is to be buried?" Fen questioned looking at the group, not noting the shock or sick looks across the faces. All he could think about was making sure the dead were not left to scavengers, all he could think about was how could anyone kill? There should be no killing... he didn't want to kill, or anyone else to kill.

"How did you know all of that?" Fayon asked after a moment. "We couldn't... there are no sounds, Fen."

"No sounds? There are plenty: the wood is still cracking from heat, you can hear as its parts thud into the dust. Those footsteps are so heavy the ground vibrates from them even at this distance. Then you can smell the burning on the wind, flesh and blood too... You really don't hear, feel or smell any of that?"

"The wind holds no smell to me. It's blowing from the west not the south..." Fayon said, shaking his head. "I do not understand how you could know any of that when the wind does not even blow from the village's direction, let alone the sounds or vibrations."

Fen of course just looked at Fayon with a small frown. He had explained exactly how he knew – was it really so strange that he could tell what they could not?

Lulen ended up clearing his throat as the two stared at each other. "While it is extraordinary that Fen was able to tell such a thing when even we could not, it is not beyond doubt that angel-blooded simply possess finer senses than we were made aware of. Instead of questioning him, what we should be doing is seeing if anyone has been left alive, aiding where we can, and burying the dead as Fen has said. It will also be useful to investigate what exactly attacked this settlement. We must know what we are dealing with."

Lulen's words immediately made Fayon look away from Fen and give a gloomy nod. The demon-blooded was still not satisfied; it was not normal by any means to know any of that. No way were angel-blooded just more sensitive to things than them.

To tell even from so far away which direction the enemy was going in, and how many there were... It was just not sitting well with him. Whatever way he looked at it, he could not find an answer as to why Fen's senses could be so refined. The uncertain feeling bubbled in his chest that, as his father's weapon, Fen had to have been engineered to become in his father's eyes perfect. That had to come with some costs if his theory was true.

For now, it seemed as if he was in fine health aside from his obvious injuries, but what if behind his smiles something was seriously wrong? Because his father had poked and prodded, altered Fen to create his ultimate weapon.

His father was ruthless; he could never put it past him to have done such unforgivable horrors when he had already committed grave acts of hatred upon Fen.

Fayon glanced at Lulen, each giving a tiny nod to the other, a promise they would figure this out, that they would look after Fen. They needed to watch Fen for signs anything was wrong, but also learn whether this was all natural for his race in general. Lulen let out a heavy sigh and looked towards the direction they were headed, chewing on the inside of his lip.

"Alright… Fen are we safe to carry on?" Fayon asked, his deep voice laced with dread. He was very much aware of what they were about to ride into, of the horror they were about to witness. The tone made Fen lean across the gap between their horses and gently pat Fayon's wild ebony hair.

"Fay… sad doesn't suit you, please smile," Fen said, looking at him with the most innocent golden blue eyes. Fayon couldn't help but smile for him. Which in turn had Fen beaming, removing his hand from Fayon's head, satisfied with the smile. Fen swayed all happy in his saddle, before seeming to remember Fayon had actually asked him a question.

"Oh! We can go, yes, I can't hear them now." Fen sheepishly rubbed the back of his head, messing the hair up slightly as he did so.

Fayon couldn't help but chuckle at the younger and made a mental note to correct the now slightly-askew bun on Fen's head.

The air that had been scented by flowers for the rest of them soon grew heavy, as the smells Fen had told them about finally hit the group full force. Nilee looked pale, turning several different shades of green as they grew closer and closer. Myst was putting on a brave face as was her personality, but she had leaned back into Fayon as if to seek comfort from the adult.

Meanwhile the three males of the group all looked grim. Lulen was steadying his breath in preparation as to what they were about to see. Fayon's face was like stone. He betrayed nothing about what he was feeling, shutting it away. Rationality was needed, not to be fuelled by wild emotions. Especially when Fen looked to be drowning in it, waves of anguish rippling around him, as if he felt the despair all the villagers had felt in the moments before their demise. That only seemed to double when they finally broke through the tree line, and the decimated remains of a once-bustling human settlement was revealed.

Hands covered Myst and Nilee's eyes instantly when it became obvious that the twisted, contorted objects in the soot were actually the bodies of this town's inhabitants.

"They shouldn't see this," Fayon spoke after a moment, hand firmly over Myst's eyes.

"Fen, you should..."

"No, I want... I want to help, I can help." Fen stopped him from speaking further. These people had died because he had escaped, because he'd refused to be used as a weapon. He heard Lulen and Fayon talking about how Aphir had likely sent all his allies out to hunt them. This had to be done by one of said allies. It had to be –

who else could be so cruel?

He needed to lay these people to rest, to promise them that they would not have died for nothing. Fen would find who did this. If this world was so cruel that this could be done with no rhyme or reason, then he would change the world. Killing, there would be no more killing.

"Killing... why can't people just *talk?* They did nothing," he whispered, for the first real time sounding completely heartbroken.

Of course, Lulen thought how naive Fen was to think this could ever come to pass. There would always be those that would rather kill first then talk. But Lulen knew all too well this would be a lesson Fen needed to learn himself - there was no changing the world. Not without fighting or war, words had done no good in history and would not in the future. He only hoped Fen realised this soon before he got hurt or killed because of those thoughts.

"Nonsense," Lulen huffed, shaking his head a little, before sighing and running a hand down his face.

"Let me take the girls then. Leave them and the horses with me. You two look around for anyone that may have survived... however unlikely that is." Lulen held his head low as he dismounted his horse, not wanting to see Fen's after what he'd said. Nor could he bring himself to fully face the scene in front of him. A glance had been enough. He felt uneasy and sick. Lulen was already having a hard time swallowing back the bile rising up his throat from this distance; up close he couldn't be sure he would succeed in keeping it back any longer. Even with all the horrors he had been witness to, this was never something that got easier.

Fayon carefully dismounted, lifting Myst, settling her

on the charred grass, making sure she faced towards the tree before he removed the hand from her eyes. Fen copied his movements.

Lulen whistled lightly to make the horses follow him before taking the twins' hands, leading them behind a cluster of trees that would hopefully hinder the two from seeing the smouldering village beyond.

"Do not look out from behind here, understand me."

Nilee clung to Myst, her face pressed into her sister's shoulder, eyes tightly closed while Myst kept her hand over Nilee's eyes for extra insurance. She just stared at Lulen and nodded her head.

"I won't move, and she won't look. We don't need you to babysit us. Go be a useful elf and help them or something." Myst spoke with sass laced through her voice, which had Lulen quirking an eyebrow. She very much had the attitude demon-bloods were known for.

Lulen crouched himself down in front of her and stared for a moment, green analysing orange.

"You are brave for one so young." He spoke softly, holding his hand up when she tried to speak. "I am aware you both are over three hundred, which in a lot of races is already considered incredibly old, and in others an unattainable age. However, within your own race and my own you are but a child. Which means whether you wish for a babysitter or not – as you have put it – you do require one. Your magic skills are lacking, you have no weapons training. Whereas I have both. My job is to keep you alive; we do not know what is lurking around us or what could arrive at any moment. This standoffish nature you possess, Myst, will get you or your sister killed. Accept help from those who wish to protect you. Let yourself be a child." Myst got all huffy and pouty, very clearly about to argue again.

Lulen simply held his hand in front of her and Myst snapped her mouth shut, grinding her teeth together, not wanting to be lectured by an elf of all beings any further. Nilee at this point gently tugged at her sister's arm, pulling it away from her eyes, looking at her pleadingly, trying to tell her she would feel more comfortable with Lulen around without saying so out loud. Myst, of course, understood her sister's gaze and clenched her fists.

"Don't leave us then," Myst grumbled, before trying to cling back on to Nilee when she crawled away from her and pressed against Lulen, little hand holding tight onto the base of his tunic. Lulen lightly placed a hand on her head and gave his best attempt at a comforting smile, something none of them had seen grace his face as of yet. Usually, Lulen's face was adorned with a scowl and a scowl alone, so of course Nilee let out a little gasp and stared up at him with amazed eyes, while Myst cringed at the awkward way he looked.

"Pretty when you smile," Nilee whispered in awe as Myst groaned and flopped sideways.

"So weird," Myst grumbled at her twin, as Lulen's ears went red with embarrassment. He was quick to busy himself with sorting out the horses so they could rest.

Fen had watched the twins and Lulen disappear behind the tree line, fiddling with the sleeve of his robe as they did, as if he was still debating whether or not he should be the one to stay with them.

"Lulen will not let them out of his sight. They are safe with him," Fayon said. Sighing, he walked back until he was looking down upon Fen, gently grasping his jaw with his index finger and thumb, tilting his head up to make his gaze meet his own. "You are very protective of them, aren't you. The best way to protect them is to let Lulen do his job while we do ours. He is a skilled warrior. Don't doubt him. Now you look for survivors, I will deal with the dead."

Fen could only give a tiny nod as he found his body not functioning in any way he wanted. The best he could do was stare into those crimson eyes until Fayon let go of his chin and turned away from him, resuming the task he'd set himself, moving the burnt and charred bodies, lining them up at the village's edge.

Suddenly Fen realised he was holding his breath and he quickly took a shaky intake of air, slowly moving through the crumbling ruins of the village, walking further and further from Fayon.

Fayon glanced up, watching as Fen walked into the distance, the corpse of a woman gently cradled in his arms. He carefully laid her down on a patch of still green grass with uttermost care and respect.

The demon-blooded prince's usually tan complexion was now pale as he stared at the few bodies he had already laid down on the grass. Teeth gritted, the pain they looked in, even in death, how tiny some of them were, they couldn't have been more than a few years into their short lives.

"Unwarranted cruelty." Fayon gazed down sadly before moving to continue to recover bodies.

Fen walked slowly, eyes burning from irritation as ash was blown constantly into his face, tears rolling down his cheeks and freezing into droplets when they fell from his chin to the ground. He listened carefully for any sounds of life that could be drowned out by the crackling of wood, his heart growing heavier with every building, every body he passed, which just held death.

Even the household pets and farm animals had not been spared, all charred beyond recognition. Blood paved the path. The ground was saturated and tacky under his shoes. Fen could tell now that those who died first had been cut down, stabbed and slashed as some tried to defend their families, others while they ran. The burning had come later. There would have been no blood if these creatures had just set the humans alight.

It was awful, he did not want to be able to tell all this. He hated that he knew the pain they felt when their wounds were inflicted on them. The pain of burning. Fen shook his head and heaved a breath, slowly coming to a stop as he reached the edge of the settlement, tears still running, hand clutching his chest.

These beasts had really spared no one, not the elderly, children or animals. How could... no one could wish this on their own people, so why had they attacked another with no hesitation? Was his life so important that anyone just in the way of finding him could be sacrificed like lambs to slaughter? He had hoped beyond anything that Aphir and his torturers were the worst beings in the world. Yet now he had realised that was just naive of him to think.

Fen did not want to believe that the world he'd wished so long to see could feel the same as being chained in that cell.

He just stood there letting his hair blow in the wind and his tears fall for what seemed like hours, just watching the distance as darkness completely descended over the landscape. Only then did Fen have the guts to turn and make his way back to his group. He barely took more than a step when he noticed another building from the corner of his eye. His body swivelled instantly to head towards the still-intact shed. How it had avoided the annihilation that the rest of the village had succumbed to he did not know. But maybe, just maybe, it held something more inside.

The pounding of his heart filled his ears as he finally picked up on faint, almost non-existent sounds from within. His walking turned to running, leaping over ruins. The moment he reached the door he stood frozen for a second.

Slowly Fen lifted his hand, pressing it flat against the rotten wood, it gave way under the light touch he exerted. The door swung open loosely on one latch before landing with a thunk onto straw laden ground. Fen's gaze focused on the blooded floor below, and the two shapes that lay concealed by the darkness. One's arms were wrapped tightly around the other smaller body, seemingly trying to protect them.

Chapter 11

Save Him

Fen rushed forward, boots and the bottom of his robes splattered with blood as he did so, his robes twisting around him as he manoeuvred his body, fingers finding themselves under the nose of the woman. Given the state of her body, it was clear she was not the one he'd heard making small noises. The fact her clothes were nothing but blood made that obvious, but still he checked. He carefully unwrapped her stiffened arms from the small figure tucked protectively in her grasp, revealing a young boy maybe a little older than Nilee and Myst. After a short examination, Fen found that his head was bleeding sluggishly but other than that, there didn't appear to be a single other mark on his body.

Gently he cradled the boy's injured head against his chest, hand protectively shielding the boy's face. He used his other arm to support his legs, tucking the child safely against his body as he stood. Fen's eyes momentarily widened when the child shifted with a grumble before going limp again.

Fen found he did not like how uncomfortably hot the tiny human's skin was against his own. He remembered how Fayon spoke of illnesses and how it had been a miracle Fen had no infection or fever from the state his body had been in. They all assumed it was Fen's blood that made that possible. But this child had just a mortal's blood – a fever could be deadly to them. If Fen was correct this child had a high one. His heart was into his throat in an instant.

The teen took off with incredible speed, not stopping for a moment. He simply leapt over anything in his path, ducking and weaving through the village to get back to Lulen with his precious cargo cradled in his arms. He moved with such grace and elegance it would be near impossible for anyone to believe he was in a panic as he ran.

"Lulen?!" Fen's voice filled the air, shouting, not even considering any danger that could be around them, his sole focus on this child. Fayon looked absolutely bewildered where he stood. All he'd seen was a blur of grey and white as the angel-blooded flew past him.

Lulen of course had his daggers out the instant he heard the panicked shout, fearing the absolute worst. He had no idea what was coming his way. He hadn't heard anything, but for Fen to sound so panicked maybe he had sensed something that Lulen could not. Surely it wasn't something that Fen could not defend himself against. He was made to be a weapon for hell's sake. So Lulen assumed that there was a large ambush headed their way.

That was of course until a dishevelled, wild-haired Fen slid to a stop in front of him, robes stained with blood from running and where the child's head pressed to his chest.

"Save him, please..." The tone was so pleading and broken that Lulen had to remind himself that there was no way Fen knew this child, despite the image his appearance and voice created. It was like a father pleading for his son.

"Lay him down here," Lulen said, focusing himself on the boy. The elf made quick work of gathering their limited medical supplies, a vast majority already having been used up on Fen's injuries, but he would make do.

Fen was on his knees beside the pair, grey outer robes haphazardly laid across the mudded ground. The angel-blooded had found himself with the child's little hand in his own, cupping it in his, eyes closed, lips moving in a wordless prayer. Lulen forced himself to pay little attention to him as he ripped up strips of fabric, eyes going to the two girls. Fayon couldn't use magic, so he couldn't ask him, but maybe one of the girls could.

"Are either of you able to use the fire ability?" Lulen asked, unaware he could have asked Fen to do just that, and he would have no issues. Instead, he waited for Myst to nod. The girl came right over, not waiting a second or saying anything snippy when Lulen held out his water skin to her.

"The water needs to be boiled. Find a pot in the saddle bags and use it to hold the water. Once it's boiled bring it back. Be careful not to spill any on yourself. I do not need a second patient." With that his attention went right back to the injured child before him. He gently pressed on his stomach and limbs, checking for other wounds as well as broken bones, finding none other than the obvious injured head. By the time he had done this Myst had come back, cupping the steaming pot in her hands, brow furrowed in concentration as she walked, making sure not to spill it as she set it on the grass.

"Thank you," Lulen said softly as he dipped some torn fabric into the water, ignoring the scolding of his own hands. Now the strips were sterilised, he moved to gently clean the wound on the boy's head.

With great care he wiped the blood, muck and ash contained within the injury to get a good look at what they were dealing with. The tension in his shoulders dissipated as he finally got a good look. It was nasty to be sure but it was not deep. There was no white of the skull showing and he could not feel any indications of it being fractured or broken beneath the tissue. He discarded the dirtied strip to one side, reaching for his herb pot instead, selecting ones best suited for pain relief, fever reduction and numbing as well as warding away infection. Lulen spent the next few moments crushing them together with a little water to create a paste he could smooth into the wound.

Scooping the paste into his fingers he applied it to the flesh wound before securely covering it with the several strips of fabric they had left.

"There is no need to worry. The child will be fine – it is barely even a wound. Heads just bleed a deceptive amount." Lulen spoke when he realised Fen had not moved from his position. He still did not move much once told, but he lowered the child's hand, removed his outer robe and gently placed it over the boy's unconscious form.

"What of his fever?" Fen whispered brokenly, smoothing the cloak down.

Lulen watched the movements, a soft look on his face for a fleeting moment before he quickly hid his thoughts with his usual scowl. Looking away, moving instead to clean up the mess he had made while Fen sat beside the child as a father would a son.

"His temperature is barely above normal. I will watch it, but with the herbs I have given him, he is in no danger. I can promise you that." Lulen huffed a little, almost sounding insulted that Fen might think he had forgotten something like a fever.

Nilee moved to sit beside Fen, giving him her cloak to put under the boy's head. Then she herself snuggled into

Fen's side, holding his hand comfortingly. Lulen's lips treacherously twitched into a smile yet again, as he thought about what a ragtag family this group really seemed to have become. That was when he noticed Myst was helping him clean, chuckling when she turned her nose up to ignore him when she realised he had noticed.

The moon was starting to descend in the sky when Fayon eventually returned. His face was covered in black from the ashes, his robes greyed out in the dust as well, a grim look on his features, defined harshly by the cracked soot lines.

"They are all dead." His voice was low and dark, eyes casting to the side where Fen had Nilee and Myst curled up asleep on either side. He noticed there was a boy asleep in front of him, so maybe they hadn't all died. Fayon was, however, more concerned that the child was covered by Fen's outer robe.

He frowned deeper on seeing Fen in only an inner robe. It was not a warm night; he shouldn't be in such a thin layer of clothing. He knew that was exactly why the child was covered with Fen's robe, and he could not fault the teen for doing as he had. But that did not mean he had to like the idea of Fen freezing.

"Not all. The child survived, with very little in the way of injuries," Lulen piped up while he watched his friend just stand there, like a lemon.

"His mother was shielding him," Fen whispered softly, opening his eyes. He carefully laid the two girls down, making sure to cover them under his cloak before he moved to stand, white inner robe covered in grass stains. His gaze lingered on the sleeping face. He couldn't imagine the pain the boy would feel when he woke to learn everyone he knew – his whole life – was gone. His fists clenched lightly as Fayon moved towards him, about to take off his outer robe to put over the angel-blooded.

"I want to bury them; may we go and do that? His family, these people should have a proper burial." Fen spoke with such compassion, eyes moving to meet Fayon's.

The demon-blooded stopped in his tracks, moved yet again by Fen. He could only nod to his question. Of course they would bury them. A proper burial was deserved by everyone. But first he finished loosening the sash that held his outer robes secure and shimmied them from his shoulders, holding the thick robe out towards the angel-blooded. "Alright... but put this on first. It's too cold to have just that on."

"If I wear it then you will be cold. Do not worry; I do not feel the cold." Fen tilted his head with a smile. Fayon frowned a little but slowly put on his outer robe again, standing there silently after his gesture had been rejected.

Lulen was now sitting on the branch of a tree, bow in hand, above the three sleeping children. He stared down at the two, inwardly cringing at how awkward his prince was as well as how oblivious Fen seemed to be. Finally, he broke the nearing unbearable silence. "I guess that means I am watching the children again," he sighed, looking down at the pair, a smirk on his features. "Do try to keep an eye on yourselves. I don't want to have to watch them and come to your rescue."

Fayon chuckled at Lulen's words. "I seem to remember coming to your rescue far more than you have mine, elf," Fayon said, smirking right back.

Lulen flushed red and cleared his throat a little, looking away, while Fen just looked curious between the pair wanting to know the stories behind their words.

"I'll tell you later," Fayon chuckled as he nudged Fen's shoulder and started walking to where he had laid all the bodies out.

Their moods instantly changed back to sombre as they let silence envelop them. The taller man moved to go and see if he could find anything to dig with, while Fen held his pale hand out in front of him. His gold markings over his body and forehead glowed lightly as his hand frosted over, slowly spreading out and creating a shovel of sparkling ice. Fayon had stopped in his tracks when he felt the cold and heard crackling, his head turning back to witness Fen creating a perfect shovel.

His eyes widened in surprise. Fen had used light magic before, how was it possible for him to also use ice magic? Surely angel-blooded couldn't use both elements at once when demon-blooded could only use fire *or* darkness elements. Not both. Never in history *both*. He almost pinched himself just to make sure he wasn't dreaming. Fen never ceased to amaze him; he wondered if he would ever truly know everything about him.

After his momentary staring, Fayon slowly turned to walk back towards Fen, arriving just as he started creating a second shovel, the first jabbed into the soil ready for use. Perhaps his use of two elements was the reason why his father had sought him as a weapon in the first place – he had never heard of any person of any race with the ability to do so. It would certainly make a useful skill in battle after all.

He was slowly coming to realise even Fen was likely still learning things about himself, and that the only person who knew his father's plan for Fen was his father. Finding Fen's family could give answers, but who even knew if they were alive. And his father was certainly out of the question. That left figuring things out on their own, which was always difficult.

The two teens worked in silence as they started digging graves, Fen's eyes dull as he stared at the death before him. Fayon could not stop his mind from asking more questions about Fen, as usual. Fayon just dug as he thought, not paying attention to their surroundings or much to what Fen was doing, lost in a world of his own.

Fen carefully placed each person into their own grave, refusing to put them all into one mass grave. He moved the bodies with great care, gentle even when covering them with earth again. Neither he nor Fayon stopped until each human had been laid to rest within the earth.

Fayon moved to collect sticks, stones, anything he could find to at least leave burial markers for the lives that had been lost. It felt like something they needed to do, when the reason these people died was, in all likelihood, because they had no idea where a runaway demon-blooded prince and a weaponised angel-blooded were.

Fen fell heavily to his knees, again gently clasping his hands in front of his face as if in prayer, closing his eyes so long black eyelashes rested against the beautiful porcelain skin, gold mark pulsating faintly.

Fayon stopped to watch Fen, admiring the younger before he carefully started creating grave markers. His eyes were soft and sad. Fen was treating the humans as if he had known them his whole life. Fayon couldn't help but want to weep with him. The younger had a pure heart, a beautiful soul inside and out. One this world would crush at a moment's notice.

He watched in growing surprise as slowly each grave

started to give the same faint gold glow as Fen's marks, the air around them suddenly feeling warm, enveloping Fayon and everything around them in a feeling of comfort.

"Please be at peace. I will protect the boy, let your spirits pass on to rebirth." Fen's soft words reached his ears, making Fayon freeze, eyes slowly growing round as saucers. He couldn't believe it, *was he communing with their souls?* He knew of course his own kind could commune and corrupt souls – his father had created an army of them. They were vicious and scary. He had never thought that angel-blooded would have the same ability. But instead of corruption, Fen seemed to be helping the souls pass on. Compared to the red vengeful energy released when his kind did such a thing, Fen's was simple and yet undeniably beautiful.

Their races truly were created to be opposites in every way shape and form.

Fayon sat and watched as the glow brightened, almost blindingly so, before disappearing in a flash. Fen's eyes slowly opened, the colour completely dull, showing exhaustion as he fell sideways. Fayon's own eyes widened, startled. He reacted in an instant, skidding across the soil and catching the younger before he could connect with the ground.

"Fen?" Worry laced the deep voice as he carefully raised him back up using his own body to support Fen's.

"I am okay... it was just... so many voices." He blinked slowly. They had all been screaming in pain as he sent his energy into the ground, trying to calm their souls. It had been too much, to reach them all, to make them hear his voice and know they would be okay, to know that the child would not be left alone. Convincing them it was better to pass on to rebirth, than to stay a wandering soul on Aleria's lands. It had been no easy feat, yet in the end he had managed to do so. The quiet left behind as each soul passed through the light was almost as deafening as their screams had originally been.

Fen slowly brought his fingers to his ears, pulling back when he felt wetness, silvery blood staining them. Maybe that was why everything felt so muffled.

Fayon of course was alarmed at the sight, spinning Fen to face him as he used his own sleeve to wipe away the blood and examine his ears. Relief flooded him when he realised there was no more blood flowing. Fen had heard him so nothing had been too damaged.

"Don't do that again, that was too much for your body," Fayon said, holding his shoulders tightly to make his point. "Risking yourself is not what anyone wants. Don't be so foolish again."

Fen just gave a slow nod to Fayon, eyes looking up to meet his. "I will be more careful. I didn't mean to make you worry. I apologise." His voice was so small as he whispered.

Fayon just gently patted his shoulder in comfort, giving a small squeeze, not daring to let go of the other in case he fell again. Neither said anything more, remaining in silence, one watching the other for signs of weakness, while the other gazed at the graves, thinking about the promises he'd made.

~

Meanwhile Lulen was watching over the three sleeping children, staying on his branch until he saw the boy's face scrunch up, and eyes flutter a little. Immediately the elf leapt from the tree, landing silently on the grass below. In a few large strides he was crouched beside the waking child. He knew he was a stranger, a stranger not of his race, but Lulen had not expected frightened brown eyes to snap open and scream the second he saw the elf.

Lulen found himself scrambling up and backwards fast, the boy's chest heaving heavily in fright. The screaming woke the twins, and when the human boy saw the glowing red marks on their foreheads, his fright only increased, as did his screaming. The boy clawed his way to stand, robe ripped off and thrown to the side as his breathing rapidly increased by the second.

Fayon came running back on full alert the second the scream sounded, sword drawn, ready to kill whatever had caused it. Except there were no orcs or other creatures in the small clearing, just those they had left there. Unfortunately, Fayon's sudden appearance, coupled with his own glowing red mark *and a sword* had the boy trying to run. Lulen, of course, stopped him, a grip on his shoulders.

"Stop. It's okay – we aren't your enemy, you're okay, you are safe." The elf tried, but the child was terrified, and the stern look on Lulen's face coupled with all his ear piercings and weapons did not help. To him he looked like a trained killer, a monster like the ones who had been hurting his papa, hurting everyone. He struggled violently, so much so Lulen had no choice but to let go in fear the boy would twist and hurt himself. It was at that moment that Fen arrived, eyes wide.

The child took one look at the newcomer and immediately fled to him, screaming and crying as he latched himself onto Fen's leg. He had seen the beautiful face, the gold marking and immediately assumed it was an angel like in the stories told by his mama. He knew that he was safe, so he dived for him, *he was safe, stories said so.*

Fen's gaze was soft, looking down at the small child, ignoring everyone else's bewildered looks as the child sobbed. Fen lowered himself, placing a hand under his bottom and easily lifting him into his arms, spare hand rubbing the child's back as he buried his snotted face into his neck, arms and legs wrapped securely around him.

"Your safe, Clanne, no one here will harm you," Fen soothed. "I promised your mother that I would protect you. You are safe, little one." The child squeezed closer, while everyone else moved away to give the boy – Clanne – some space.

"How did he know his name?" Nilee whispered, looking at Fayon, then changing to look at Lulen because he always had all the answers to everything. Fayon looked rather offended when she looked at someone else.

"He communed with the child's family." Fayon looked smug because he answered a question Lulen couldn't. He chose to ignore Nilee's surprised look.

He of course was the only one present to witness what Fen had done, so it wasn't a hard guess as to how he knew the boy's name. Fen seemed to have become this boy's family. Clanne was under Fen's care now, it seemed.

It was a good thing Fen couldn't look scary if he tried. Fayon huffed at the mere thought of a scary Fen, it was just so impossible to imagine. Even the kid could see he wasn't mean by a glance. Fayon chuckled because those thoughts just didn't work. Evil, scary or mean were not words to describe Fen, especially not watching him now.

Fen did not move when the others did, he just swayed with the human child in his arms, rocking him until Clanne's cries turned into hiccups and eventually into silence. Never did he loosen his grip around Fen's neck. Only when he was sure he had cried himself off to sleep did Fen venture to sit them down, Fayon carefully wrapping Fen's discarded outer robe back around the pair to warm them until the sun rose in a few hours' time.

Chapter 12

You Are Safe with Me

Fen sat almost unmoving for hours. The only movement he made was a gentle sway of his body when Clanne whimpered in his sleep, or to press his hand to his forehead checking that his fever had not grown. Thankfully, as the sun had reached its midday peak, the child's fever had broken, which had seemed to ease his sleep greatly.

Just after the sun had started to descend after the marking of midday, Clanne had stirred to consciousness, face nuzzling into Fen's chest as the angel-blooded just gently smoothed his hair down. Everyone drew near at seeing the human start to wake. Lulen sat himself on a boulder sticking half out the ground, while Fayon sat down at Fen's side, one leg crossed, the other bent up, arm resting on it. He watched intently as the girls came to sit across from Fen and Clanne.

Clanne opened his eyes, his face very much concealed by Fen. He made no movement, breaths picking up a little as he remembered what had happened the night before. The boy jumped in fright, shooting into a sitting position when a hand brushed his hair from his face. Clanne made to scream yet again when he finally noticed everyone, realising that it hadn't been a dream as he had hoped. The only reason he did not scream was because that meant the angel had to be real as well. Sure enough, that was who had brushed hair from his face. The soft smile on the angel's face was enough to make the scream die on Clanne's lips and the child to sink back into his embrace.

His eyes wandered over everyone else, distrust filling his gaze.

"Who are you?" Clanne's voice was slow and filled with a level of caution not suited to a tender-aged mortal. Fen patted his head a little, gaining his attention so he would listen to his words and know the truth in them.

"I know it is scary for you right now, but I promise, they aren't scary at all. I am sure they may look like it, because of their weapons or frowns. But they aren't, they are all my friends, and incredible people." Clanne gave an unsure look at that but was listening to him at least. "See the girls? Their names are Nilee and Myst. Don't let Myst fool you; she may act all tough but she's very nice," Fen whispered dramatically. "She can use fire magic too, but don't worry she won't hurt you with it. Nilee is really sweet and will definitely tell you all kinds of stories. She has a special magic that helps her see the future. They saved my life – they won't hurt you ever."

Clanne looked to who Fen pointed and talked about, slowly sitting up further so he could see them. Myst was sat cross-armed with an annoyed look on her face. He didn't think he liked her very much. But when Nilee elbowed her, she did smile, and she looked nice when she did that. He looked a little excited when he heard Nilee liked to tell stories. He would sit around the campfire and listen to his uncles and father tell all kinds of stories, adventures they'd had or tales of great heroes. Maybe she knew ones he had never heard before.

Fen carried on talking when he saw Clanne was sitting himself up to listen and look. "The grumpy-looking one there is Lulen. He is an elf. I had never met one before until a few days ago. He is always looking grumpy and grumbles a lot, but he is very nice and knows a lot too.

Sometimes he smiles, but it's very rare. I made a game out of trying to make him smile. Myst is winning so far."

Lulen looked shocked. When had he made that game?

"But word of warning," Fen continued, "he doesn't like it if you touch his ears... I tried that and he got very grumpy."

Lulen looked highly embarrassed. That was how Fen chose to describe him to the child. He had to mention the ears, didn't he.

"He is helping us all get somewhere safe, which means you as well, so if he ever snaps or seems grumpy to you, just know he has all of us depending on him to get us there unharmed, so we have to make sure we are always nice and help him however we can, okay?"

Clanne nodded quickly at that, looking over to Lulen. Now, instead of terrified, he looked at him with amazed eyes, wondering how one person could be so strong to get everyone here to safety.

"Then the tall one there is also demon-blooded, just like Nilee and Myst, but don't be scared. I know you have likely been taught that they are bad and to never go near them. But they are not. Every race has bad and good people. Some demon-blooded are mean, yes, but not these three. Especially not Fayon. He has a very big heart even if he doesn't show it. He named me, you know. He called me Fen because I don't know my birth name. He helped us all escape even though he didn't know who we were, and he is very kind to me although I am an angel-blooded. From stories I know I am not supposed to get along with him or the girls and they shouldn't get along with me, but we do. Fayon worries a lot, even if he doesn't show it, and will protect everyone no matter what." Fen spoke in a soft voice the entire time, his words conveying nothing but the truth. It was plain to see Clanne had absolute trust in every word that left Fen's lips. The bright smile he gave Fayon after Fen's words was incredible, and the small boy started to relax around the group.

Fayon's ears had gone very red at hearing how Fen described him, knowing what he really thought of him. Well, he had that funny butterfly feeling in his stomach, but a smile on his lips all the same. It was evident that those words meant more to Fayon than Fen knew.

"I promise you, with us around you will be safe," Fayon said, bowing his head a little to the child.

Clanne stared at him. His voice was very deep but it didn't sound scary or mean like the monsters had – they had yelled and cursed in languages he didn't know. But this man seemed nice; his face wasn't nasty and his voice held no malice in it.

He glanced up at Fen for reassurance, and the warm smile he was met with was enough to make the small child relax.

"Hello," he whispered, reaching to squeeze Fen's arm, nerves evident at the gesture before finally relaxing when he only received smiles.

Nilee even bounced over with a massive smile. "You want to play?"

Clanne had pushed himself back into Fen's chest when Nilee had bounded over, pressing his bandaged head close, looking scared at the sudden movement. But with one glance up at Fen, who gave a soft smile and nod, the human boy slowly unpeeled himself from Fen, shuffling his feet as he stood up, giving a tentative nod to the slightly smaller girl.

"Come on, we can look for bugs!" Nilee beamed at

him, grabbing his dirty hand and tugging him along with her, the three adults of the group moving to catch Clanne when he seemed to stumble, but the child caught himself and followed along quietly. Myst got up to go after her twin, because no way was she leaving her alone with a boy. A boy!

The three children ended up crouched around a dead log trying to roll it over to see what creepy crawlies were hidden beneath, Myst poking at them with a stick she found, tongue sticking out of her mouth.

Lulen, Fayon and Fen all stayed seated where they were, watching the three young children play. Even Lulen's gaze had softened for a moment before it went to its usual furrowed brow.

"Grumpy? Really? You had to describe me as grumpy?" Lulen huffed at last, gaze shifting to the side to see Fen, who was just smiling innocently.

"Well, you are grumpy."

Lulen looked so offended while Fayon covered his mouth to try and hide the fact he was laughing at his friend. Which just resulted in Lulen throwing a stick at the prince's head.

"What? It's true! Don't throw things at me just because you always look like someone stole your sword." Fayon let out a deep chuckle as he threw said stick up and down in his palm, as Lulen just growled a little at the pair of teens. They were definitely far too childish, despite the fact they counted as adults in most races.

"I am sorry – I didn't mean to cause you offence with my words," Fen spoke after a moment, bowing his head to him in apology. Lulen just waved him off and glanced back when he heard Nilee say *eww* as Myst held a worm up for them all to see on the end of her stick.

"Alright, since the boy is injured, we will make camp, we should allow him another night's rest before moving. We will spend our time scouting and watching until tomorrow. Let us hope whatever attacked this village stays away." Lulen looked at the sky. It was early enough to be considered afternoon and not yet evening. The boy was showing no signs of infection and his fever had broken. One more night's rest should be good enough for humans. So instead of worrying about the boy, he needed to worry about whatever was out hunting and destroying.

"The pack you heard was moving south, correct?" Lulen asked after a moment. Fen responded with a short nod. If that was the case, they could still travel at the tree line westward as planned.

It seemed Aphir had the same plan as Lulen and was sending his raiding parties towards the mountains. After all, the mountain range was vast. Climbing or crossing the valley Revel bordered were the fastest ways to flee south. The only other ways were to go around, which would take weeks in either direction; it was just not possible.

Lulen had to hope that with Revel being the largest human city of the north, that it would still be standing by the time they reached its gates. He held no doubts it would be crawling with people Aphir had under his thumb, though. They had to be incredibly cautious from now on.

"We need to disguise ourselves, you, the girls and Fen specifically, your markings are too obvious." Lulen tapped his own forehead as he spoke. Fen pressed his hand to his, looking up, making his eyes cross as he tried to see his own mark.

"Do I just put mud on them?" Fen asked, fully

scanning the area to find mud to do so, ready to scoop it up when Fayon put his hand on top of his, shaking his head.

"There are far more clean ways of hiding one's identity, do not worry about it. I will work on the things we need. For now, we take turns to rest – one of us awake at all times to keep watch. If we are staying until the next moon's pass, then we should take the opportunity to gather our strength back."

Fen's ears went a little red, embarrassed that he had thought to just smear mud on himself when Fayon already had a plan. Of course, a prince wouldn't want mud all over his face. He nibbled on his lip a little. He still knew nothing, for all he had soaked up these last few days, for all his improvements, he still didn't think like Fayon or Lulen did. He felt so far behind, a child left to drown in the water while the adults swam to shore. He clenched his fist a little. He needed to learn, so he could be more than the burden he was to the group. He jolted suddenly when a hand patted his shoulder, whole face turning red when he saw the two men looking at him.

"Were you listening at all?" Lulen asked, eyebrows twitching in annoyance.

"Y..yes! I was listening: stay here and rest, Fayon will work on disguises and one of us will keep watch at a time while the others rest," Fen said rapidly to prove he really had been listening.

"And?"

Poor Fen blinked owlishly. Had Lulen said more?

"Lulen, stop teasing him, he missed nothing." Fayon sighed, shaking his head disapprovingly when the elf gave a chuckle. "If you're going to just tease, why don't you go do something useful like find us some food."

130

"Alright, Your Highness, I shall be useful as you request." Lulen sprang to his feet, snatching his bow from the tree he had propped it against before he'd disappeared into the trees.

"Don't mind him, Fen, he's just teasing you for calling him grumpy. You rest up first or keep an eye on the little ones if you don't wish to. I am going to see what is salvageable from the village." He needed to find some things to disguise themselves with. Cloaks they had already, but he could do with finding head coverings – Fen's hair was too obvious. The markings he could cover by ripping more fabric to wrap around their foreheads, but it would be less suspicious if he could find themselves some ribbons or even leather. He could twist those into decorative headpieces. He doubted the ruined village would have anything of value but there was little harm in checking. He could always hunt game for the skins if the village had nothing fruitful.

~

The group spent the daylight hours as such, Fayon climbing through the wreckage searching for anything that could have survived, Lulen hunting for game, foraging for berries as he found them. The more they could fill their saddlebags now the less they'd need to stop and the faster their journey, although with the heat of the day their rations would perish fast no matter what they did.

Fen spent the last daylight hours watching over the three small children as they played, constantly enquiring as to how Clanne's head felt. Trying his hardest to get the boy to talk more, Nilee and Myst spent the day trying to get smiles or laughs from Clanne. But he gave none, which did not surprise Fen, he had witnessed such horrors. What reason could he feel he had to smile or laugh when he was alive but the people he loved had been murdered and burned?

By the time night fell Fayon was given first watch. Fen took the second after much convincing he was capable of keeping watch on his own. This gave Lulen the sunrise watch. It was agreed Lulen needed the straight rest the most considering he was their guide. Lulen argued nought about the schedule and simply lay himself down onto the grass to sleep. Fen lay down the twins and Clanne beside him, the three children definitely gravitated to the angel-blooded for comfort. Fayon sat himself on top of a mossed-over rock, one leg crossed, the other bent up for him to rest his arm over, sword placed beside him.

Fayon's eyes scanned all around them. At times he would close his eyes and simply listen, trying to pick up on the vibrations through the ground like Fen had. He was doing just this when a gentle tap came to his shoulder.

"Fay, it's my turn, you should sleep." Fen's voice was soft, keeping his tone low to avoid waking anyone, the three sleeping children all now curled up under Fen's larger cloak instead of snuggled against him.

"Right, thanks… nothing to report. It's been silent apart from a few snores." Fayon slowly stood up and stretched, his shoulders and back popping after staying sat as he had for half a night, like a statue. Fen simply gave a nod and took his place on the rock, while Fayon chose to lie down near to the children in case of attack so he was close.

"Sleep well." Fen's warm voice drifted to Fayon's ears as his eyes fluttered closed.

Chapter 13

The Demon and The Angel

Fayon's eyes sluggishly opened, hand reaching up to rub the sleep away. When he did, he found himself not where he had fallen asleep. Before him were humans all cowering in a corner of what he guessed to be a tavern, judging by the bar and the stench of cheap ale.

The people had all crammed themselves into a corner of the room. After a moment he followed their gazes to something he really had not expected.

Eyes widened as he took in the man before him, sat with his muddied boots on the table. Sharp teeth chewing lightly on a stalk of straw, his blazing gaze bored as he watched the humans, black hair long and unruly, half covering his face, a scar over his right eyebrow. Then there was the horn extending from his right temple, curling back in a sweeping motion behind him. Parts of the skin on his arms were cracked and almost scaly in texture.

Fayon didn't have to look for the bat-like wings that were surely dragging on the ground behind the man to know this was a demon. One of the races that had created his own people. His heart was pounding in his ears. This wasn't possible; they had gone extinct in the Angel-Demon wars... They had finished annihilating their creators, the Elementals. Then went to war and slaughtered one another. One being here now, it just couldn't be possible.

Fayon could not help but take a few steps back, especially when the man let out a snarled laugh, much larger pointed canines then even he as a demon-blooded had. It gave his whole face a murderous glint. Fayon wanted to run, to hide, be anywhere but here, but found his feet were rooted in place.

"What a pleasure. I didn't expect one of your kind to see me away personally." The man's voice was smooth and deep, immediately sending chills up the spines of everyone in the room. Before Fayon could open his mouth, he felt like ice. Someone had just walked straight through him, gracefully taking a seat across from the demon. The room immediately filled with a calming aura, the cowering humans all visibly relaxing. Fayon realised at that moment he must be dreaming. He was standing in his dream, without control and apparently invisible. Someone had just walked through him, after all.

His heart calmed down as he thought rationally about the situation. One, there was no way he could have awoken here without knowing how he came to be here. Secondly, demons had long been extinct, even the oldest angel or demon-blooded had little recollection of their creators.

A dream though it was, it felt so real. He couldn't help but wonder if this really was what a demon had looked like, then his attention went to the new male now sitting across from the demon. Fayon tested his feet again, finding himself able to lift them this time. He slowly walked around until he could see the face of the newcomer.

Fayon fell to his knees in an instant as he stared at the man before him. Sat with a warm expression on his face, it was... it was *Fen*. No, an older Fen – his features had sharpened out, eyes becoming more golden, the blue deeper. His white hair was intricately braided with gold chains hanging from them, with beautiful golden leaves woven into the chains. Even his ears had beautiful golden earrings decorating them. Then there were his robes – there was layer after layer of fine material, blue and white, with large open sleeves that hit the floor, a thick sash around his middle securing everything in place. The mark on his forehead was gone, which had Fayon frowning, until he realised, he had missed something. Fen's whole body let off a soft golden glow, and folded upon his back was one wing of white and gold speckled feathers. Just the one wing. This wasn't Fen.

Fayon sat in awe as the original ethereal beings of light and dark sat before him at opposite ends of a small rickety circular table.

"You are scaring the humans. Please leave." The angel spoke in a calm tone, that already had the humans slowly leaving the corner they had been crowded in.

"Tisk, so much for the politeness of angels, not even asking my name before asking me to leave. I haven't even been served a drink yet. It's not my fault they cower like mice – I would have already been gone if one would serve me." The demon chuckled, smirk never leaving his face. It only grew when he flicked the straw he had been chewing into the face of the angel.

Fayon felt anger when that happened. How dare he flick something at... no, it wasn't Fen... he had to force himself to slowly unclench his fists. This was not someone he knew, it was a dream, not a real person. Still, it did not help that he looked so much like Fen.

The angel did not react, breathtaking eyes never leaving their point of focus, before suddenly the man stood, robes flowing as if in a gentle breeze. The angel Fen, as Fayon had decided to call him, moved with grace towards the bar. To the astonishment of everyone in the room, including the demon, he poured a pint of ale into a tankard, leaving a golden piece as payment. Then he set it down in front of the demon, sitting himself back down in his chair.

"What is your name then?"

Suddenly the demon erupted into howling laughter, feet leaving the table and he hit his leg in amusement. "Now I never expected that! Alright then, Mr Goody-Goody, since you so graciously poured me a drink with those dainty hands of yours, I suppose I can tell you my name. Irden. I assume you have heard of me?" Irden leaned forward with a cocky smirk, lifting the tankard to curled lips, downing it in one large gulp. He ran his tongue across his teeth as he slammed it down, quirking an eyebrow when he realised the angel's expression hadn't become one of horror. "What's with the blank look? I just told you I'm Irden, the angel hunter. I have killed more of your brethren than any other of my kind, yet you're sitting there like it's nothing!" Rage laced his words as he blasted the tankard in his hand to ashes, causing screams from the humans who once again cowered away.

The angel simply let out a cold sigh and waved his hand, icing over the smouldering table. Fayon tried to move closer, eyes wide with worry.

"You fool, why are you just sitting there? Run, leave! Don't just stay sat with a killer. He is clearly deranged!" Fayon waved his arms as he yelled, trying to get the angel's attention, before realising, ah yes, he was invisible in his own dream.

"Should I fear for my life over a name? Over a demon with the temper of a child?"

Irden's whole right arm became engulfed in flames. The demon lunged over the table, fist about to connect with the pale unmarked skin, before Irden was on the floor, flaming arm twisted behind him, a foot pressed in the small of his back, flames extinguished by ice slowly creeping down his side. Irden let out a grunt as he smacked into the floor, his body twisted in a way it was not supposed to. Now *this* was a surprise to him. He hadn't expected this one to be a fighter, he definitely didn't carry or dress as one.

"You should know who your opponent is before you try an attack. You were careless and forgot to ask my name." The angel's expression had turned ice cold, piercing down at Irden, who felt the air shift around him. Now that was interesting, this one was more than he seemed.

"I will humour you. What is this angel's name, hmmm? I bet it's pretty." He laughed, twisting his body hard and fast, making the angel jump backwards, landing with no sound, back bent slightly back to avoid the flash of fire that came from Irden's kick. The demon flipped himself to stand.

Fayon himself had ducked in reaction to the arch of flames, not knowing if the attack would pass through him or burn him. He had no intention of finding out.

"Go on then, what's the name I will be adding to my wall?" Irden laughed, eyes crazed with bloodlust, hands both igniting in blue flames.

"Theliel." The cold response came, and in the instant the name was announced, the flames that had been building in Irden's hands extinguished themselves. Fayon watched as the demon's face turned into one of horror. He slowly started backing up, eyes darting towards the door. Before he could even take two steps, Theliel had appeared in front of him, moving in a flash of golden light.

"I did not come here to kill you, simply to ensure you left this village alone. Agree to leave the humans of this region in peace and you may leave here alive." Theliel's voice held so much authority as he spoke.

Fayon watched in amazement as Irden lowered his head and gnashed his teeth together as if speaking was causing him agony.

"You will not see me here again. I will do as his lordship wishes."

"Then leave." Theliel flicked his sleeves as he stepped to the side, holding his arm towards the door, gaze locked on Irden as the demon stormed out, footsteps cracking and splintering the wood as he left into the darkness outside. His silhouette became quickly lost in the night.

Fayon stood there having watched his dream unfold, a confused look on his face. What had his subconscious come up with? It did not feel like a dream, more like a recollection. Because although he was sure he had never heard either the name Irden or Theliel before he felt familiarity with both.

Theliel simply stared out into the darkness, a small nod to the humans who rushed over to thank him before he himself left into the night. Fayon went straight after him, engulfing himself in the darkness.

"Fay...Fay...Fayon!" The voice was quiet in his ears until suddenly the yell brought clarity to his fuzzy mind and his eyes snapped open.

~

Meanwhile in the Valyn Mountains, a new being was awakening, Fayon's dream causing a ripple through time and space, setting in motion events that had long been predestined.

~

Amber eyes slowly opened, light hitting the honey tones that encircled the serpent pupils. Short, spiked strands of charcoal hair blew gently in front of a handsome face, a smile forming to reveal sharp canines and a scarred lip, a slicked back grey horn glinting in the light.

"You're finally awakening." His voice was like a pebble dropping into still water, deep and soothing, incongruous to his intense looks. Slowly he uncrossed his legs and stood from the stone throne he had sat upon for the past twenty thousand years. Sleep left his frame in an instant as he took slow steps down from his throne, a dark smile gracing his face, hand running along the deep red of the cave's walls.

"Zydrina, come, our time to descend into the world has come." Eyes glinted with excitement as movement surrounded him all of a sudden, the cave lighting up as its entrance was revealed. A large red dragon stretched her limbs, jaw opening in a yawn, rows of sharp teeth exposed.

"Finally." To this man the dragon had the sleepy voice of a young girl, but to the outside world it was nought but a terrifying growl.

He tilted his head with a smirk, hands clasped behind his back, posture elegant and proper as he watched his dragon stretch. "You cannot emerge like that, my dear. We wouldn't want to scare the humans, now, would we? That would give us away far, far too soon." He pointed two of his fingers, pooling magic at the tips before he touched her side then ran them down his own form. Shimmering black ripples cast over the pair. Suddenly the once giant dragon shrank rapidly, the sounds of bones popping and cracking echoed throughout the cave system.

She stood there in tattered clothes, ripped leggings, with a leather-striped skirt around her waist, a pale fabric top hanging loosely around her frame. Messy fiery red, waist-long hair stuck out at all angles, her skin tanned and dirty, striking icy blue eyes making the beauty beneath painfully obvious.

Where the demon once stood was a far shorter man, dressed in traditional human hunting garb, tight leggings, and a long brown tunic, paired with leather bracers and boots, a quiver and bow on his back, bone knife secured by a leather belt around his middle. His long dark hair turned to shoulder length mousy hair, a braid on one side where his horn used to reside, eyes a deep brown hiding the amber that lay beneath.

"It seems your clothes will need to be rectified." A chuckle came as he stared at the red-faced girl as she pulled on the disgusting garb.

"You better get me nice things, Varys!" She crossed her arms, sticking her lip out in a pout, making Varys chuckle and catch her chin, before he gave her cheek a pinch and a squeeze.

"Of course, anything my little dragon desires. Come. We have a mountain to descend." He released her chin, the red-haired dragon-shifter quickly following her master, running to match his long strides. The pair exited the dark cave and met the light for the first time in twenty thousand years. Varys stopped a moment, closing his eyes, humming in delight as the sun beamed down on his skin. He had missed this feeling very much. Finally, everything was beginning, a plan he had waited centuries for was here. Things would be right this time, they had to be.

Chapter 14

A Rude Awakening

The second Fayon's eyes snapped open, all his senses came back to him, pain shooting through his leg, smoke hitting his nostrils and growling filling his ears. It took all of five seconds for Fayon's mind to catch up. The growling came from a pack of white wolves, known for their giant size and vicious attacks, the pain from one biting into his leg, and the smoke from fires that blazed in Myst as well as Fen's hands.

Fayon would question that later, right now he needed to move. The children were screaming, Fen yelling, waving his hand rapidly in different directions, pleading for the wolves to leave them alone, crying out for Fayon to wake up.

"Fay!"

Fayon ignored Fen's almost relieved call and focused on getting himself up.

Fen was filled with relief when Fayon finally woke up – it had been like he was cursed, nothing could wake him, no matter the screams, or the shaking they gave him. Not even when the wolf started chewing on his leg after Fen and the children were forced backwards away from him. But whatever had kept him asleep was thankfully over now. Fen could feel his heart rate slow. Just seeing Fayon's eyes open, seeing him move made it feel like he could breathe again.

Fayon wrenched his free leg and sent his foot crashing into the wolf's nose, causing it to whimper and back away. He used that chance to push himself around and up, ignoring the pain and dampness of blood against his leg. Right now, he needed his sword. Thankfully, he had fallen asleep with it beside him. He spun, grabbed it, and was up closing the gap between himself and the children.

"Where is Lulen!?"

"We couldn't wake you up... Lulen diverted half the pack's attention, he hasn't come back yet!" Fen yelled, his hand still held up, ignited in full orange flame, waving wildly any time a wolf so much as stepped forward. The children clung to him, tears running down their faces, Nilee and Clanne letting out screams of fear while Myst tried to copy Fen, screaming at the beasts to go away.

Guilt was plastered over the angel-blooded face. He had been on watch, now Fayon was hurt because he hadn't reacted fast enough. He hadn't been able to alert Lulen, wake Fayon, or get the kids anywhere safe. He had thought he could reason with the wolves, talk to them and send them on their way... He hadn't wanted to hurt the wolves, they were just hungry. So, he had tried to protect them all, the people and the animals, even after Fayon wouldn't wake up and Lulen went to attack.

He remembered how Lulen had been so incredibly angry at Fen as he had stopped his knife from hitting the pack leader. Begged him not to kill them. So instead Lulen had to try and drag half the pack away in order to get rid of them.

Lulen had been thankful that when he had drawn some away the leader of the pack and its strongest chased after him. All he could do when he diverted some of the pack was hope Fen had the balls to kill what remained or Fayon would wake up to save the kids.

"Fen! Get your head out of the clouds and listen to me, you ass! Use your fire and burn the bastards before they attack!"

Fen looked completely startled at Fayon's anger-laced words and heated look, the angel-blood looking at him with wide eyes, trying to shake his head. But instead he held back a whimper as the glare hardened. He threw his hand out at the same time Myst did. Their flames collided, neither hitting any wolves but instead igniting the ground, causing screams of terror from Nilee and Clanne. The wolves circled to get around the flames.

Fayon grabbed Fen by the collar, dragging him close so their faces were nearly pressed together, crimson eyes ablaze in anger.

"You did that on purpose," he hissed, pushing him away, spinning around, sword thrusting out catching a descending wolf dead between the eyes. The beast died instantly, red blood spraying out as it fell with a thump to the ground. The three children gasped and cowered beside Fen, while Fen let out a heartbroken sound at the dead creature.

"Get a grip! It's kill or be killed, Fen – they are starving, and we are food." Fayon slashed out again, another wolf jumping back snarling, its canines showing, drool splattering the ground. Fayon's steps were careful and calculated; he'd manoeuvred them against a tree. He didn't have to watch their backs and could focus on the sides and front. His eyes darted constantly to watch for attacks from three sides. Unfortunately, he was too slow when the next wolf bolted forward from the shadows, heading straight for Clanne.

Fen moved on instinct, his arm going right between the beast's jaws as they snapped closed, puncturing the flesh beneath. Fen gritted his teeth, but he even extinguished his fire so as not to hurt the wolf that was literally clamped down on his arm.

"Fen!" came three whimpered cries from the children.

Fayon moved to swing his sword down, to chop the thing's head off, when Fen gripped his wrist in a death lock.

"Don't! Enough killing!" he yelled, eyes clenched shut, hiding the tears that were threatening to spill at all this violence.

"Let go! Fen you need to let go!" Fayon yelled frantically, trying to pull free of the iron grip he had on his wrist as the circling wolves moved to attack. The first to jump hit the ground hard after a whizzing sound accompanied by a thump penetrated the air, an arrow buried deep in its side. The wolf gnawing on Fen's arm soon fell to another arrow as Lulen appeared crouched on a branch above them.

"Stop messing around and fight, Fen, or stay back! You're a danger and a burden like this!" Lulen snapped down at him, not caring as the youngster flinched as he held his injured arm close to his chest. He simply nocked another arrow while Fayon finally ripped his arm free and pushed forward to kill the remaining wolves.

The demon-blood and elf worked together, Lulen guarding Fayon from above as he moved to fight through the pack. After he had slain another two of the white wolves, Fen intervened. He couldn't stand by and watch the creatures die.

"Enough." Fen's one word travelled through the air with such force it seemed to physically stagger the humanoids and animals alike. His left hand waved in a sweeping motion, eyes and markings all lighting up bright gold as the ground below all their feet frosted over and turned into a sheet of glistening ice. The second the

145

ice spread past Fayon and towards the wolves, it spiked upwards massively, in deadly points, thousands of them blocking the wolves' path but also blocking Fayon from moving forward and Lulen's line of sight.

"Fen, what are you doing?"

"I told you to stay back!"

Fen simply ignored both the men, moving forward, the children scrambling to stay clung to him. "Leave, all of you. All that awaits you here is death. I am giving you all the chance to survive. Run now. *Please*, run." Fen's words were soft, carrying the beauty of his heart with them.

The wolves slowly stopped their growling. No longer did they look menacing, heads tilted as they stared at the swirled blue and gold eyes. Everyone was still for a breath's moment. Then, just like that, the pack each bowed their heads and raced off into the darkness, and then distant howls were all that they could hear.

"You really are insane," Lulen huffed angrily as he jumped down from his branch, shouldering past Fen to make sure the wolves they'd injured were in fact dead. Fen found himself looking down at his feet, holding his injured arm close.

"They are gone, aren't they... I wasn't a burden." The whisper was so silent it was almost impossible to hear. But it received frowns from both Fayon and Lulen, who said nothing in response. Fayon just limped away to search of their horses, just praying they had not been killed.

Fen stood rooted where he was, Nilee and Clanne soon appearing at his side, both their faces tear-stained and eyes puffy as they hugged onto his leg.

"We don't think you're a burden, Fen," Nilee said

146

quietly, Clanne nodding in agreement. Myst meanwhile was poking at the dead wolves, following along behind Lulen. She let out a very girly shriek when one of the beasts with an arrow to its side let out a small growl as she touched it. Lulen's knife was immediately drawn, ready to put an end to its suffering, when yet again Fen got in the way.

"It's hurt, we can't save it – why do you want to just leave it to suffer, Fen? You have already caused Fayon to be injured and very likely lost us our rides because of your incapability to keep watch. Do you really want to be the reason another animal suffers? Get your head out of your ass. I do not care if you were tortured and God knows what else. You have to kill in this world! It's kill or be killed. No one is going to stop to talk in the middle of a battle, and the sooner you get your head around this the better. Because otherwise you're going to get us all killed. Now move, you useless angel!"

"NO!" Fen all but screamed out, body covering the injured wolf. "I can help her! Just because you believe this world can't be saved from conflict doesn't mean I have to. I won't kill, but I can still defend better than you. They all left, didn't they?" Fen glared hard at him, as if daring Lulen to try anything.

Lulen let out a loud sigh. "By the Lord give me the strength… Do what you wish, Fen, but do not expect me to help when she tries to rip your throat out." Lulen crossed his arms, leaning against the tree and watching close. Poor creature, suffering because of a deluded angel-blood.

Fen slowly lifted his body up when Lulen moved back, a light frown on his features as he studied the wolf's injuries. He nervously chewed on his bottom lip as

147

he started easing the arrow out, cringing at her whimpers.

"Shhh, you're okay, you will be okay, the pain will be gone soon." Fen kept whispering words of encouragement, the arrow discarded to the side the second it finally came free. Both his hands cupped the bleeding wound in an instant.

"Please work. Please," he chanted under his breath, focusing all his energy into his hands, watching as they started to glow a beautiful golden light.

Lulen kicked off the tree, eyes wide when he felt the healing warmth of magic in the air. Healing arts were rare enough in the fae races, angel-bloods were no exception to that. This was the fourth magic Fen had shown an aptitude for now. Lulen was very much beginning to realise why Aphir had chosen Fen as a weapon.

Fayon returned to the clearing at this point, with three horses in tow, all three having bolted into the ruined village long before the wolves could grab them. The horses had saved themselves as well as their journey. They would never have made it to Revel on foot. Of course, the second he arrived the reigns were dropped yet again as he stared in utter shock at Fen.

The rest of the group gravitated closer to Fen and the wolf, everyone highlighted in a golden glow, looks of astonishment and wonder gracing all their faces. Fen however took no notice of the rest of the group and focused on the injured wolf.

The glow grew brighter and brighter, until it seemed like his whole body was made of shimmering gold. Even the wolf just stared at him from where her head rested, blue eyes never leaving her healer's face.

As fast as the light came it receded back into Fen's hand. Gone was the matted bloody coat, back was the brilliantly stark white fur. The wolf sprang up in an instant, snarling when both Lulen and Fayon made to pull their weapons, causing the children to whimper and cling to any leg that was closest to them. Myst however went to create a ball of fire.

"Stop. She won't hurt us. Hands off your weapons, okay?" Fen spoke softly, still holding his hand out towards the wolf.

"Are you insane?" Fayon hissed.

"He's completely insane," Lulen huffed out, but removed his hand.

"Trust me… please Fay."

Fayon heaved a giant sigh, but slowly withdrew his grasp from the hilt of his sword, nudging Myst with the heel of his boot to make her extinguish her fireball, which she did with a very snarky mutter.

The second that all hostility was removed from the group, the wolf slowly walked forward and nudged her head against Fen's outstretched hand, before flopping down completely onto his lap. Fen laughed loudly and stroked her.

"Such a good girl," he cooed as he rubbed her side, laughing hard at the happy yips and licks he received. Fayon and Lulen were just staring at each other with the most dumbfounded expressions. The snarling starving wolf that was trying to eat them was now acting as like a common household pet. Fen truly was something.

"Come pet her; she's friendly." Fen motioned his hand to the twins and Clanne, who all swarmed instantly to love on the wolf, already forgetting how fearsome of a beast she really was.

"Does she have a name?" Nilee asked softly as she slowly stroked along the wolf's nose.

"I do not think she does, no. Why don't you all name her?"

Nilee and Clanne both let out little excited gasps, instantly whispering between one another. Myst spent the whole time rolling her eyes.

"Oo ooo what about *Flair!*"

"Kia?"

"No, that's not right, ummm... Bunny?"

"She's not a Bunny, she is a..." Clanne was cut off by Myst.

"Your ideas are dumb. She's obviously a Moon," Myst snapped at the pair, the wolf licking her cheek in response. "See, she likes it," Myst said, all smug, hugging the creature around its neck. Moon wagged her tail happily.

"Well okay then," Lulen said. "Now that you have all done... whatever this was, we need to leave. The sun is coming up, there is no point in trying to rest here any longer, so pack up. And say goodbye to Moon, you won't see her again." He briskly walked away to pack up their things. Myst tightened her hold and Moon actually whimpered. Fen stood up fast, glaring at Lulen.

"If Moon wishes to come, then she will, she can keep up. Do not decide for others."

Lulen just stared in shock. Fayon even backed away slightly. Never had they heard Fen sound so stern, it was honestly a little scary. All the elf could do was swallow and nod, while the three children cheered and carried on cuddling and petting a very happy Moon. Said wolf seemed to very much agree with Fen's words – it was freaking Fayon out how much that creature seemed to understand, as well as how much she instantly attached herself to the group.

150

Satisfied, Fen turned to Fayon and stalked over, kneeling down and hovering his hand over the still-bleeding leg, gold light returning instantly.

"Wait, it's not that bad, you don't need to... oh, you already did." Fayon looked baffled at how fast his leg went from a gnawed mess to healed, smooth, scarless skin.

"Thank you... Your arm," Fayon whispered, gently grasping it before Fen could pull away. "Can you not heal yourself?"

Fen shook his head in response. His body healed fast enough; he did not need to heal with any magic. He just covered it up with his sleeve and went to his horse.

"Lulen is right, we should get going. Clanne, come on, time to get up," Fayon called, waving the child over and lifting him up onto their steed.

Nilee scrambled over to stand by Fayon's horse while Myst sauntered over to Lulen, holding her arms up, Moon at her side.

"Lift me then." Her eyebrow all raised, like *what are you waiting for, elf?*

Lulen rolled his eyes at the girl as he lifted her up, mounting behind her, staring down at the wolf who stood beside them. His steed treaded nervously. Letting out a sigh he looked back at the two other pairs. Seeing everyone was ready to leave, he started riding with no words, a prayer in his head that Moon would lose interest in following them after a few hours. He did not want to try and get a wolf into Revel. The demon-bloods and angel-bloods would be difficult enough.

Soon enough the group of six had picked up speed and started their race against time, to reach Revel before their enemies could.

Chapter 15

Enter Revel

The group had finally set off again, led by Lulen. Three horses, six people and a very persistent wolf, their destination Revel. One adult, two teens (adults in other races yet still young in their own), and three children. They moved obscured through the forest, keeping hidden and silent, off roads, away from settlements, stopping only for water, to eat, barely resting, the children sleeping upon the horses as the oldest slept only when they could stay awake no longer.

The next stage of their journey was crucial. Lulen couldn't let them be found, tension was high but they encountered no signs of raiding parties. There was always smoke in the distance but none ever close to the group, thanks to Fen's incredible senses telling them when to stop, wait or change direction.

When they would stop for a night, Fayon would teach the children about combat, teaching them to defend themselves with small daggers - Clanne even learnt to use a bow. Moon would sit like a sentry beside Lulen, who over the days became rather fond of the white wolf. Their days solely consisted of training, movement and teaching Fen more and more as they rode.

Clanne slowly came out of his shell. He said few words but became more comfortable around everyone, not just Fen. The young boy still did not smile unless playing with Moon and the twins. But for now Fen was just glad he ate, drank and interacted, not sitting there traumatised, lost to the world. He was what Fayon told him a child should be like.

Their travels lasted like this for more than a week. By the tenth day Lulen was at his wits' end. They were taking far too long – they still were at least two days away from Revel, and who knew what the city would be like by the time they arrived. What if it wasn't even *there*? The elf made their stops shorter after that, saying they could travel two days with no sleep. Their bodies were built for it after all. No one dared argue with him as his words were short and sharp. They knew wasted time meant more danger.

With this new pace set, the group made it to Revel's walls by midday on the twelfth day of travel, horses stopping alongside the river that ran through Revel's centre.

They looked at the imposing grey walls, the top lined with patrolling guardsmen, and its archers just peeking through the crenellated battlements. The only road in was through a large wooden gate at the heart of the curved wall, its ends digging into the mountain side. The portcullis was half lowered as a group of guards stopped each person in the long line of what they could only assume were refugees from entering the city. They were inspecting everyone before entry.

Lulen's throat bobbed as he swallowed and looked at his companions, their hoods all up over their heads.

The one thing they had going for them was that originally demon and angel bloods were created from a mix of angels or demons and a race of elves. This meant the slight point to their ears and looks could be explained away as different races of elf. For example, Lulen had instructed Fayon and the girls that they were to say they were dark elves. Although feared, they were not currently at war or allied to demon-bloods, so entry should be permitted. The plan was to say Myst and Nilee were Fayon's sisters and that their parents had been killed by orc raiding parties, like most of these refugees, he guessed.

Lulen of course was obviously a forest elf. His people lived on the other side of the valley and often traded with the human settlement. He should have no one questioning him. Clanne being a human child was likely to get in with ease also.

Lulen had instructed Fen to say he was a celestial elf – or a moon or sun elf would work just as well –as long as he said any of the three his white hair was easily explainable even if slightly rare. Lulen had told Fen to say he was travelling with Lulen to learn about scouting and forest environments, and they just happened to come across Fayon and his siblings in the ruins of a village.

Lulen had tested them all repeatedly and their stories were rehearsed. All he could do was hope these humans were not suspicious in any way. Moon was coming no matter what, Lulen had decided. He had fallen in love with the beast as a hunting, scouting and patrolling companion. She would get in as his familiar, he wouldn't take no for an answer.

The elf gave them a slight nod, Fayon taking it as a signal to disguise themselves now. Fayon leaned over his saddle and opened one of the smaller leather pouches he had attached. He pulled out several braided headbands he had been working on over their days of travel, all made from the pelts of animals they had hunted for food these past weeks.

He pulled down Myst's hood and carefully placed it over her red mark, braiding the ends into her hair in an elven fashion.

Fayon fixed Nilee's band next in the same fashion as her twin's, then his own also matched, making sure their braids were uniform: elves often kept braid styles the same throughout their families, so Fayon had made sure to follow the tradition.

Finally, he moved to Fen, who pulled his hood down. Unlike the leather he had managed to find to create his and the girls' headbands from, he used fabric instead for Fen. He had ripped apart some of his own white inner robe, because it was a silk fabric that matched better with Fen's appearance and story.

Fayon had woven Fen's far more intricately than the others, making it larger than theirs were as well. The fabric at the back was long and trailed down to the base of his spine even when tied and woven through his hair. It made for a more graceful look, rather than the roughened look the leather bands provided the three pretend dark elves.

"Are you all ready?" Lulen glanced at Fayon as he finished tying the intricate knot of Fen's head piece, all forehead markings now covered.

"As ready as we can be." Fayon nodded as Fen gently trailed his hand over his head piece, a small smile on his lips. This was the second thing he had ever been given that was all his – the cloak and now this. He was completely in his own world, so much so the teen nearly got left behind as Fayon and Lulen kicked their horses' sides into motion, riding along the grass plains towards the dirt-worn road that hundreds of refugees now queued along. The group of six found themselves further from the city than they had been before when they reached the back of the line.

Lulen shifted uncomfortably in his saddle. It would take hours, maybe even a day before they would be inside these walls. Until then they would be sat here in the open, exposed to any malicious creature that was out hunting for them. They were sitting ducks, and there was little he could even do about that. It was all up to the speed of the guards and fate now.

~

After sitting on his horse for two hours, moving slowly along with all the refugees, Fen dismounted, wiping his brow. He was too hot under the blazing sun with no shelter to cover them. The heavy cloak felt far too suffocating, and for the first time he was not glad to possess it. Fen wanted nothing more than to take it off, but hiding their identities was important so he couldn't. He was used to the cold of his cell. Even if it had been in the fire and ash-filled demons' realm, his cell had always been cold. Used to the shade of trees, he had never stood out in the open under the blazing sun before.

The heat could almost be compared to what he felt when flames were pressed against his skin. It was stifling, unbearable – all he wanted was to get away from it. He lightly pressed his head against his saddle, ignoring the burn it gave as it had become scalding under the sun. At least where he stood he could bask in what little shade his steed provided.

Fen closed his eyes, trying to focus on anything but the fact he felt like he was cooking under Caru's cruel grasp, eyes clenched shut, trying to blot out those memories that surged into his mind. Of course, that was until there was a gentle tap on his shoulder. Fen spun around fast, eyes wide, breathing a little erratic as he at first saw Caru's harsh face. That face soon melted away, his mind clearing of distortions, making him see clearly again.

A young human girl stood in front of him, red hair pulled back into a high ponytail, her eyes a little wide and her hand hanging in midair from where she had tapped him.

"I'm sorry, I didn't mean to scare you. You just didn't look well. I thought you might need some water." The redhead held up a water skin for him, a gentle smile on her face, words sweet like honey. Fen looked at her warily from under his hood. He didn't sense that she was harbouring any ill intentions, and he did desperately want some water. But as he lifted his pale hand to take the offered water skin, a thank you about to cross his lips, a far more tanned hand pushed his back down.

"Don't accept things from strangers." Fayon glared down at the redheaded human, distrust in his eyes, his hood not even over his face. Fen had not realised Fayon had dismounted his horse. The redhead tutted and put her hands on her hips.

"So distrusting." She pulled the cap from the skin and poured some into her mouth, swallowed easily and wiped the corner of her lips. "See? It's perfectly fine. What human is going to try to poison an elf? That's just bad karma. We have enough trouble here as it is without you lot getting angry. *I* was just trying to be nice." She huffed, blue eyes rolling dramatically as she shoved the now open water skin into Fen's hands.

Fen glanced up at Fayon from under the shadow of his hood. His mouth was pulled into a grim line, crimson eyes still glaring at the girl, but he gave Fen a slow nod after casting his eyes towards him. It was clear that the younger one needed water; he could see the beads of

157

sweat running down his face.

Fen looked so relieved as he took a gulp of water. It was cold on his parched throat, instantly filling him with relief. "Thank you." He gave a small bow as he held the water skin back towards its owner.

"No problem, you looked like you needed it." The petite redhead grinned as she took the skin back from him. "I'm Rina by the way!" She bounced on the balls of her feet, waiting expectantly for them to give their names in return, but Fayon just moved himself to be in front of Fen. He was not giving off a friendly aura in the slightest. Rina huffed and crossed her arms, muttering under her breath about how snotty elves were, thinking they were better than everyone else.

Of course, Lulen's eyebrow was twitching away from where he sat. Fayon wasn't even an elf, and yet he was apparently fitting right into the stereotype humans had conceived about his species.

"Rina, you should not mutter such things under your breath. Everyone here has been through hardships to get to safety, it is only right to be distrusting in the current state of our world. Not everyone has your uncanny ability to stay positive," a smooth voice said, as an older man appeared. He was not old for a human, but he was far more aged in appearance than the girl. Fayon reckoned he must be at least in his thirties. His garb and body structure implied he was trained in combat and had seen it, but his face, although plain, was warm and welcoming, with a soft smile lighting up the hardened features of his face. Rina ducked her head in embarrassment, making the older man chuckle.

"Sorry, Uncle Varys... he just looked unwell."

Varys patted her head. He was barely a head taller

158

than her. Rina immediately smiled, jumping up and down again as it meant he wasn't mad.

"I apologise for my niece's comments," Varys said, "she has never been one to hold her tongue. Please forgive her, immortal ones." He bowed his body down, hands folded out in front of him as a sign of respect that Rina quickly copied. Fen pushed past Fayon and gently grasped each of their arms, hood falling from his head as he lifted them up again.

"There is no need to bow. Thank you for offering me water, I was in need of it. Nor is there need for forgiveness; my friend is distrusting, making him seem like he dislikes you. It is not the case. We are simply wary, for the road has not been easy, as I am sure it has not been for you either. So, I apologise for any unwelcome feeling he may have given."

Varys stared at Fen, nearly letting his eyes widen before he schooled himself. This he had not expected. How interesting, he thought to himself, as he smiled in acknowledgment to Fen. *It seems I have found more than I was expecting*.

"You grace us with such kind words. I am humbled to have met someone such as yourself, when I myself am not worthy of it. My name is Varys. If I may ask the young master and his companions your names?" He watched in amusement as Fayon moved to go back in front of Fen.

Fayon disliked the aura this man was giving. He was too friendly, too trusting, too keen to know things. But Fen just pressed a hand to his chest, pushing him back.

"The pleasure is ours. My name is Fen, the glaring one behind me is Fayon. Lulen is the blond scowling at us all, then there is Myst, Nilee and Clanne." He pointed to the three children respectively. Fen smiled at Varys. The angel-blooded knew that this man felt off, that there was something hidden. He did not know what, but he could tell from feeling alone that neither he nor the girl harboured evil intentions. In fact, it felt to Fen as if this pair had come to protect them.

As Fen had felt no issue in sharing their names, as well as stopping Fayon from being rude, Varys and Rina both smiled. Varys had a subtle smile while Rina's was bright and toothy, like she was excited to know even that much about them.

"You all need to move, stop holding us up!" A gruff growl came from a haggard-looking gentleman from behind them, leaning hard on a wooden cane, his clothes torn and stained, a small sack tossed over his shoulder and a dark scowl on his face.

Both Fayon and Varys looked forward to see Lulen had moved with the horses and there was an increasing gap between the four and the rest of the line. Fayon grabbed onto Fen's arm instantly dragging him to close the gap.

"Why did you not tell us you were moving?" Fayon snapped, eyes filled with annoyance as he looked at Lulen.

Lulen just leaned forward, elbow propped up on the saddle, head resting on his fist, staring at Fayon with a raised eyebrow and bored eyes. "You were too busy trying to look scary and guard Fen to even look in my direction. You noticed eventually."

"Our goal is to travel together... what if our group got split or if an attack happened?" Fayon growled, to which Lulen just narrowed his eyes and sighed.

"Me and the children were barely three horse lengths

away, Fayon. My, you are touchy – is someone trying to make friends with your precious Fen really that horrible?" Lulen teased, a sly grin on his face as Fayon shot red in embarrassment.

Fen was tilting his head looking as confused, the three little children all staring at the arguing adults.

"Why *his* Fen?" Clanne whispered to Nilee, who shrugged, looking at her sister who was just frowning away.

"Grown-ups are just weird," Myst finally said, and the other two nodded their heads solemnly in agreement.

Behind them all Varys was smiling to himself watching the group. When he had come down the mountain, he had expected to find only one person. Instead he'd found a lively group, one of which he had not expected to be protecting yet. But here they all were. Perhaps he was not needed as of yet – there was no need to force himself into the group until it was time. For now, he would watch and protect only if needed. He moved his hand behind his back, holding out two fingers and drawing them in a horizontal line.

When Rina saw them, she held herself back, falling into line beside her master, staring at him.

Varys gave a small shake to his head. "*Not yet,*" he whispered. The one he wanted to protect was not travelling alone as he had thought. For now he could watch from afar, keeping them safe that way for now. "Focus on getting into the city, where we will be safe. Then you may make friends." Varys spoke in a low voice to his dragon. After all, it would be another few hours before they were inside the walls of Revel, which meant it was time to listen for attacks, not distract and make friends.

His gaze lingered on the arguing group in front of them, lips twitching at Fen's attempts to calm everyone down, before he turned to look at the horizon. Watching, waiting and listening for what was coming.

Chapter 16

What's Wrong?

Dusk was settling in by the time the group made it to the imposing wooden gates. Up close you could see the wear through time. Deep splintered chunks were missing in places, from where axes and the like had hacked at it, in a desperate attempt to get access to the city. It truly showed the might of this human nation and their ability to defend what was theirs.

Outside the gates were four knights, spears in hand, stationed two to a side, watching the horizon, while on the inner side of those gates more knights stood. A few were seated on horses, all with swords at their sides. Several had scrolls and quills, writing names and checking lists as refugees filed through.

Each group was stopped, two at a time as they filed through. Few questions seemed to be asked – the majority of people were spoken to for mere seconds before being admitted through into the cramped streets within the walls. Occasionally the guards held people back and seemed to question them as if they had committed grievous crimes, but in the end everyone got through. They had seen no one turned away, which meant when it came to be their turn, Lulen had little nerves left about their plan.

"Names, where you're from and your destination." A bored voice of a guard came, not even looking up from his scroll as he spoke. Which almost made Lulen laugh, feeling as though they need not have hidden all the marks, for they weren't even given that much attention.

How human, he thought.

"Our group consists of three children, Myst, Nilee and Clanne; two teenagers, Fen and Fayon; and myself, Lulen," he said, tone stern as always. He held the reins of his horse just as Fen and Fayon did, while the children all sat or rather lay in the saddles, all but falling asleep. "We have travelled from different locations. Three of us have come from Nueay, one is a human child we found in the wreckage of his village, and two are from Fareen Woods. We are travelling back to the Woods." The guard's head snapped up from his scribbling when he heard *Fareen Woods*, his eyes widening under his helm as he took in the pointed ears, his posture immediately straightening.

"My apologies for keeping you, oh immortal ones... enter, enter," he said quickly. His orders had been clear; the elven lord of Fareen Woods had promised medical aid and supplies to the humans in return for any of his race being granted safe passage through Revel. No one wanted to anger the lord. This guard was almost shaking with nerves for just having asked the questions.

Lulen looked at him curiously, confused by the sudden change in demeanour, but giving a slight nod in thanks before he continued walking. The horses pulled along behind, with the children safely upon them. The moment they passed through those gates and into the lantern-lit city within, it became a whole new world.

Horses and carts, stalls, vendors yelling for last sales of the evening, hundreds of people hustling and bustling around, shouldering their way through the overcrowded streets. Homeless people lined every street, most refugees from the destroyed villages, sweat rolling down their faces from the heat of the evening and overcrowding.

Fen had tension written all over his features as they

walked. He kept himself sandwiched between Fayon and Lulen, eyes darting constantly to make sure the three children were safe. He had never experienced anything like this – the sounds, smells – everything was completely overwhelming for the captive-raised angel-blooded.

His ears pounded, blood rushing through them in painful waves. He wanted to close his eyes, to hide somewhere quiet, where he couldn't hear the breaths of hundreds of people, couldn't smell the rivers of waste that travelled in stone gutters throughout Revel. One hand reached out, slowly fisting into Fayon's cloak.

Fayon looked to the side instantly when he felt the extra weight, brow furrowed when he saw Fen walking face scrunched and eyes screwed closed. He was holding on in order to be guided and to try to stop the overwhelming feeling that was washing over him like waves. Fen felt like he was drowning, it was too much.

The small screams or yelps of terror that Moon brought with her did not help Fen find calm either. Her presence just made the crowd louder, even though the wolf was walking like any common household dog beside her masters.

Concern instantly replaced his frowned expression, and he cleared his throat to get Lulen's attention, eyes darting to Fen to get the elf to look. Instant understanding dawned on the elf's features. Fen had never been around more than a few people. Even the line outside had been single file and almost silent apart from wails of grief. Inside the walls he was cornered at every turn, there was no relief. He had overlooked this issue, everything else he had planned to a fault but not this. Lulen looked around them, trying to gauge where the least amount of people seemed to travel. It was a large city; there had to be a quiet corner somewhere he could get them to.

Clanne leaned forward on the saddle, his small hand holding onto Fen's, trying to comfort him. The boy had a terrified expression on his face – the man that was his protector, that he trusted more than anyone else, was in pain and he didn't understand why. It made both men's hearts ache, especially when Fen squeezed the hand back, grounding himself on Clanne and Fayon.

"Lulen," Nilee whispered, leaning to try and tug on his tunic. She could only reach his hair, so she tugged that instead. "Go that way." The girl pointed down a smaller alley between the butcher's and what looked to be a tavern. It was barely wide enough to get a horse down, and the floor unevenly cobbled with a sewage gutter running straight through it. But there were hardly any people using that path, making it ideal.

Lulen instantly started fighting through the flow of the crowd to cross the street, one hand on Fen, guiding him while Fayon watched close behind. Lulen felt himself gagging at the stench that instantly enveloped them as they stepped into the alley, the children all pushing bundles of their cloaks against their faces to avoid the smell. Fen looked positively green, making Lulen hurriedly lead them further down, hoping it would open up into an area they could rest in, before Fen decided to experience what vomiting was.

"Disgusting," Fayon muttered. "How can humans live with this?"

"Not everyone is as advanced as your race, Fayon," Lulen called from the front.

Fayon sealed his lips because clearly that was true. Even the building style was different, no black stone buildings that towered over everything. The humans seemed to prefer grey stone, with wooden-beamed tops. Very strange.

Lulen was relieved when he found that the alley did indeed open up to a small, grassed area, housing a well that seemed to have been swallowed by the city as it had grown. It was clearly out of use. But it was a large enough area for the three horses, a wolf and the six of them to wrest away from the hustle and bustle that was now muffled by the stone walls surrounding them.

"Fen?" Clanne's small voice called out, almost in a whimper, causing Fayon to let go of his horse and move to gently grab Fen's arm.

"It's alright, let go now, let's sit you down." With a firm tug and words of reassurance Fen allowed himself to be guided, the reins slipping from his fingers. Fayon slowly sat the younger man down with his back against the moss-covered fountain, moving with him so he was crouched at his eye level. Fen curled in on himself, hands covering his sensitive ears, face burying itself into drawn knees.

Both Fayon and Lulen had faces drawn into grim lines watching their friend. Fayon stayed crouched, unsure what to do, his hand reaching out and drawing back repeatedly while Lulen was lifting the three children down. They immediately moved and all curled around Fen, making Fayon back away. He wasn't needed; the little ones seemed to know what to do. Instead, Fayon focused on the horses and taking their burdens from them. They needed to be rested for the next leg of their journey.

Lulen gently patted Moon's head. "Guard them, okay?" the elf whispered softly, the beast instantly lying in front of the group, head looking at the entrance, eyes locked on. Nothing was getting past her.

"What happens now that we have made it this far?" Fayon looked at Lulen. There were so many people looking to do exactly what they were doing. It was feeling like an impossible situation.

"Now you all stay here. I will find some food and learn what the situation is with accessing the valley. I am hopeful that it has been fully opened to at least my people. Judging from the guard's reaction to us it would appear likely. We should get out of the city fast – the valley will already be dangerous to cross and take a few days. We can't risk Fen becoming unable to do anything by being in this situation for too long."

Fayon gave a nod of understanding. Fen could become sick if he stayed like this, and neither of them knew anything about the constitution of angel-blooded. It couldn't be risked. After a pause Fayon responded. "Alright, stay safe… Come back, don't do anything to get in trouble."

Lulen gave a chuckle and patted his back, hard. "It is you who always gets in trouble, not me, my friend." He flashed a rare smile before he made his way back down the small alley, disappearing into the sea of people beyond.

Fayon ended up sitting himself down opposite Fen and the children, a worried look in his eyes, growing worse with every moment that Fen stayed in the foetal position. All Fayon wanted to do was surge forward, envelop Fen into his arms and tell him he was safe, yet he did not, he couldn't move. He and Fen had known each other for just over two weeks, although they had spent every one of those days in each other's company. Teaching things, seeing new sights, learning about each other. It still felt like he had no right to comfort Fen in a way that was so familiar, despite the urging in his heart to do so. So, he sat there, never reaching out, not saying a word, letting the three children comfort and curl around him.

Lulen, meanwhile, was effortlessly weaving between humans, making his way towards the rear of the city and the gaping gap between the two halves of the Valyn mountains. The crowds, he noted much to his displeasure, only grew thicker. This was not what he wanted. Dusk was finally creeping into night by the time Lulen had shoved himself past the mountain of humans, ignoring comments of *stuck-up elf* and the like. He just wanted to get to the pass gates and find out if they could travel through.

His heartbeat increased when he noticed the portcullis was down, several guards stationed in front of it and a mass of people camped out, waiting. That would explain the thickening of the crowd in this area. Still, he maintained his course until he came to stand right in front of one of the knights, all of them straightening up the moment they saw the elf.

"We apologise to the immortal one, but the pass is closed for the evening per His Highness's orders." The poor boy couldn't be more than seventeen in human terms, his voice shaking as if he were talking to an enemy he couldn't defeat. Lulen tried to look less stern and more approachable, having remembered Fen's description of him earlier, when he heard the nerves in his voice, and the others shifting uncomfortably. He realised maybe Fen had been accurate in his description.

"I see. May I enquire when the passage will be open? Me and my companions wish to return home as soon as possible. We have children and sick among them." Lulen laid it on thick – they did have children with them and currently Fen was unwell, so it wasn't necessarily a lie.

"As soon as the knights taking the last group through the valley return with the supplies promised by your lord. We do not have the knights to spare to guard another convoy." The young boy's voice was meek, almost cowering in on himself when he saw the frown on Lulen's face.

"How long do you expect that to be?"

"Five days at most, sir." The voice almost a squeak at this point.

"What if our group is able to protect ourselves and require no escort? May we leave sooner?" Lulen enquired, head tilted a fraction to the side as he stroked his chin.

"Well… I do not know, none of the refugees so far have been able to protect themselves. W…we would have to a...ask our captain." The poor boy was becoming a stuttering mess while Lulen frowned away at this information.

"I would appreciate it if you could find a way to ask this of your captain. I shall return tomorrow for your answer." Lulen gave a bow to him in thanks before turning on his heel. That was not what he had wanted to hear but it couldn't be helped now. All he could do for the moment was purchase food for them all while awaiting for dawn of the next day to acquire his answer.

Lulen made his way back through the crowd, eyes peeling for any food stalls that might still be open, eventually coming across one that was. The meat looked dubious and nothing that Lulen would normally eat at all. But needs must when you are on the run, and he was able to purchase six donkey meat sandwiches, steaming hot and wrapped in wax paper, with a few scraps extra for his beloved Moon. It cost no more than four copper pieces, a steal on the limited coin they had thought to bring with them. Even if he had to sit and stomach meat which was not typically in his diet. He only hoped that Fen would be able to stomach it; it was more grease than he had likely ever had, and the angel-blooded was already unwell from the overwhelming feeling of this city.

A feeling that he was unhappy to see hadn't changed. If anything, Fen seemed to be curled even further in on himself than when he had left, three scared children and a frowning Fayon all watching him intently. Lulen sighed heavily as he sat himself down beside Fayon and untucked the sandwiches from under his arm.

"Here. Everyone eat," he said in a very quiet voice, handing a package to each child first, then Fayon. Fen's sat in his lap untouched as the angel-blooded made no move to uncurl or even acknowledge that a word had been said to him. This did nothing to ease their worries, but Lulen motioned for them to eat and ate himself. Even if Fen would not eat, everyone else needed the food. As he ate, he threw the scraps he'd procured to Moon who, true to her name, wolfed down her meal with great enthusiasm.

"Sleep once you have eaten. It will grow quiet soon enough, so make the most of it. Tomorrow will be a long day for everyone." Lulen would keep watch; he felt too tense to sleep as it was, and he had enough medical knowledge to at least help Fen if he did grow sick from everything he was going through. No one argued with him, and the three children fell right asleep snuggled to Fen, bellies full.

Fen was next to fall asleep. Tension went from his body as people turned in for the night and the chatter of the city fell silent. Fayon was last to sleep – he found it difficult to let tiredness win when Fen had been in pain like that. But it was like a switch the second Fen had fallen asleep: Fayon was right behind him. Lulen was left, with Moon sat diligently beside him, watching over their companions – not their friends – as well as guarding their horses and belongings. They sat in silence – well, as silent as it could be inside a large city.

Tomorrow, he would get them out of here. He had no choice, not if he wanted to keep Fen healthy. Not if they wanted to get away before the inevitable attacks on Revel's walls began. The elf sighed and dragged his hand over his face. He could be sick from the stress he currently felt. Everything was too unknown for his liking. All he could do was sit and wait for tomorrow to come.

Chapter 17

Greatest

Aphir lifted his onyx eyes from where he had been gazing down at the procession currently making its way through Nisha. At its centre, an obsidian coffin, polished to perfection, sealed with magic never to be opened again. Carved deeply into the lid was his son's name and titles.

He had intended for the funeral to be a quick affair. Something that lasted a day at most. However, his people had called for the coffin to be taken around the realm. All wanted to mourn the loss of their prince.

Initially Aphir had opposed the idea with a passion. He wanted to get his army ready to move within days of Fen's escape. But then he had realised; if he wanted his entire realm to fight in revenge for their prince, his body needed to be seen by all. So, it had been, in all its mangled glory. The uproar had been far more delicious than he could have ever hoped for. When the coffin had finally been sealed just moments ago, the cries for revenge and death to the angel-blooded had been like a bloody melody ringing in his ears.

A perfect symphony of outrage, a compendium of emotions. His people all united under one goal. It was their time to rebel. To escape this unfair truce and the confinements it had placed on them all these last eleven thousand years. No longer would they limit themselves to this sorry piece of land while the angel-bloods had free reign.

This was the beginning of the era of demons. No-one would be defeating them in battle this time. Those angels and their supporters – those that allied with the side of "good" – they would know nothing but the bitter taste of defeat this time. Blood would flow like rivers until every last person, animal or thing that stood against them – be in the past or the present – was dead beneath his feet. Revenge for the pain they had caused his people, caused *him*, paid back in full.

Aphir's lips grew into a crooked smile at just the thought of all those dead under his boot. The thought of smushing that smug bastard angel-blooded king's head into a pool of bloody mud. It had his body shivering in excitement.

The demon-blooded king stood, lost in his own destructive thoughts, when he noticed Halki, his new captain, saluting at his side. Halki stood tall and thin in stature, garbed in impressive scaled black iron armour, her hair short, spiked and burgundy in colour. The captain had piercings through both her ears and lips, a deep scar through her left eyebrow, narrowly stopping before her eye. The bright red and yellow-flecked eyes she possessed could make her stand out among any crowd.

She was a beauty by any standards. Deceiving many, she was a black widow in a butterfly's skin. There were few who could best her in battle. She was swift and deadly, a truly brilliant tactician, and eager to prove herself worthy of her newfound position.

"Have you found out their location yet?" Aphir's gaze returned to the procession below as he awaited his answer.

Halki finally dropped her salute, facing the king as she opened her mouth to deliver the intel that had been gathered by the Valsar Plains orc packs. "The reports

174

have been coming in hourly. Any settlements they came across have been raided and destroyed as you requested. Those orcs have served us well, torturing those inhabitants for information, but so far none have seen Prince Fayon nor the escaped angel-blooded." Halki paused when she saw Aphir's jaw go tight, his knuckles cracking as he pulled his hands into fists. She took a deep breath before continuing. "We have, however, come to the conclusion their aim was never to climb over the mountain range. They have not gone in that direction. Which leaves them with one option. The human capital within the plains. It is known as Revel. Built around the old dwarven valley, the Valyrine pass. I have alerted the giants, goblins and trolls residing within the mountain caves. There is little point in having the orcs trying to raid Revel; they would take too long to get past the city defences. If the group do travel by way of the pass, an ambush is already set, they will not make it through the pass to the forest beyond. If they are hiding, waiting to climb the mountain, the orcs will keep them trapped. No matter what, they will be captured soon, my King." Halki spoke with a clear confident voice, showing no fear in front of the man who had murdered her predecessor, despite his tightened jaw.

This was one of the reasons Aphir chose her. She had spirit. The confidence of youth could not be compared – the young were a different ball game and he admired it. He slowly nodded his head, working his jaw a little, fingers clenching and unclenching behind his back.

"Ensure those in the pass attack no one but them. They must remain hidden – an unnecessary battle may lead to us losing them to a different route or them travelling with a bigger party for protection. I want them caught swiftly.

175

My angel-blooded must be unharmed, alive and whole. If my son is lost, it is of little concern to me... after all, he is already dead to his realm." A shiver of joy ran through his frame at the thought of having his weapon back. His most prized possession. Soon everything would be in place, his oh so sweet weapon back where it belonged and used to destroy the race it was born from.

They thought they were so strong that they could never be bested by Aphir and his people. Wait until they saw he had the child of prophecy all along. Instead of bringing peace to the world, he would use the child to destroy it. Poetic justice. The weapon was born to them, but he would be the one to wield it.

"Of course, my King. I have already taken the liberty to tell them this in the raven that was sent out. All current caravans that have travelled through the pass in the last few days have not been attacked, only observed. They have so far not attempted to enter it. I estimate if they are to use that route, we will see them enter within the next few days."

Aphir actually returned his gaze to her, a hint of fondness in those dark eyes. He liked her forethought and planning – that she had done what he wanted without coming whimpering to him for permission.

"You are far more reliable than Caru was, I chose well with you. Go, oversee the preparation of my army. I want seven battalions ready to descend within the week. Try not to fail me, Halki."

She immediately stamped her foot and slammed an arm to her chest, bowing heavily. "As you wish, my King." With that she turned fast. Moving with long purposeful strides across His Majesty's balcony and through his office until she was descending the halls to reach the training grounds, which had now been repurposed. Gone were the large empty plains that had resided for horseback training. In their place now were war tents, more and more added by the day, as flocks of their people filed in from all over Prophet to join the king's crusade against the murdering angel-blooded.

In just a matter of days, since the coffin had officially begun to circulate the realm, hundreds and now thousands had come to sign up for war. They had an ever-increasing number of blacksmiths, slaves running backwards and forwards from the mines. Mine carts full of black iron, to forge into the black steel weapons. Armour of all conditions and make were piled high behind these tents. The blacksmiths worked all hours of the day to create their weapons of destruction, beautifully sharpened blades, horrid, spiked arrows, thick movable armour.

Not only did they have blacksmiths working all hours to equip the soldiers, but they had carpenters making shields for those who fought without magic. But not only that, they had engineers creating massive siege weapons to bulldoze any gates or walls that stood in their way. No magic was going to be wasted on such trivial tasks. Their strength needed to be saved for when the angel-bloods descended, not spent on mere useless mortal races.

They had Velka, who had recruited any able-bodied alchemists within their realm to help her brew poisons to dip arrows and soak blades. This would be a bloody war, there was no doubt about that. It made Halki smile twistedly, excited to see fields of green painted crimson as their foes fell endlessly to their blades. She had yearned to be part of a war as long as she could remember, and now she was getting her chance.

Halki glanced around what was left of the training grounds, and no matter where she looked, she saw people training. The archery ranges were completely packed, the combat rings full of knights, training normal civilians to fight. As usual, their kind picked up such skills with ease.

Then the magic circles were no less packed with demon-bloods, all practising their fire or darkness magic. Lines upon lines everywhere, to get armour, weapons, to train and even to just sign up. She knew Aphir would be very pleased with this. Forget only seven battalions ready to go. She could have ten at least. This was by far the most united their people had been in thousands of years.

Halki worked her way through the crowd, shoving over a small slave child as she went, not caring that she was the one who walked into him. He was in her way; he was lucky he only got shoved to the floor and not whipped for standing where he had. She just left him there sniffling away, scrambling to get up before someone else stepped on him.

Eventually she made her way to the registration tent, a massive imposing black and red tent, set up at the heart of the fields. It had officers of all levels inside signing up and placing people into rank and unit. The man in charge of overseeing everything was an old demon-angel-blood war veteran. He was a legend known for killing over a hundred angel-bloods single handedly. Saren was his name, and since the wars had ended he had become the trainer of all their realm's knights. He was her teacher, her mentor, her father.

"Our king has requested I aid in overseeing the recruitment and creation of his army. Where would you like me, old man?" If she were anyone else, he would have set her ablaze on the spot for talking to him in such a disrespectful manner. But she was his youngest child, as well as his greatest warrior. If anyone could get away with it, it was her.

The two looked incredibly similar. Both father and daughter had deep red hair, Saren's darker with age. He, like his daughter, had a scar, only his ran the whole length of his face. Their eyes were both enchanting, hers with colour, his an endless black. Both had the same stern face. Even the way they carried themselves was scarily similar. It was why they were known as the Twin Beasts of Prophet.

Saren let out a huffed laugh, smacking her on the back, making Halki stagger forward a little.

"You can help by making sure those good-for-nothing smiths keep making us weapons. I got nearly five hundred still waiting to be armoured and armed. I want that number halved in the hour, you got me, girl? We ain't messin around here. This is a war, we got to be prepared for when those angels make their attack. They ain't nothing to mess with." He looked grave as he spoke, as if remembering the past battles with those animals. He would not send any of his men or women into harm's way unprepared. Mortals called them devils. Those angel-bloods were no better, they were just as ruthless.

"Yes sir! If they are not working fast enough, I will ensure that changes or they will regret it." Halki cracked her knuckles, marching off to go and crack the whip on these smiths. She'd find more ore, the people to help, whatever they grumbled about needing they would have. In order to create the greatest, most unstoppable army the world has ever seen.

If that still wasn't enough, she'd make a grizzly example out of one of them.

By the end of the week the demon-bloods would join the world again, with more than three thousand five hundred descending their borders in the first wave of troops. They would cover the world in fire and darkness, and anyone that dared oppose them or side with the angel-bloods would be slaughtered. Only those that bent to their will would survive.

If everything went to plan, then the angel-bloods should have received their king's declaration of war by now and be frantically arming themselves up after years of peace. The fools. They'd probably got fat; got lax with the thought they were safe from war. Halki could bet they didn't have a single trained soldier.

She very much hoped she got to kill a hundred herself just like her father had. Halki arrived hands on her hips to the smithing area, gazing around, glad to see everyone was working, that no one was standing still.

"Alright you lot, why have we got so many unarmed and without armour? What do you need to get this done faster?"

"More hands!"

"Moulds, if you can find em."

"Lava – running low on fresh stuff."

"Ore! You got more slaves? Get em working, lass."

"If that is all you require you should have had the sense to ask before! Your lack of foresight is unacceptable. I will get what you need. If you have not made progress after that I shall see that you are made an example of for your inadequacies," Halki snapped, causing flinches from the smiths, who all started working faster as she left to get everything they needed.

~

Back at the castle Aphir had officially ended the procession of his son's coffin. The stone casket now lay in the royal mausoleum, beside his mother and his twin. Of course, he would ensure one day the body was replaced with his real son. His wife would not rest well in her coffin until Fayon was safe beside her. But he would have that done in secret once the war was underway.

Aphir slowly placed his hand on the words engraved into his wife's casket, fingers tracing her name: *Queen Aarin Phet of the Realm of Prophet. Beloved Queen, Wife and Mother.*

"Soon, my love, I will have revenge. I could not prove they killed you and Engel, but now they will pay for it dearly. Just wait a little longer." His words were uncharacteristically soft. The king stayed there in silence, fingers gracefully tracing her name over and over until Culvat cleared his throat and announced his presence.

"My King, I have received a missive that you will want to know about… it is from Elyon."

Aphir's whole being changed at the mention of that name. His body became tense with anticipation, spinning around fast, a wild excited look in his eyes, fists clenching and unclenching.

"And? Are they in panic? Mobilising whatever pathetic army they have left? Do they regret thinking there was lasting peace? Come, Culvat tell me!" Aphir sounded positively giddy. However, that look and excitement slowly vanished as he took in Culvat's pinched expression.

"What is it? Spit it out, Culvat!" Aphir snapped, as the man in question heaved a heavy sigh.

"Elyon returned our raven. His missive states that he has decided to keep his realm locked and sealed away.

They are making no moves to arm or prepare for war. They are keeping themselves from the affairs of the outside world still, my King." Culvat remained still and unflinching when Aphir let out a scream of rage, his arms igniting, fists making contact with 'Fayon's' coffin repeatedly as he vented his anger, leaving scorch marks all over it.

"Then we will make them come out! We will turn the world against them until they have no choice to come out and protect their name! Get everyone ready! I want as many of those shits ready to march into the mortal realm as soon as possible. We will burn it all to the ground! They will come out to protect those wretched mortals they hold so dear!" Aphir screamed, rage not dying down for a second. The building was even trembling at the sheer power of Aphir's anger.

Culvat knew better than to stick around. He bowed and backed out of the room slowly, leaving Aphir and his anger alone, in favour of making sure as many people were ready to march as demonly possible by the end of the week.

They had four days to become a great army. He would make certain of that. Not only to ensure his king's ambitions were met, but also to ensure that he remained alive to see the end of the war. To assure the creation of the greatest demon-blooded army to ever march this earth.

Chapter 18

New Allies

It was at first light that Lulen got up to return to the gates, hoping to have his answer as to whether they could travel through the pass without waiting. He was certain they would since they were able to protect themselves. That would not be an issue but only time would tell if his thoughts were correct.

Before he left he had woken Fayon, telling him to wake Fen before it grew loud, to try and get the now ice-cold donkey meat sandwich into him. Then he left Fayon with Moon to watch over everything in their little area. Lulen hoped he would not be too long, but he also knew there was every likelihood he would need to fight to gain the access they needed before the five days were up.

By the time the sun had just started to light up between the crammed together buildings of Revel, Lulen had made it back to the gates that separated the pass from the city. There today were faces he did not recognise from the night before, but clearly they had been told to expect him, because a finely-armoured young man was walking towards him. His armour, unlike the others, was all silver; there was no mix of leather or steel. The armour itself was incredibly crafted as well as intricately patterned. His sword had a blue tassel hanging off the end of it, differing to the red or green that the others had. Lulen assumed he was of high rank. He just did not know how high.

"You must be the elf that terrified my guards yesterday." The man gave out a hearty chuckle and held his hand out. "I am Prince Beau. My father sent me to discuss with you about your group's traversing the pass without guards."

Lulen shook his hand after a moment, not wanting to offend the human prince. "My name is Lulen, son of Lufen. It is my pleasure to make your acquaintance. I apologise if I scared your men yesterday. I have been told repeatedly I just have that kind of face."

Beau let out a belting laugh upon hearing that and waved his hand. "Nonsense! You look no sterner then their captains – they're just still green to the gills is all."

Lulen's lips twitched a little at the corners. He had to admit, for a human this man was not half bad. "Alright then. Not to sound rude but you said about gaining access to the pass – is it possible for my group? We do not want to wait five days for an escort." Lulen watched Beau's face for any indication for what he would answer.

"How many are there in your group? Children and sick you told my men you had. How many of each?"

"We are a size of six. There are two elven children within our group who are travelling with their elder brother, who is combat trained. The other child is a human who has been adopted into our little family. Then there is me and my cousin. He is currently sick from the noise; he is not used to being in crowded places. He should recover once we get into the quiet of the pass." Just like before, Lulen's eyes never left the face of this prince. He did not like the frown that appeared there as he spoke.

"With only two adults to protect three children and a sickness-stricken elf, I cannot permit you to pass. It is too dangerous."

"We also have my companion – or familiar, if you will

– who is a white wolf. Will that not satisfy you? We have enough horses for us to ride. None of us shall be walking, we will be in the pass far less time than any of the caravans you send there and back." Lulen tried to reason but Beau just shook his head in response.

"I'm sorry it is far too risky."

"How many more able-bodied adults do you suggest our group have for you to let us pass?" If he had to find warriors he'd find them, they needed to leave. He could feel the winds turning, almost taste the iron in the air. The demon-bloods had to be nearing, ready to intervene soon if their orc and other allies couldn't capture Fen. Of course, Lulen could not know how correct he was.

Beau looked hard at Lulen. The look honestly did not suit his features. The light brown hair and soft blue eyes just made his gaze soften, likely no matter how hard he tried. Lulen had to admit he was impressed this young man had the respect he did without being able to use such looks.

"If you are able to find two more companions, each with a horse and combat training or experience also, then I will allow your group to pass."

"Two more, each with a horse and experience in a fight. Done." He could do that no problem, with the sea of people around them, finding two that had horses, combat experience and did not want to sit around waiting for four more days just to hope they got in the next caravan would be easy. There had to be at least a hundred that fit that bill.

"I will return with my group as soon as we have the extra two people. You give me your word we will be allowed to pass?" Lulen made sure to question this; he had been let down by mortal kinds before. It was how he came to be trapped as a slave in the demon-bloods realm after all.

"You have my word. Take this, show it to whoever is stationed here upon your return. I will pass my order on. They will count your numbers and if correct they shall let you pass. On my name I swear you this." Beau spoke with such authority and promise that Lulen had no problem in believing him. The elf reached out, grasping the small blue metal shield that Beau had held out. It appeared to have on it two mermen facing each other, likely a family crest of the royals here. That would explain why presenting it should allow them through.

"Thank you, Your Highness, your generosity is highly appreciated. I shall remember this." Lulen gave a bow to the prince who smiled softly, his whole face lighting up as he did so.

"You are welcome, my friend. I truly wish you luck in your journey." With that the prince turned away, giving a slight nod to his men before moving off back towards the main gate, the crowd parting fast for the young man.

"Right, two people, all you need is two people, Lulen...Two people you can trust." He heaved a sigh and ran his hand down his face as he thought about how he could even judge whether or not anyone here was trustworthy. *Surely no human here was helping the ones responsible for destroying their lives. Unless of course they were told this was because of Fayon and Fen. Then maybe they would?* This was going to be impossible to do fast now he thought about it.

Just as his thoughts began to spiral he was tapped upon the shoulder. Lulen turned around, hand slipping fast back to his dagger, ready to attack, to dash backwards in case this was a trap. But when he turned, he found himself face to face with Rina and Varys.

"Overheard you needing one or two more people to join you in going through the pass." Varys spoke in a matter-of-fact tone, as if to make sure that Lulen didn't deny his words in any way.

"You heard correctly," Lulen spoke after a long pause, silently trying to debate whether he was mad about the fact they'd eavesdropped on his conversation, or relieved that he didn't have to go looking for people.

"Then you should bring us!" Rina piped up, bobbing on her feet with a real bright smile on her face.

"She is right, we would be happy to accompany you. Both of us have seen real fights and are able to protect ourselves as well as others." Varys stared at Lulen, shouldering his sword as if to draw attention to the fact he had a very fine weapon.

Lulen looked between the two. Admittedly the man looked to have seen combat, but this young girl? She did not seem like a fighter to him – she did not carry herself, or act like someone who had witnessed the horrors of battle. She was far too young, too bubbly for him to believe that she had the necessary experience. Even with the spear she carried.

"I am really sorry, but I do not believe I can take you two with me. Neither of you has a horse." *And I do not know if I can trust you,* went unsaid.

"We have horses," Rina piped up, hands on her hips.

"I do not believe that is his issue, Rina," Varys said. "Am I correct in saying that, Master Lulen?"

Lulen blinked in surprise for a moment, before recalling that it was Fen who had introduced them to this pair.

"Yes, you are correct... May I ask why you wish to

travel with us, when a safer option is only four days away?"

"I could ask you the same thing, young master," Varys responded, making Lulen scowl.

"I asked you first," Lulen growled a little, getting rather defensive very fast.

"That is true, you did ask first. Very well then. I wish to accompany you because, within your group there are people I would like to see protected and away from the ones currently hunting them. Is that satisfactory?" Rina's eyes widened when Varys said that. She looked at him like he had grown two heads. That was supposed to be a secret was, it not?

"Protect... from those hunting..." Lulen could not help the stunned look on his face. He had expected many responses, and for them to be lies, but not this one. Nor had he expected it to sound so honest.

"Correct. I can promise you that neither of us mean you or your group any harm, but I cannot explain things more than I already have. For now, at least. Just know that you could not be any safer than with us as your extra protection."

"Varys is right, you know. You won't find anyone better than us, and anyway Fen trusted us, so you should know we aren't hiding any malicious intent."

Lulen stood there in silence for a long time contemplating their words. Clearly, they were hiding things, they knew things that no one here should know. Not unless they had been told by evil forces. Yet it didn't seem like that was the case at all. He could sense no lies in their words. He watched their faces with each word they said. No clues to indicate deceit had been present on their features.

"Oh, come on Mr Uppity Elf, can you just say yes already? Standing here is getting old now." Rina poked his chest with her pointer finger repeatedly, not caring at all that Lulen was looking more and more perturbed by the minute. His left eyebrow twitched relentlessly as Varys pulled Rina back a few steps, giving a disapproving look.

"And you have your own horses as well as weapons, correct?" Lulen asked warily after a moment, having decided to trust them for now. But he'd keep an incredibly close eye on them. However, they had found out about Fayon and Fen, and the fact Varys said he couldn't tell him things right now put an uneasy feeling in the pit of his stomach. But at this point, what *didn't* make him feel that way? At least they had been forthcoming about their knowledge.

"Yes, we have two horses as well as our own weaponry. As I previously said, you will be hard pressed to find two comparisons more suitable than us." Varys stared at him as he continued to hold Rina back, smiling a fraction when he knew Lulen had given in to reason.

"Very well. If you two are sure about this, you may accompany us through the pass."

"WOOOOOHOOOOOOOO," Rina practically screamed, jumping up and down, fist punching the air in excitement. People all around them turned to look at the commotion.

"Calm down, would you? You're giving me a headache," Varys muttered, rubbing his temple.

"Sorry Varys." Rina was giving him a sheepish smile.

Varys turned his attention back to Lulen. "We are sure. You will not regret this, I promise. When are you and your group intending to leave this place?"

"As soon as possible. I need to get a few supplies then bring everyone to the gates. If you would meet us back here by midday, we shall leave and get as far as we can before the sun sets, and the trolls and goblins come out."

"Yes, nightfall will be a dangerous time, but do not think the day will be any easier. This pass is notorious for bandits as well as those foul creatures." Varys was confident in his words, making Lulen sure that this man knew his stuff.

This made him believe Varys was not some normal human. This man knew things, he had a way with words. He had an air about him, and not one he would ever associate with a mortal. It made him trusting and wary of him all at the same time.

"I am less worried about the bandits." *It is the ones Aphir has hunting Fen and Fayon we need worry more about*; he added in his head. Varys just gave a small nod, pulling Rina away before she could open her big mouth and say something to upset the elf for a second time.

"We will be waiting for you at noon," Varys called behind him as they left, leaving Lulen standing there alone beside the gates.

Eventually Varys stopped pulling Rina along when they made it to a rather grand-looking stables, its ceilings vaulted with great thick oak beams. It smelt fresh, as if it were cleaned daily. Definitely not somewhere you would think they could afford to house their horses by the looks of them.

"Cassian," Varys' voice boomed. Soon a short wart-faced man came scurrying over, head bowed a fraction.

"Y...Yes oh esteemed one?" He stumbled over his words, shoulders shaking a little.

"Still afraid of me?" Varys sighed, shaking his head,

lifting his hand, making Cassian flinch violently. However Varys just gently patted his shoulder.

"No matter, we shall be leaving today, you will have to fear no longer. I need you to saddle the two fastest horses as well as purchase the supplies necessary for supporting, say, eight people for a few days."

"B...But Sir... the silver pieces..." The poor man seemed to cower in on himself with every word, until Varys just pulled a pouch from thin air, setting it into Cassian's hands. The small man nearly toppled under its weight.

"Will this amount of silver be sufficient for you to do as I have asked?"

"Y...yes Sir! Right away." The warted male scurried off, dragging the silver pouch with him, to purchase all the best supplies for his guest. When Varys was sure Cassian had left ear shot, he returned his gaze to Rina.

"I want you to stay with Fayon, make sure he is not hurt." He would not lose him again.

"But what about you? He's your brother, why do I have to protect him?" she whined loudly. *Fayon was mean and grumpy. Why did she have to get stuck guarding him of all people?*

"Me? I will be protecting what was most precious to him, both in his last life and it seems this new one as well."

Rina blinked at him for a moment, before crossing her arms and pouting. "I suppose that's acceptable," she murmured, much like a child who has just been bargained with. Varys hugged her close and patted her head, chuckling a little.

"I only choose to protect him myself, because unlike Fayon, he does not seem very strong yet. You do better being able to move freely, my little dragon."

"I suppose… Fayon's still grumpy and mean though. I better get treats every time he's mean to me, Varys!"

"You always get treats." Varys chuckled and shook his head before sitting himself down, hands behind his head, eyes closed.

"Rest until we leave. Do not argue," he said just as Rina opened her mouth to argue. The dragon girl slumped down, hunched over, arms crossed, massive pout on her lips just glaring over at the relaxed Varys.

That is how the pair stayed until the sun rose towards noon. Only then did Varys move to take the two saddled and packed horses from Cassian, heading off straight towards the gates to the Valyrine pass.

~

Meanwhile Lulen had found himself wandering the streets of Revel, trying to purchase any supplies he could with the few pieces of silver he had left. They needed as many provisions as possible, so he spent his time finding different stalls, assessing their prices, aiming to locate the best deals. He was after three hours able to leave the market area with arms full of wrapped goods.

He had been able to get dried meats, several jars of pickled vegetables and a plethora of cheap dried fruit. He had even been able to snag a jar of rum with an incredible amount of bargaining. It was not bought for drinking, no. He had it for antiseptic in case anyone else decided to pick up an injury up before they reached his realm.

By the time he got back to the rest of his companions, the only thing he was vaguely worried about was whether they would be able to find water in the pass. He had no doubt there would be plenty of grass patches for their horses, or things for Moon to hunt.

"So, are we able to leave?" Fayon asked the second he saw Lulen. Lulen did not reply straight away, because he was chuckling and ruffling Moon's fur, rubbing behind her ears after the large white wolf had come bounding over to him.

"Yeah, I missed you too," he whispered, although not quietly enough because he heard a gasp from Nilee.

"So, you *do* like her! I knew it! Lulen loves Moon. Lulen loves Moon," she sang as she skipped around them. Fayon burst out laughing, watching as Lulen went a little red.

"I don't love her… she's just a good companion."

"Who you wanted to get rid of," Myst oh so helpfully pointed out, causing Clanne to actually snicker beside her, hugging on to Moon who came right over when she heard him sounding happy.

"Alright, alright, I will admit I was wrong. What's with you all ganging up on me today?" He huffed as he came to sit down, depositing his goods onto the grass. The elf glanced over at Fen, glad to see he seemed much more relaxed, albeit he was asleep.

"Lulen? Are we getting through?" Fayon asked again after waiting for the children to get distracted by a playful Moon.

"We were allowed to pass if we had two more combat-trained adults with horses. I found those two people, so we will leave around noon."

"You already found two people? Lulen, how do you know we can trust them? You said yourself anyone could be here... what if they are playing us?"

"Calm down, they are the two that gave Fen the water yesterday. He trusted them, did he not? And I saw no deceit in them when I questioned why they volunteered. I

193

considered our options carefully, Fayon, I promise you."

Fayon looked no more happy hearing who Lulen had chosen to accompany them but did not question him any further. "Alright... if they can help get us to safety then very well. But that does not mean I trust them."

"Nor did I say you have to. How is Fen doing?" Lulen changed the topic as soon as he felt he was able to. He found himself more than anything wanting to see how their angel-blood was doing.

"He woke briefly, maybe ate two bites of that sandwich. After that he just slept." Fayon reached over, gently brushing a strand of hair from Fen's face. Lulen watched in silence. At least Fen had something in him.

"Let him stay asleep until we leave. It is going to be louder than even yesterday, so best not overwhelm him for too long."

Fayon nodded in agreement instantly, staying sat watching him for a moment, before Lulen tapped his shoulder.

"Help me pack everything." Lulen did not need any help really, but he did not particularly want Fayon to just sit there and watch Fen sleep.

It was two hours of packing, the children and wolf playing games like tag and fetch, and Fen lay sleeping the entire time. Only when that sun was reaching its midday peak did Lulen lift the children onto horses and Fayon wake Fen. The angel-blood was immediately in pain.

Fayon lifted Fen into his arms, getting him seated upon his horse, a pained expression on Fayon's own face as he watched Fen hunch over, hands clamped hard over his ears. Fayon walked on foot through the crowd, leading Fen and his own horse, following after Lulen to go and meet Varys and Rina. Then they could finally enter the pass, and get to the elves, where they could live a peaceful life.

Chapter 19

The Valyrine Pass

Lulen led his group through the stifling crowd, managing to get them to the gates just after the sun crossed over its noon peak. Rina and Varys were already sitting on their steeds, saddle bags packed full of various supplies. Varys waited patiently for their companions, while Rina half hung off her horse, letting out loud bored moans.

"I was beginning to think you had replaced us," Varys joked, before his expression turned grave upon seeing Fen hunched over. "What happened to him?" His voice was laced with worry, sounding more like a friend than a stranger. It made Fayon shift uncomfortably in his saddle; he did not like how familiar he made himself sound to them.

"Fen sick," Clanne whispered sadly, his little hands clinging onto Fen's.

"Sick?" Rina's interest peaked, watching as Clanne nodded his head in response.

"He doesn't like the sound," Nilee informed them next.

"He will be alright once we get away from the city." Lulen watched as Varys and Rina shared a look before nodding.

"Very well, let us be off then, with haste if it means he will recover sooner." Varys would not be losing Fen. Even if they thought it was just because of the sounds of the city, he needed to test it to be sure. No one was dying on his watch, never again.

"Why are you coming with us? I don't want you to

come!" Myst yelled, sticking her tongue out at them. She didn't like them one bit, nope.

"Myst, they are gonna help us," Nilee whispered, eyes round like saucers, not understanding why her twin was so angry.

"We don't need their help."

"Why you little... What are you gonna do, huh? You're too little to fight, that's why you need us. Stop being a brat," Rina snapped, glaring at Myst who just glared right back. The two clearly were not getting along already. They could expect plenty of childish arguments from them.

"Rina, you are an adult, do not argue like a child."

"Enough, close your mouth, Myst," Fayon snapped, giving the girl sitting in front of Lulen a pointed glare. Rina gave a smug *I won* look, before she was slapped upside the head by Varys.

"I told you to stop."

Rina received a smirk from Myst at that, causing Rina to just glare harder.

"If you two are quite finished we will leave," Lulen said in a bored tone. He nudged his horse toward the guards, digging into the inside of his tunic to pull out the token Prince Beau had given him. He held it in the palm of his hand, holding it up for all those stationed there to see. Instantly the knight in charge of this watch shift moved forward.

"Master elf, we were told to expect your group. We were informed you could only pass if your group consisted of five adults at least."

Lulen nodded to the man and motioned his head behind him. "If you could not already tell, we have the two extra required by your king and prince for us to pass without waiting. I would appreciate it if you opened the gates now. We are expected back." That last part was of course a lie, but with how the guards at the entrance had reacted to him, he safely assumed no one here wanted to anger his lord or the elves of Fareen woods.

The knight instantly bowed, taking quick count of the group one last time before turning to his men. Cupping a hand over his face in an attempt to make his voice travel further, he yelled over top of the crowd: "Raise the portcullis! Open the gates. Group passing through, by order of his majesty Prince Beau."

Almost instantly every knight present was moving, several stepped to the side, spears held upright in front of them. Two went to pull on a massive wheel, a chain attached, winding repeatedly around it. This was used to slowly raise the heavy iron portcullis that lay on the inside of the wooden gates. The two strongest knights present were in charge of lifting it, and even then, it took several minutes to fully raise it. Once locked in place another order was barked, and yet again knights ran forward, sliding the locking bars from the thick oak gates, two shouldering each side, pushing with all their might to slowly open the way.

There was a great creaking sound as the old hinges were forced to move, and every second more of the other side was revealed. It was a crevasse, maybe thirty people wide, running the entire way through the Valyn mountains. The sides were completely sheer – the chunk had quite literally just been carved through what was once a whole mountain.

You could not see one end from the other. All that faced them was chopped cliff sides, patched uneven ground, consisting of stone and now grass. The light of the sun did not seem to reach it – the mouth was as light as day, but the further you looked or travelled in, the more you realised it was perpetual dusk and night once inside, making it perfect for ambushes that often occurred in the Valyrine pass. No matter how many torches, magic or any other form of light one could create, it made no difference to the deep dark of the valley. It made it the perfect refuge for evil to make its mark.

If you travelled this path, you did so as a large caravan or with a band of fighters – travelling without was suicide. The pass had claimed enough lives to make it regulation to have such things now.

"Good luck," the knight said, looking at them as the gates fully opened, the crowd behind them all standing wide-eyed as they were readying to leave.

"Pass through now; the gates are not permitted to stay open long!" the knight snapped.

Lulen wasted no time in kicking the sides of his steed, spurring them into motion, Moon hot on his heels as he raced over the rickety wooden surface and onto the stone-laid ground beyond. Soon after, Fayon and Fen's horses followed, Varys and Rina bringing up the rear.

Behind them they heard the yell of "Close the gates! Lower the portcullis!"

The sounds of uproar followed. A yell for guards to stay in formation as hundreds of refugees tried to surge forward into the pass before the gates could be sealed, knights' shields going up, spears pointed outwards to stop people in their tracks.

All that could be heard in the air were cries of outrage.

"You can't keep us here!"

"The king prioritises elves over his own people!"

"Why let them through!"

"Hold them back, men! No one gets through till our boys get back from the other side! Steady!"

"It's our lives, our choice! Let us through!"

"Bastards! There are children here! Let us leave, by the demons damn you!"

Then came the heavy slam of the gates and the crash of the portcullis coming down fast, scraping back into its stone grooves on the ground. The uproar, although still heard floating over the top of the walls, almost seemed to be completely muffled now. The pass seemingly blocked out all sound of the city behind it. An eerie silence awaited them in the gloomy passage. They sat side by side, horses all lined up in a row as they stared at the dark expanse in front of them. Lulen clicked his tongue against the roof of his mouth, considering the best way to go about this ride.

"Fayon, ride up front with me. Fen's horse will follow yours. Then Varys and Rina, if you ride behind him, that should cover us in terms of vulnerabilities. When Fen recovers his senses, he will give us an advantage over anything trying to sneak up on us. Everyone agrees? Good." He gave no one a chance to even answer whether they agreed with his plan. That's what he wanted doing, that's what was going to happen.

Myst looked rather smug that she was going to be up front, while Rina was going to be stuck behind looking at horses' asses the entire journey. Yeah, the little girl was snickering away to herself.

"Very well, it seems like a well thought-out arrangement," Rina said. "Putting those who know each other's strength together is ideal. Two at the front and two at the rear provides ample cover. I must say, master elf, I am glad to see elves are not as the people of

Revel described."

Lulen gave a funny look. "And pray tell, what do they say about my kind?"

"That you're arrogant, self-centred and think of no one but yourselves. Oh, they also say that you're glory seekers, stealing fame from others." Rina was all too happy to pitch into this topic of conversation.

Varys shook his head. She seemed a little too giddy to be making Lulen's anger rise. However, the elf did not defend himself. It was Myst that did.

"He isn't any of those things! If you can't be nice, you shouldn't say anything."

Fayon, Nilee, Lulen and Clanne all looked at Myst a little shocked. Here was the usually snarky and mean demon-blood child telling a human adult to be nice. It was a little ironic.

"Alright, as much as I would enjoy seeing where this argument goes, let's at least do it while riding so we can get Fen away." Fayon had already started his horse into a trot as he said this, meaning they had to start moving no matter what anyone wanted to do. His only priority in this moment was to get Fen far enough away that his sensitive ears unfocused on the sounds of the city that he had hyper fixated on the moment they went inside the walls.

Before they went in, he seemed to be able to select when he wanted to expand his senses, but once inside he hadn't been able to shut them away. Everything seemed to be unfiltered, just assaulting Fen from all five senses. Fayon was getting him away, even if it meant they hadn't actually finished their conversations.

Lulen soon fell into line along the right side of Fayon, Rina lining herself up behind him, Varys behind Rina. This left Fen and Clanne sandwiched between the four warriors. It also meant, unfortunately, that two of the children were at the front, the first targets. This had Lulen and Fayon on high alert; both had an arm protectively crossed over the child in their care, a measure to ensure they were not the easy target.

"How long will it take us to get through the pass?" Nilee asked curiously after several minutes of only echoing steps ringing between the cliff walls.

"The last time I travelled through it took me nearly three days."

Clanne actually groaned in response to that. "Three days? I don't want to sit on the horses that long again," he whined, not that Lulen could blame him – riding a horse for so long made even his legs hurt. He imagined the children were in quite a bit of pain by now.

"Once we arrive, I promise you will not have to ride a horse again. But until then you have no choice."

Clanne crossed his arms with a hmph, but said nothing further, while Nilee leaned to the side to try and look at him, nearly falling off in the process. She would have if not for Fayon's protective arm.

"Clanne? Wanna, play 'I see?'" She grinned excitedly. Clanne's face instantly brightening as he nodded.

"Hey I wanna play too! I'm going first, okay? Good. So, I see… ummmm something starting with... L." Myst smirked away because they would never guess what she had seen. Sure, enough both littles were occupied for a good ten minutes coming up with all manner of words beginning with L. It got to a point where even the adults joined in to try and help. No one had been able to guess the small girl's word.

"May I ask, Myst, is it something only you know?" Varys asked, voice laced with amusement. He may not be able to see her face but judging by Lulen's slightly annoyed grumble he knew he was right.

"You weren't supposed to know that," she whispered under her breath.

"Myst, no fair, that's not how you play the gaaaameee," Nilee whined out.

"Cheater." Clanne pouted heavily, he didn't like letting Myst play now. She cheated. Lulen looked down at the girl in front of him with a frown on his face, trying to think what she could possibly know that they did not.

"Alright, since we will never be able to guess, why don't you tell us all," Lulen suggested after a moment.

"Lucky," was the only word that came out of Myst's mouth, making the two children as well as Rina just tilt their heads in confusion.

"Lucky?" Fayon questioned this time.

"Yeah, Lucky… Fen's horse."

The entire group sat there in silence for a moment staring at Myst, who started squirming in her seat.

"Who names a horse Lucky?" Rina blurted out, eyes rolling. It was such a childish name.

"I named her." Myst glared around Lulen and back at Rina, who just stuck her tongue out at the small demon-blood.

"Explains why it's so childish," Rina retorted. If Lulen hadn't been holding onto Myst the little girl surely would have jumped off or alternatively tried to throw a fireball towards Rina's face. The glint in her eyes was absolutely murderous.

"Enough, all of you!" Lulen snapped after grabbing a hold of Myst's raising fist out of fear she would try to attack.

"Now is not the time, playing a game to entertain

yourselves is fine, but stop arguing. You, Rina, are supposed to be on guard. So do your job and stop arguing with a child."

Rina looked down guiltily at that, shifting uncomfortably in her saddle. She didn't like being reprimanded. She definitely would have been mumbling under her breath if there wasn't a hundred percent chance everyone in the group would hear her.

The whole group was silent after that. None of the three children tried to start another game, not with the angry-looking faces on both Lulen and Fayon. The only sounds to be heard other than the clipping of hooves against stone was the occasional whispered word between bored children. This was how they travelled for the remainder of the day and well into the night.

The already-dark valley became shrouded from any light at all as night fell. It seemed as if no moonlight could penetrate past the imposing cliffs that towered over each side of the valley.

This meant each of the adults had gone from high alert to completely on edge, bodies tense with their vision being impaired by the darkness. Even the elf and demon-bloods' vision was compromised. They could most reliably use their hearing at this time, but even then with Fen still unconscious they wouldn't have as far advance of a warning from him to prepare if they were attacked.

The children were shushed by Lulen, who now had taken to listening not to the rocks around them, but to Moon. The wolf was his key to knowing when they were safe and when danger was lurking.

Fayon's knuckles slowly became a stark white due to the tightening grip on the reins, as he constantly listened to the crackling of rocks as they rolled and shifted around them, his head snapping to different directions every few seconds. From the sounds of it Varys and Rina were all doing the same, the three of them trying to catch glimpses of any kind of movement at all. A pointless task when you could barely see the path ahead, let alone the walls of the valley.

It wasn't until the moon reached its peak that light filled the valley, but what should have been a momentary respite from the tension they felt did not occur.

Seconds before the light beamed down from directly above, Moon snarled, body taut with tension, tail pointed behind her as she lowered her head in an aggressive manner. Lulen's hands nimbly pulled the bow from his back, notching an arrow before the soft light of the moon illuminated what Moon had been alerted to.

The moment the valley was bathed in soft light Clanne let loose a terrified ear-piercing scream, making those with sensitive ears flinch. Fayon's horse reared up at the startling sound, throwing himself and Nilee to the ground with a heavy thud. The older of the pair curled his body to protect her as they were thrown, making sure he hit the stone hard and not the child.

"Ambush," Varys snarled.

The group barely had a chance to react as goblins raced forward on all fours, snarling and laughing maniacally, Moon racing forward to meet them with a haunting howl. Three trolls slowly rose to stand, emerging from the very rock itself; they had blended in until they didn't. Now the great big hunking creatures blocked the entire path forward, leaving the group no choice but to fight or flee, and fleeing was not an option.

Varys kicked his horse into motion, getting himself between the fallen pair, grabbing the stallions' reins to stop them bolting before his eyes flashed forward, brown eyes, flashing an orange in the night.

Rina on the other hand had pulled Fen's mare to stand behind the group, the angel-blooded still unconscious. Clanne, who was sitting in front of him, held in his shaky hands a small bow Lulen had made in their travels, one arrow nocked and ready to use only if necessary.

"Try not to shoot any of us kids," Rina teased as she pulled her reins sharply to turn the horse, charging right towards the oncoming goblins. All hell broke loose within seconds as the small group took on the goblin pack and three lumbering trolls.

Chapter 20

Battle of the Pass

A trio of arrows whistled through the air, shot from one pull of a bow, thunking sickeningly into the skulls of three goblins. They crashed into the rocky ground, only to be clambered over by their own kind. Six more now stood in their place.

Moon raced forward, getting close enough to leap up, teeth gnashing and clamping down onto a goblin's throat. It let out a pained wail as its neck was crushed under the force of the wolf's bite. Black blood stained her beautiful white coat. Its colour made her look even more deadly as she went for her next victim. She was weaving between swinging scimitars and pointed spears, arrows taking out those around her with deadly accuracy as Lulen released arrow after arrow at lightning speed.

Fayon rolled himself up, ignoring the pain that flared down his left side. Broken bones would just have to be dealt with later, he thought to himself. He pulled Nilee up by her arm, not having time to check her for injury as she was lifted up by Varys and onto the stallion. The two men gave a short nod to one another, a silent plan agreed upon. Protect the littles at all costs.

Varys tapped the steed's rump, making it move back towards Fen, while Fayon moved towards the fight.

Fayon's hand went behind his back, pulling a shining black blade free from its sheath. The two-handed blade was dangerously sharp and wickedly thin, making it as light as the one-handed weapon still in its sheath, but with the devastating damage of a two-handed blade.

Fayon ran after Rina, who had charged forward after Moon, her spear sparking along the floor behind her. The spear appeared to come from thin air, disappearing and reappearing at will. She spun it with zero effort, the silver spear striking true and swift, skewering goblin upon goblin. Rina had the high ground, Lulen took a ranged attack, while Moon and Fayon struck at ground level.

Fayon's deadly blade sliced through bone and rock as if it were made of butter. Blood stained their clothes, their blades and their faces. A ferocious battle unfolded, one holding glory and merits, as these few slaughtered the goblins coming after them. The death toll for their enemy was a staggering amount for so few fighters.

"Are you going to help?" Lulen yelled behind him, eyes narrowed as he let loose his last arrow, bow thrown to the ground in favour of pulling free his beautifully detailed short swords. Clearly, they were of elven craft.

He had long noticed the human had hung back, watching in favour of fighting. The man fired no arrows, not moving to take up his sword. With a battle taking place, Lulen was pissed off to express it lightly.

"Just wait," Varys said, his voice oddly deeper than it had been previously.

If it weren't for the fact they were in a battle, Lulen may have looked back questioningly. But the fight took priority over curiosity. So, he stood in his saddle and leapt over his stallion's head into the battle, leaving Myst with the rest of the children and Fen. He sliced his way through the goblins that had passed Rina until he was fighting back-to-back with Fayon, who seemed to be the target of near all attacks once he had been noticed. But the prince was successfully keeping any goblin from racing past them again.

"The trolls have yet to move." Fayon panted a little as Lulen reached him, the elf giving a short nod in response.

"They are waiting," came the grunted response as Lulen crossed swords with a slightly bulkier-built goblin, taking its head off in retaliation to the small cut he'd received to his cheek.

"For us to become too tired to battle them," Rina informed them, as her spear spun at astounding speed on her forearm, creating enough wind to force those around her back several steps. She had a pile of dismembered corpses strewn beneath her feet. She fought atop the ever-growing pile.

"No, they are waiting for darkness to return," Fayon informed them. "It is one of my father's favourite battle strategies – attack when the enemy is at their most vulnerable. They attacked at light, when we will put all our effort into defeating them swiftly. They are tiring us out before the moonlight gives them back an advantage. Darkness is a weakness to us, not to them." Fayon grunted, stepping back in time to watch a blade barely miss the tip of his nose.

"Gahhhhhh," came a gurgled sound as Fayon cleaved his attacker clean in half, kicking the blade away.

"Get back!"

"Kill them, kill them all," a hiss came. The chanting of goblins filling the valley, almost drowning out the horrific sounds of battle. All the while, their field of vision grew dimmer and dimmer as the moon moved past its peak. The goblins' vision was not affected in the slightest. In fact, it only grew better in the coming darkness.

"Get to the trolls, kill them before we lose vision!"

"Everyone moves together."

"Moon!"

Heads all turning as a loud whimper sounded, just in time to watch as Moon was thrown into rocks. She had tried to jump at one of the lumbering trolls, a target too big even for the large white wolf. She thudded heavily against the jagged cliff walls, disappearing behind the rocks.

Myst leaned up, wobbling to stand in her saddle. She had heard all the yells for Moon and needed to see. She screamed for her canine friend, watching in horror as she disappeared. The child leaned further up in the saddle, desperate to try and see if Moon was okay in the ever-growing darkness. Myst was shaking, trying to let go of the saddle to raise her hand, desperate to create some light so she could see that everyone was okay. Almost instantly she rocked to the side, nearly toppling headfirst to the floor before Varys grabbed her arm. Myst looked at him startled, no glare on her face, nor did she yank her arm away with a growl. Instead, she looked thankful as Varys gave a nod.

"Myst, *do it*," Nilee shouted from behind her, eyes staring widely at her sister, a panicked look across her face as their friends disappeared into the darkness.

"Duck!" Myst yelled as loud as her lungs could manage, igniting her hand in a massive ball of burning hot red, orange and yellow fire. She drew back her arm, then threw the ball of fire over arm as far as she could, in a hope to light up the valley, but also not to hit her friends.

Varys tracked the small ball of fire with his eyes, eyebrow twitching a fraction, the ball lifting up more, soaring in a perfect arc. Then he raised both eyebrows, eyes flashing orange again. This did not go unnoticed by

Nilee, who stared at him hard, a frown on her soft features.

The moment that Varys had raised his eyebrows, the fire ball had connected with the ground, becoming instantly brighter. Almost white now, spreading along and burning the small amount of moss that covered the dewy rocks.

Varys' eyes moved along the surface, the flames following his gaze, only igniting where he looked, bathing the whole battlefield in white light that somehow spread in a way that harmed no one.

"How did I do that?" Myst gasped, her eyes wide in astonishment. Then she shook her head and gave a smug smile, hands placed into her hips. "I'm amazing."

"Yes, you seemed to be a very skilled young one," Varys said as he finally blinked, stopping the spread of the flames. He scanned his eyes over their group, taking in the situation after the momentary darkness had engulfed them.

Myst was just beaming at the praise she received. She'd liked that compliment a lot. She felt good. Someone had finally acknowledged her truly exceptional skills.

During that few minutes of darkness, the trolls had all moved from their position blocking the pass to engaging in combat. The stinking creatures swung without care, sending goblins flying instead of their targets. Rina ducked under the heavy swing of a club, spinning on her feet, fiery red hair glinting in the light. She rolled under the troll's legs, and once on her feet she ran, jumping one-legged, landing briefly upon a rock. She used her momentum to push hard and fly up, spear above her head, deadly point aimed at the troll's head.

It would have been a deadly blow had it landed. Instead, Varys watched as the creature spun faster than should have been possible for something of its size and went to grab for her. His hand flicked out, Rina went crashing down to the side, rolling across the rocks, spear lost from her grip and scattering uselessly to the side. She coughed harshly, holding her side, a small tinge of blood at the corner of her lips.

"By the hells that hurt," she muttered, slowly pushing herself up with one hand, teeth gritted as she heard the troll swing again.

"None of you move," Varys spoke to the children as he finally ran towards the battlefield. It was clear he would have to aid in this fight. He could not let Rina be hurt further. He could fight without revealing his true form, even if it brought up some questions of his strength. He could not risk that yet, even if it meant he had to take some hits that would usually never land.

He flew forward almost as if gravity had no effect on his movements, crossing the gap between the children and where the battle took place in seconds. His hand hit a goblin square in the chest, sending it crumpling to the ground. It made no sound as it just fell dead, all life leaving its eyes. Varys then stamped on the hilt of the goblin's weapon, making it arc up into the air for him to catch.

He held the weapon out momentarily in front of his narrowed eyes, before giving a few experimental swings against the charging enemy, slicing the heads off three goblins in only two swings.

"A little blunt, but you will do," he commented to himself before putting his sole focus into the battle when Rina went flying yet again past his vision. "A little more effort, Rina." The comment came as he jumped over her, making his way towards the troll who had thrown his niece for the second time this battle.

Rina of course huffed, spitting out a mouthful of blood and muttered out, "Annoying asshole."

"There's no end to these bastards!" Fayon and Lulen were fighting back-to-back at this point. They were completely surrounded. A thick sea of stinking, rotting green, brown and black was all they could see. Growling, snorting, snarling, and the clashing of steel on steel were the sounds that drowned out everything else in the valley. They could barely deal with the sheer number of goblins that kept charging them let alone spare a thought to the trolls they still had to kill.

"Lulen, down!"

The elf ducked in response, allowing for Fayon to swing in a circle, cleaving a group of five in one mighty swing. The demon-blooded prince's face blackened with the spray of blood.

"Thanks," the elf panted out as he stood back up, stabbing under Fayon's arm and into the gut of another foe. He yanked it out forcefully, ignoring the blood-curdling screech it let out as pain overcame it. The creature fell, wounded but alive until he was trampled on by his own clan mates, who scrambled to be the ones to kill their targets.

"You sound tired, my friend. Has the battle worn you out so quickly?"

"Ha! I could go on far longer than you, princeling."

"Oh really? So that's not panting I hear?" Fayon jested as the pair spun around each other, footwork perfect, blocking blows and dealing killing strikes for one another.

213

"I have no idea what you refer to. Focus on the battle before I kill you myself." That stern response had drawn a chuckle from Fayon, a grin on his face, sharp canines peeking out. No matter how dire the situation was, neither was giving up. The pair had been fighting to get to where Moon had fallen, but had quickly been locked in this stalemate. They could neither move nor escape, they simply had to defend.

Despair was not in their nature.

"Get away!" The terrified shriek bounced against the stone walls of the valley, ringing loud and clear to all in the battle.

"Nilee!?" Two yells of worry sounded in unison from both Lulen and Fayon, the pair instantly fighting with renewed vigour, determined to break free to see anything, do anything to get to the scared child.

Rina's and Varys' heads both snapped to attention, eyes wide as they saw goblins running on all fours towards the scared children.

"Go!" Varys screamed to Rina, heart pounding in his chest as the young dragon scrambled up, moving only to have all paths blocked, while his distraction earned him a hard blow to the side. He smacked into the stone cliff, head bouncing off it as water would a leaf.

"Varys!" Rina was panicking now as she watched a man she had rarely seen sneeze let alone hurt crumble to the floor with a dazed expression, unable to do anything to help as the troll towered over him. Nor could she do anything to get to the children and unconscious Fen.

"Go! Ride!"

"Run!"

"Nilee!"

"Myst! Clanne!"

"Fen, wake up!" Fayon screamed loudly, eyes wide with horror when he caught a glimpse of the children.

Clanne's arms were trembling as he fired his bow, arrows sparking uselessly off the surface, not hitting a single one of the incoming attackers. He was too scared, too inexperienced.

Their horses all moved unsteadily, not listening to commands. They looked ready to rear up or bolt, and neither would be a good situation for any of the children.

"Stay back you... you... uglies!" Myst yelled out as she threw fire ball after fire ball at the goblins. She couldn't understand why they weren't as big as before.

"Nilee, help! Do your thing again," Myst yelled, for once looking completely terrified, wanting her twin to do whatever had killed that guard again... that had been really effective, maybe it would kill all of these dark creatures.

"I can't," Nilee sobbed to her sister, tears of fear rolling down her cheeks as she tried to pull the reins to move the horse. When she couldn't she reached over as far as she could, fingers wiggling as she tried to get Fen. Managing to get the fabric of his robes between her fingers, she pulled, trying to shake him.

"Fen, please," she sobbed. "Wake up, wake up... help us Fen... *please.*" Her sobs only became more audible throughout the valley as she grew more desperate, Fen not reacting at all.

"Fen, wake the hell up you bastard, they need you!" Fayon screamed. The ground almost seemed to rumble in response to the power behind that scream.

To Lulen the next few moments felt like slow motion. One troll had picked Varys up by the throat, the other still dazed, sticky blood trailing down his face. Rina was fighting with everything she had, dicing anything that came in her way as she tried desperately to break through the hordes surrounding her. Fayon's hand pressed flat against his own chest, shoving him backwards. The spikes of a club digging into the prince's chest seconds later. The blow taking out leather armour, robes, skin and muscle with it. Spinning him with the force. Eliciting a cry from Fayon as blood gushed down his chest, causing the prince to fall to one knee.

"Fayon!" Lulen dispatched the attacker quickly, eyes darting up in time to see Clanne's horse rear, and goblins jumping up to deliver the killing blow to Myst, with cries and hisses of "Kill the witch!"

"Burn her! Burn her like she burnt us."

Then as Clanne and Fen started to fall backwards, Fen's blue and gold eyes finally snapped open. One arm wrapped around Clanne's waist, pushing off the saddle with the tips of his toes, moving gracefully backwards. His eyes darted, moving two fingers up in front of his eyes, then forward in a sweeping motion. Ice spread fast, stopping the goblins in their tracks, as well as their jumps. Encasing them instantly.

"Are you alright?" Fen's voice was so soft as he set Clanne carefully on the ground, glancing up to the girls. Worry etched into his face when he saw the redness of Nilee's face, the puffiness of the child's eyes.

"Nilee?"

"You have to help them! Help them, Fen," she pleaded, causing him for the first time to survey the battle going on in front of him.

"Stay here," Fen whispered as he took in the horror before him, the smell of blood assaulting him all too fast, as he for the first time stood in an active battle. He walked around the rather angry snarling goblins he had frozen in place. Not even their arms were able to move, but they were all very much alive, and would be freed from the ice long before starvation or the like could kill them off.

Beautiful eyes scanned the scene in front of him, black blood pooling across the ground, lifeless bodies, heads rolling across the stone. It made his stomach lurch uncomfortably. The angel-blood fought back hard against the nausea that was rising up his throat.

He took stock of his friends, those serene eyes filled with absolute anguish. Varys was being choked, Rina bleeding from her side, blood rolling down her chin. Lulen battled for his life, heavy gashes in his cheek, arm and leg, bleeding sluggishly. His heart beating faster and faster. He caught sight of Moon lying still between the grey rocks. Hands fisting up, Fen looked around again.

Where was he?

"Where is Fayon," he whispered to himself. All of a sudden that sickening feeling came back with double force, his vision growing black at the corners as he looked around frantically for the Demon-blood.

"Where is he?" Fen screamed, fear overtaking him, thinking the worst. That somewhere in the mass of gore and bodies was Fayon, lying there stiff, pale, breathing no more. The air around him started to shift. It grew colder, darker. His eyes narrowed dangerously. They had killed him, he was dead. Swords of ice started to grow in his hands.

It looked very much like Fen was about to join the fight. Not in a pacifist way either.

To Lulen it was a terrifying sight, to catch a glimpse of Fen with an absolutely murderous look in his eyes.

Lulen had to blink a moment and try to wipe his eyes. He was sure... no, those eyes were *definitely* flickering red.

The air felt ominous, cold and unforgiving. Suddenly Lulen felt like death was coming. He knew in that second why Aphir called Fen his ultimate weapon now. If this was just the feeling Fen could create with the mere building of power, he did not want to find out what would happen if he used it.

Suddenly the idea of never letting Fen kill anyone seemed like a much better plan than this. This person, this teen stood there, a look of pure hate on his features. That was not Fen. Fen was kind, soft to a fault, and Lulen was sure now he would rather him no other way.

Rina had heard Fen's scream and she instantly started to press forward. She needed Lulen to hear her. She had seen that look once before in her life. The owner of that look had massacred the entirety of his own race and the Angels in one battle, and he had not known friend from foe.

"Show him Fayon! Lulen! You stupid big-headed elf, listen to me! Show him Fayon's alive!" she bellowed at the top of her lungs; she could have drowned out the entire battle with how loud she had managed to get her voice.

Lulen of course was confused as hell for a moment, until he noticed the desperate look on Rina's face as it appeared and disappeared between the swarms of goblins. That look had him instantly spinning, swords whipping out deadly fast, un-noticeable until it was too late. In that one massive spin attack he managed to give himself the room and time to haul Fayon, injured as he was onto his feet.

"My apologies," he gave a guilty whisper at the pained

groan the teen gave him as he pushed him away to stand on his own two feet.

"I'm not dead yet, Lulen. Give me some credit." He gave a cheeky smile. But it was clear from the way he held himself, the sweat on his brow and the pained creases in his face that he was far from okay. The blood was a good indication of that fact.

"Don't ever die," Lulen said with all seriousness before he glanced nervously over towards Fen, just as nearly every goblin had by this point. The air had become so thick with power that even the trolls had stopped their attacks to see what was happening. Varys found himself dropped ungracefully to the ground, coughing and spluttering for air.

Fayon stared at Lulen a little shocked, but smiled a fraction.

"I knew you liked me more than you let... Lulen?" He paused mid-sentence, finally noticing what was going on around him, causing him to actually shiver at the awful feeling the air carried. The energy made his body feel heavy. Slowly he moved his throbbing body around to see what everyone had stopped fighting to stare at.

"Fen?" Fayon whispered. No longer was he worried about fighting but taking stumbling steps to try to get to his angel-blood, blade tight in hand as he got ready for the goblins to stop him.

"Fen!" Lulen yelled loudly, when the ground quite literally shook, and small rocks started crumbling from the sides of the cliffs. "Look over here! Fayon's here." The elf found himself nearly toppling over when the ground trembled again. This was not good. Fen didn't hear him.

Fayon realised at that point what was happening. Fen

was like this because of him. He drew all the strength he could muster and started to battle his way through the hoard. Most backing away and not even engaging, the stronger the energy became the faster the goblins started to move. The aura around Fen becoming darker and darker by the second, eyes glowing an eerie red for longer and longer.

Fayon struggled to remain standing as whatever Fen was doing caused earthquake-like movements in the ground, and bigger and bigger rocks starting to crumble from the valley's walls. Every few seconds the power Fen was building seemed to increase beyond anything Fayon would have thought possible, and clearly their enemy agreed with that sentiment as they started running, not even looking to try and stop Fayon.

The goblins trapped in their ice shackles cried out for help, desperate to get away, all sounding far more terrified than even Nilee's earlier scream.

Finally, Fayon managed to stagger himself over to Fen, leaving a trail of dark maroon blood behind him, his hands, body, face all stained with both his own and goblin blood.

"Fen, I'm here, I'm right here, come on, look at me," Fayon whispered, noting that Fen seemed to look right through him as if he were not even there. He gritted his teeth, taking another step forward, and slowly reached out a hand. Just holding it there mid-air, letting it shake. He had intended to hug him, pull him into his chest and yell at him to snap out of it. But when he moved to do so, his heart started thundering against his ribs, his stomach churning at the thought.

Whether it was because hugging Fen was wrong or because it would be so right, he couldn't handle the thought of being pushed away. It was a battle Fayon would have in his head later.

Instead, his hand fell onto Fen's left shoulder, his other hand soon gripping onto his right and he shook him hard.

"Snap out of it, you big angel-blooded asshole! If you keep this up, we all really will be dead. So get a grip and actually help us, Fen!" His grip on those strong shoulders of Fen's tightened and tightened with every word. It wasn't until he looked into his eyes and said his name that he saw recognition within them. Flickering, disturbing red vanished in an instant. The shaking stopped, the rocks no longer clicking or thudding against the valley floor. Everything became so still as the suffocating power build-up dissipated into the wind.

Fayon huffed out a laugh and smiled when he saw those dazzling blue and gold staring back at him, so wide it was almost impossible.

"Fayon," Fen whispered, hands reaching up slowly to touch his bloody chest, eyes widening more than possible when he saw the damage. But underneath his palm and the blood, he could feel the strong heartbeat.

"Yeah, who else, you stupid angel. Don't go trying to kill us all next time over… over…" His words went unfinished as the adrenaline keeping him on his feet started to fail. The world around him was spinning and before he knew it everything was black. The last thing he could hear was several cries of his name. Funnily, he could have sworn Varys' voice was the loudest. He must have lost far more blood than he thought; how could someone he barely knew cry out the loudest?

Fen's arms easily slipped under Fayon's shoulders as he staggered backwards to catch the slumping taller man.

In the end he fell backwards, pulling Fayon down with him, landing with a thud. Fayon landed awkwardly on top of him. Fen had to shift him slowly, carefully laying his head on his lap, a panicked look on his features as he gently tapped his cheeks. Tears filled his eyes when Fayon just stayed limp.

"Fay? Fay? Wake up, please." To say the younger sounded anxious was an understatement. He was trembling as hurried steps reached them and Lulen landed on his knees beside the pair. The elf ripped away at the armour and robes to treat the wound.

Fen was trying to control his breathing as he watched Lulen's every move like a hawk, until he finally noted the cries of Nilee, Myst and Clanne, all pointing ahead of them. His ears finally noted Moon's scared growls, and the sounds of goblins returning in full force. His head snapped up to see Rina and Varys, the humans from the gate, out there on their own, illuminated only by the fire.

Rina had Varys with an arm around her shoulder trying to keep the concussed male standing upright. The rage in his eyes could kill as he stared at Fayon bleeding out on the ground. He was pushing himself to get to the teen fast. He wasn't losing him again.

Moon, who had been lying still all this time, was finally pushing herself up onto her paws, a pronounced limp as she tried to walk. Everyone was taking the chance of their enemy racing away to try and regroup. But now they were stranded, wounded, too far away from their only capable fighters.

Sadly, with the stopping of the earthquakes, the goblins quickly started to screech again. They were far more afraid of leaving and facing Aphir than going back towards a weakened foe.

"Crap," Varys growled, trying to push himself up on his own, but quickly started teetering to the side. He wanted to, *needed* to get to Fayon. But he couldn't. Not with those foul creatures racing towards them once again.

"Don't do that!" Rina scolded him as she looked back to the returning enemies, her teeth gritted as she tried to walk faster to get Varys to the rest of the group. The young girl released a yelp when Varys pushed her to the side, his body sagging as he turned around to face the incoming hoard for the second time.

"Alright, this time you all die," he growled darkly, eyes starting to glow red, as Rina grabbed his arm, shaking her head. He would destroy their cover if he exposed himself now.

Before Varys could do anything but raise a hand his vision swam, and he went off kilter, barely kept up by Rina. Her breathing picked up; she was not in a good situation. Varys couldn't fight. Fayon was down with Lulen keeping him alive. She couldn't do anything in this form.

"Okay, turn me back, turn me back, Varys, *come on*." She poked his shoulder repeatedly trying to focus him on her, before she threw her arms around him in a protective hug, the pair falling backwards onto the ground as the goblins neared attacking range. Her eyes squeezed shut waiting for pain to overwhelm her, whether from being trampled or stabbed, she would endure to protect him.

Pain never came.

223

Chapter 21

Fields of Gold

He was getting rather annoyed waking up like this. That was the first thing that came to Fayon's mind when he opened his eyes to completely different surroundings. He had never had such dreams before, so why now had he had two in such a short space of time?

Fayon slowly turned himself around. It was nice that he was able to move freely this time at least, without his feet stuck to the ground. For now anyway. The sky above him was almost green in colour, very few white puffs of cloud even visible. The breeze hitting his face was gentle, carrying the sweet smell of cherry blossoms with it. He inhaled deeply; the scent was so familiar yet he was not sure why.

When he looked in front of him, he found he was standing on the edge of a field of gold. He had never seen farmland quite this beautiful before. It was rare in his heat-encased homeland, and the fields they passed during their travels had been far from lush. He took note that there were only a few houses in the distance, and other than that it seemed to be quite an isolated place.

"Alright... why here?" He was honestly dumbfounded. He had been in the middle of a battle, wounded, and this is where his clearly delirious mind decided he needed to be standing. Alone beside a field.

"I am going mad," he muttered with a heavy sigh. He went to pinch his arm to wake himself up – it supposedly worked, according to Myst, who he had seen repeatedly pinch herself when she thought she was dreaming. But he stopped short. He could have sworn... Fayon stood in silence for a moment until he heard it again. Then he started walking, jogging, and running through the hay, until he came to a half-harvested section of field and found Irden sat against several bales of straw.

"The demon again?" Fayon whispered to himself. Said demon had his eyes closed, arms behind his head, taking in the warmth of the sun. A sprig of straw hung loosely between his lips.

Fayon knew that if this was like his last dream, this demon would not see him. With that fact in mind, he could not help himself take a closer look. Circling the seemingly sleeping demon he took him in. On closer inspection he realised two things. One, his horn and hair were considerably larger and longer than the last dream. And two, his face. Minus the horns and scar he could not help but think of the similarities between their features.

They had the same straight nose, the curve in his lips, shape of his eyes, even the way the hair fell across his face. All eerily familiar between the demon and demon-blooded.

"I know you're there." A deep voice startled him from his trance, causing the younger to jump and fall back onto his behind.

"I..." he started only for another voice to fill the air.

"Even in your sleep I find myself unable to sneak up on you." Theliel smiled softly as he stepped into sight from behind the straw pile.

Fayon found his breath catching in his throat as he looked upon the angel for the second time. Time had clearly passed between his two dreams, and somehow this Fen lookalike had become even more beautiful.

No longer was Theliel in elaborate robes, no more

golden leaves or flowers decorating his hair. Now he stood in a simple white robe, that like his loose hair gently moved with the breeze. In that moment Fayon could only see Fen, not a literal angel. Fen. Every part of this look screamed the teen he knew and it made his heart pound wildly in his chest.

"Fen." He truly hoped that maybe it was Fen this time, that he would hear him and smile his way. That was not the case.

Irden smirked, fangs showing as he turned his head to the side and opened stunning crimson eyes. "If it were anyone else, I would have attacked before you realised I'd heard you."

"Oh really? Well thank you for being kind enough not to attack me, in our own field." The angel laughed softly before he sat himself down beside Irden, head tilted to the side as he smiled at the other.

Fayon blinked. Wait, their own field? As in the angel and demon together? His mind was already reeling at that little piece of information.

"Attack you? I would never," Irden said, his voice to Fayon's ears unusually soft. Theliel gave Irden a pointed look that had the demon letting loose a hearty laugh. Irden lifted his lips into a cheeky smile, while Fayon stood there blinking, rubbing his eyes to make sure what he was seeing was correct. Then he smacked the side of his head.

"If you're going to make up weird dreams at least make them make sense. They hated each other last time, what the hell is this?" He waved aggressively in their direction as if someone would actually answer his question. His arm waving paused as he watched Theliel lean down over the demon, and Irden reached up. *Oh, okay here they go, the demon's going to try to kill him now*, Fayon thought to himself. Until Irden simply took a few strands of white hair and ran his fingers through them.

The look gracing Irden's face was not one of hate as his last dream had been. No, this time there was something much different.

"I seem to remember several times you attempted to attack me," Theliel spoke, watching with gentle amused eyes. There was no tension in his body.

"Hmmm, I have no recollection of being anything but chivalrous to you."

"Ha, is that so. Shall I remind you where this scar came from?" Theliel laughed, holding his wrist up, allowing for the sleeve to fall and reveal a nasty jagged scar down his arm. Usually, an angel would hold no scars on their bodies, or so the legends said. But it seemed that, like most creatures, both angels and demons kept their serious scars.

"Hmmm, must have been an accident," Irden said softly, as his fingers moved from the hair to gently trail down the pale skin of the scar. Theliel's body shivered lightly in response to his touch. Then he did something that made Fayon's mind stop. The demon placed a soft kiss on the scar. Theliel bit his lip as Irden kissed the scar several more times.

"But if I really did cause this — not that I admit to anything — I will make sure you love this scar as much as I do," Irden whispered softly against the skin before he pulled away.

"I do. Because it reminds me of the day we truly met each other."

"Heaven's, you angels are so sappy," he teased.

227

Theliel snorted before he moved his head down, while Irden leaned up. The pair met in the middle. Theliel held back slightly, their lips almost touching. Crimson, gold and blue staring at each other for a few seconds. Which seemed like an eternity to Fayon who spun around, face burning red. He did not need to see what was about to happen. His heart beat uncomfortably fast in his chest at the image of a face like Fen's and a face like his own leaning into one another. Like a husband would a wife. It was extremely intimate. Full of love. All Fayon could think about in those few seconds was how would Fen's lips feel against his own if he were to lean in so close.

He did not think about this long. Seconds after he turned away, pain hit him like an iron hot knife in the heart. He gasped, grabbing his chest, falling to his knees, panting, sweat beading on his forehead, dripping from his nose, before he collapsed face first into the dirt, screaming.

His hands moved from his chest to his head. His skull felt as if it were shattering into a thousand pieces, as if a giant was crushing its foot down on his head. He was desperately clutching at it as if to try to keep everything in place.

Fayon writhed in agony on the dusty ground, his body contorting and stretching in all kinds of awkward ways as he was overwhelmed.

The world around him swirled and changed, he could feel it spinning, moving, shifting. Even with his eyes closed he could feel himself falling. He felt how cold the air became. A feeling of terror, of cruelty lapping over him in waves. He could smell the iron tang of blood, hear the clashing of swords, the crackling of magic colliding. It was overwhelming, all of it, flashes of colour pulsating inside his own head. The voices of others rung through his mind. He would sometimes hear Theliel, but mostly he heard Irden's voice, his shouts, cries, his anger.

Images flashed before his eyes, but he could make little sense of them. Images of Irden and Theliel fighting, of them trapped together. Theliel looked like he was dying. Irden carried him on his back. The images swirled around again until he saw them meeting at different times, different places. The feelings of Irden within these images overwhelmed him. Then everything turned dark. Irden looking crazed. Blood and bodies was all he could see. The scream that Irden released was the most heartbreaking thing he had ever heard.

Emotions just crashed over him, drowning him. Suffocating him. Driving the air so forcefully that his lungs hurt. Until finally everything blanked out, and this time he welcomed the darkness that drew him in. His exhausted body gave in to whatever was happening, images of what he saw forgotten in place of a welcoming release from the pain.

Chapter 22

A Treaty Broken

Fayon's eyes felt heavy as he tried to open them. It was almost as if thick fluid held them together. His head throbbed from the pressure. It was so quiet around him. There was no smell of blood, no clashing of swords or screams, no immense pain in his head. He found himself almost afraid to open his eyes, fearful of experiencing whatever that was again. Getting lost in a world that was not theirs. It took him minutes to gather the courage to pry his eyes open, to finally see whether he was in a dream or reality.

Slowly, tenderly, the demon-blooded forced his eyes open. He cringed at the almost ripping sound they made, before hurriedly closing them again when light assaulted his sore eyes, making his head pulse horribly. Wait – *light?*

The valley had barely let moonlight in... even during the day it had been dusk-like, so how was there so much light now? He swallowed thickly. He was now terrified to open his eyes again. What if he really was still in that dream? *Was he going to wake up in that field again?* He desperately hoped not. He needed to get back to his friends. They were in a battle. He could not afford to be a hindrance to them now.

Fayon gritted his teeth as he tried to feel around, frowning when he felt a soft surface under him, and the scrunching sounds of fabric moving. *A bed? It certainly was not dirt or straw, at least. But what was going on here? Where in the hell was he?*

With great effort, Fayon finally forced his eyes open for a second time. He had to blink several sluggish times to adjust to everything around him. When he could finally see more than just beams of light, Fayon found himself dumbfounded.

What was before him was beautiful carved wood that seemed to curve naturally as if they were within a tree. Pale marble made up the walls, with so many windows he could see how the light had been overwhelming. White silk curtains flapped gently in the breeze and the whole room was full of every kind of herb possible, stored in all manner of jars on shelves, as well as hanging in bunches on the walls. Water was steaming away over a fire to one side, seemingly filled with cloth for bandages judging from the white he could just make out.

"Ah, you are awake," a soft voice came as the door pulled open.

Fayon's gaze darted over instantly, eyes widening. There stood with a basket of herbs in hand was an elven maiden. She had a light tanned complexion, cheeks a natural dusty pink colour. Her ears were sharply pointed; he could see them poking out between the braids in her hair. Hair, which was sandy brown, accompanied by the palest blue eyes he had ever seen. He continued to just stare at her as she smiled and walked closer.

"Everyone has been very worried about you. May I?" she asked, motioning to his chest. Fayon nodded numbly as he stared at the thick bandages. How had he forgotten he had been wounded – *was his head really so messed up?*

"How?" His voice cracked, he had to lick his lips to try to get moisture into them, realising just how thirsty he was and how dry his throat had become since his last waking moments.

"Questions can be answered later." The maiden spoke as she peeled back the bandages, a satisfied smile gracing her features as she moved to grab a bowl of green paste from the bedside table.

"This may sting." That was all the warning Fayon received before the paste was spread across his chest, drawing a hiss from his parched throat.

"Torturing him already, Enlynn?" came a chuckle from the doorway, causing Fayon's gaze to instantly fly over, a smile on his face at seeing Lulen standing there seemingly unharmed.

Lulen let go a relieved sigh at seeing Fayon finally awake. It had been a tense two weeks of waiting for any signs that he would survive. Now that he was finally awake, alert and not screaming incoherent nonsense, Lulen felt like he could finally breathe normally again.

Lulen made his way over to a pitcher, carefully pouring water from it into a crystal glass. Fayon could not help but lick his lips for a second time upon seeing the clear water. He was incredibly thankful when Lulen brought it to him. The elf carefully lifted him with one arm and pressed the glass to his friend's lips, monitoring Fayon to make sure that he could not glug it down too fast and make himself sick.

"Try not to move him so much while I'm working, Lu," the she elf huffed out, not admitting it had made it easier to change the demon-blood's bandages, but that was beside the point. Lulen, knowing this, just chuckled as he lowered Fayon back down.

"Yes, Dear."

"Dear? Enlynn!" Fayon seemed to suddenly realise where the hell they were, and to say he looked a mixture of shocked and bewildered was an understatement.

"Oh, he at least told you about his wife then."

"You're really holding that against me, Love? We were on the run."

"And you were running here, Lulen, here to me. Do you not think that's a good reason to tell people you had a wife waiting for you?"

"En, my love, my sweet sweet flower, it was not a priority at the moment."

Fayon cringed for him at those words.

"Not a priority?" Her voice was deadly low, those pale blue eyes narrowing. The hands on her hips were never a good sign.

"No...nonono... that's not what I meant, of course you're my priority." Lulen waved his hands around frantically, trying to dig himself out of a rather large hole as his wife pointed a finger at him. "My top priority always and forever... please don't hurt me," he weakly joked.

Fayon, although amused at the state his friend had found himself in, did not particularly want to listen to an argument he was sure the couple must have already had when they first arrived here... whenever that may have been.

"Where..." A cough followed the word, cringing at a needle-like feeling in his throat. "...Is everyone else?" He finished his question after a few short breaths, trying to ease the burning left in his throat.

Enlynn glared at her husband one last time before she spun sharply on her heel, hair whipping around and smacking Lulen across the face. She gave a humph sound as if to tell the male he deserved that, before moving to wash her hands of the herbs.

Lulen let out a breath when she did move away, only blinking rapidly a few times when the hair smacked in his face. The normally very composed and closed-off elf definitely didn't live up to that image right now. Not when he was sending a look of thanks in Fayon's direction, for distracting his wife from committing murder. His murder to be precise.

"Varys and Rina have taken it upon themselves to help guard the valley's entrance, much to the annoyance of several of my people." Lulen's lips twitched a fraction at the look he received from Fayon, before flinching when a bundle of rags hit him in the back of the head.

"You know he wasn't asking about them," Enlynn scolded, shaking her head at her husband's childish torturing. Fayon gave a grateful smile. Although he was glad to hear the two humans were alive and well, he barely had any connection to them.

"I was getting to them," Lulen muttered, ducking down when she threw something else his way.

"Are they okay?" Fayon's voice was definitely getting hoarser than when he first spoke, the lack of use finally catching up with him.

"Clanne, Myst, Nilee and Moon are all exploring the woods with my older brother Luven… and Fen." He couldn't help but leave Fen's name last. He had to get back at Fayon somehow for making him lose his composure and worry so much. Fayon, whose eyes had shone with a little more desperation at each name that wasn't Fen's, filled with so much relief. He squeezed his eyes closed, suddenly feeling an overwhelming need to cry. He did not cry. He did not let himself.

"They are all unharmed, before you ask. You and Varys were the only two that received more than a glancing blow." Lulen spoke before Fayon could do more than open his mouth to ask just that question.

"How," a lick of his lips, "did we get here? The goblins..."

"Ah that." Lulen looked back at his wife, catching her gaze and nudging his head to one side. Enlynn put down what she had been cleaning and left the room. She was fully aware that secrets were being kept from her. But it was by the order of their Lord and Lady at Lulen's discretion.

Lulen sat there in silence. Fayon looked at him, a frown growing ever deeper between his brows as he waited. A feeling of unease was washing over him. Why had Lulen sent his wife away?

"Don't look like that, this is to keep Fen safe."

"Fen?"

"He... his being your father's weapon of war. After you passed out, I witnessed just why he was titled as such."

"Lulen, what happened to Fen?"

The elf gave a long sigh, rubbing a hand over his face as he recalled the events just after Fayon had passed out from blood loss.

~

Rina had thrown herself over Varys in an attempt to shield him, while Lulen looked on with a cursed cry, hands still pressed firmly over Fayon's bleeding chest. They were going to be killed. He was preparing to abandon the prince to try and save two lives instead of the one before him. But before he could do so Nilee let out a cry for Fen.

Lulen's head snapped back to his side, to find where Fen had once knelt with Fayon's head in his lap was now an empty space. The elf looked startled to find the angel-blooded had moved without him hearing or seeing anything. He knew where to look, his eyes widening to find where Fen had positioned himself. His body stood at an angle, right between the oncoming horde of goblins and trolls and their two downed allies.

"Fen, move!" Lulen instantly moved to stand.

Rina's head whipped around, eyes wide as the person she was supposed to protect was now right in the line of fire. She rushed to stand to pull him back, to do anything to keep him from danger.

The two were frozen in place. Before they could even stand, Fen's hand lowered from behind him as he kept his gaze forward.

"Are you insane, Fen? Get rid of the ice! You can't fight alone!" Lulen yelled, the anger on his face directed at the angel-blood. He was a pacifist going against bloodthirsty creatures... what on earth could he be thinking?

"Do not let him die," Fen said, and Lulen shivered in response, gritting his teeth but then pressing his hands back down hard on Fayon's chest. His gaze never left Fen.

Fen stared ahead for a moment longer, seeming like he would just stand there to be grabbed, just as these creatures desired. To please their lord, to win favour of Aphir. He blinked slowly, hands moving in a graceful arch to meet together in front of his chest, thumbs pressing together, fingers also to create a triangle. He then bent his ring and little finger down on each hand, moving his hands forward away from his chest.

As he moved green light ignited under his fingertips, the eerie glow emitting not only there but from his eyes, forehead, and rippling up his arms also. The air like earlier became heavy with magic, although this time there was no sinister feeling accompanying it. Instead Lulen, Rina, the children – they all felt inexplicably safe.

The breeze around them was gentle, yet around Fen it seemed to be a whirlwind. His hair and robes aggressively moved, dust picking up, circling around him the further his arms moved out.

The goblin hoard seemed to not know whether to keep rushing forward or retreat. Their ranks became chaotic as they scuttled. Some tried to escape whatever was happening, while others chose to race forward still. After all, the last time the angel-blooded did this no attack ever came.

Fen finally moved his hands apart, creating a large pulse. It blew out in all directions, shattering the ice he had created before. Including the enemies, he'd frozen earlier. The force sent even the trolls staggering for balance.

The pulse was followed with momentarily stunned silence. Had that been all his attack was?

That silence did not last. Fen flashed his eyes and haunting cracking sounds echoed throughout the valley. The ground beneath them rumbled, cracks appearing, growing larger by the second, spanning only underfoot of the enemy. Fen pointed forward with his right hand and back with his left, index and forefingers pointed on each hand, the green light becoming brighter by the second. Until out of the growing fissures erupted giant angry vines. They twisted and curled fast, weaving underfoot of the startled hoard. They whipped weapons from hands, wound themselves around limbs until even the lumbering trolls were pulled hard to the ground by the sheer force of the plants.

In a matter of a minute, Fen had created a single attack that took down every single goblin as well as the three trolls. Without any blood being split. With his task complete he lowered his hands back to his sides. Fen stared at the screaming, wiggling goblins, listening to their rancid curses as the vines kept them tightly bound against the cold stone floor.

The onlookers from his own group could do nothing to hide their shock. Rina held Varys against her – the man had his eyes half open, but he was fully focused on Fen. The sight before him was incredibly familiar, he could not help the smile that spread across his features. It was not the magic that was familiar, but the hazy figure of Fen.

Lulen's fingers trembled a little against Fayon's chest. He had never seen, had never even *heard* of one person being strong enough to do that. The little ones had cried out in amazement; even Moon had howled in response to the display.

~

"After that, he wasted no time. For as little as he is, he's incredibly strong. Picked you up like you were nothing. Took off with you on that horse of his. We didn't catch him until we arrived. He got you medical treatment just in time. You barely survived that wound, Fayon."

"He... Fen?" Fayon couldn't find the words. Fen had ended the battle with one attack. With plant magic – not ice, not light – and he had not killed one beast.

"He will not speak a word about how or what he did." As Lulen spoke those words, Fayon's frown came back in full force. He worried that Fen thought of himself as something dangerous, or worse: that he was a weapon.

"Frown like that and you won't keep those immortal good looks of yours." Lulen flicked his head to make a point. "He is fine, Fayon. Still happy-go-lucky, in awe of the world Fen."

"Is he really, okay?"

"Yes, or he would not be out climbing trees with the children and my enabling brother."

Fayon had to let out a small laugh. "Sour because they like him more?"

Lulen narrowed his eyes at that. "For that comment you can wait to see everyone until they come back in their own time," he huffed, back to his old grouchy face. Clearly, he was very much sour because his magic-using older brother was cooler than him to a bunch of children.

"Let them explore." Fayon closed his eyes. In the rush he had managed to ignore the pounding in his head. But it was definitely not forgotten. His eyes pulsed along with his head at this point. "Enjoy their freedom, now they're safe." He sighed quietly. Finally no more running, safe away from his father's reach. Nothing dared come through this forest. Not according to Lulen. His father's minions feared the wood elves.

Lulen however made a rather tense sound with his throat at the words *freedom* and *safe*, which had Fayon forcing his eyes back open.

"Lulen?" Fayon kept his eyes narrowed as the elf refused to look in his direction. "What aren't you telling me?"

Lulen's throat bobbed a little. He refused to speak — that was until the prince grabbed his arm in a bruising hold. Rather impressive for someone who was weak from injury.

"Tell me."

The elf finally looked at his friend, peeling his hand off his arm, rubbing it a little to get blood flowing again. "It is your father... He has broken the treaty."

"He what!?" Fayon shot up, then doubled over in a pained gasp, holding onto his chest, panting as sweat beaded his temples.

"Are you crazy, lay down!" Lulen snapped as he shoved him rather harshly back onto his back and started to inspect the bandages for fresh blood appearing.

"Lulen," Fayon growled through pain-clenched teeth.

"Fayon... you have been unconscious for two weeks."

"What? Two? Why did you not..." Fayon stopped himself talking when Lulen glared at him, his look conveying: 'if you want to know what's going on stop interrupting'.

"In that time, the humans have been sending messenger birds to my lord. Aphir broke the treaty with the angel-bloods. He sent ravens out with a missive of war, stating the angel-bloods... well, stating they assassinated his beloved son."

Fayon let out a huffed laugh at that. Beloved was not what his father ever thought of him.

"In response the message stated any being that is allied to the angel-bloods shall be judged as if they are angel-bloods themselves. Fayon... he left Prophet's lands. He left the confines your race was banished to eleven thousand years ago... and he did so with an army."

Fayon looked even paler now, going almost green with the sickening feeling building up in the depths of his stomach. How... his escape was supposed to stop his father from being able to rally the support of his people. It was supposed to cripple his army recruitment. Yet he had convinced... he was still declared killed. His father was not trying to get him back to start his plan. He was trying to kill him so he didn't ruin it now. If he was seen still alive, his plan would be ruined. His father feared if his people saw Fayon they would turn on him. They wouldn't wage a bloody war.

But even then, Fayon had never expected his father would start this without Fen, a war without his prize creation. Fayon gritted his teeth. His father was coming himself to get Fen now. To many failures by others, matters were in his father's hands. It would not be the wild cards of goblins and orcs hunting Fen now.

"Where is he?" Fayon growled, fists tightening at his sides.

"We received word from Revel two days ago. All their civilians are being evacuated as we speak. Your father's army is preparing to siege them."

Fayon was pushing himself back up the instant he heard that, smacking Lulen's hands away when he tried to stop him, throwing the covers off himself and moving his feet over the edge of the bed, panting heavily.

"Try and push me down and I'll stab you," Fayon growled, baring his slightly-pointed teeth at the elf who quickly raised his hands up in surrender.

"Just take it slow. I'm not getting yelled at for your dumbass choices." Lulen stood and grabbed a pile of robes, throwing the grey inner robe and black outer robe at the prince. "Put something on before you try to leave, would you. I don't need you scaring the children."

Fayon said nothing in reply as he rather aggressively shoved his arms through the sleeves, tying the sash roughly around his middle. "What is the plan," he panted, wobbling badly as he pushed himself to his feet.

Lulen caught his arm to steady him. "Evacuation. The

humans will not be able to hold your people back for long. While those who need to flee do so, we will hold them as long as possible if it comes to that."

Fayon closed his eyes again, anger rippling through him, muscles tensing. "I left to stop this, and it did nothing! Nothing."

The pain in his voice at that moment broke Lulen's heart. He had never seen his friend like this. No matter what he'd seen thrown at this prince, he had overcome it all with confidence, never a doubt in his mind until this moment.

"No, it was not for nothing. If you had laid down and died, who would have saved Fen, the girls, Clanne, me? Who would know your father's plans? Who else would be able to tell my people how to combat what's to come? With you here, we have a fighting chance to hold on until the angel-bloods arrive. Now is not the time for you to wallow in pity! People are counting on you, Fayon. Not just Fen and our group anymore, but thousands of humans, elves and whatever other race your father will displace in this crusade of his!" Lulen gripped his shoulders tightly, fingers digging harshly to his flesh, leaving white imprints in the sore skin.

Fayon stared at him, eyes slightly dull, but there was not an ounce of pain in his gaze from his abused flesh being pressed into. He did not seem convinced by his friend's harsh words. The guilt of this war was weighing on him, like a cloud covering him and only him in gloom.

"Don't," Fayon snapped when Lulen's mouth opened again, shrugging his shoulders, ignoring the tight pulling of his skin as he got himself free from the elf's grasp, forcing himself to stand, to walk on his own.

"Fay... it's not..." Lulen ducked when the demon-blooded swung around, fist nearly connecting with his skull.

"No! Not that name." The growl came as a surprise. Lulen wasn't sure why the nickname Fen had been calling him by for the past weeks had brought forth such a strong reaction.

"Alright… if you insist on walking around in a foul mood I might as well take you to give useful information to my lord."

Fayon stood, a frown on his features, staring hard at Lulen, who just passed him and waited at the door, arms crossed, eyebrows raised as if to say 'are you coming or not?'

"Look, you couldn't stop a war but you can damn well help fight it, and until that grim face of yours is gone, don't think I'm taking you to Fen or the kids."

With that Lulen just started walking, not looking back. He knew Fayon had followed. Being injured, Fayon's footfalls were far from being the typically silent of his race.

Chapter 23

The Fall of Revel

Aphir stood, hands clasped behind his back, staring down the plains towards the city blocking the passage through the Valyn mountains. It was a shame really, to have to destroy something the mortals had clearly struggled against the passage of time to build. But they were just not surrendering.

"Halki, why are you holding the troops? They surely cannot still need more rest." The king's gaze was hard as his eyes shifted to look at his new general. He had conceded two days' rest for his men and women, seeing as he had marched them here with little time to take sleep. But now his impatience was reaching an all-time high. Every second was another that his weapon could be lost from his sights. He had no information on the boy anymore – the elves could have whisked him far away by now if they realised what... or *who* the weapon was.

His knuckles cracked violently as he squeezed his fists together, jaw tense as he watched Halki shift from foot to foot. The younger demon-blooded moved in front of him and instantly bowed to her king.

"My Lord, we are just waiting for Velka to arrive with the explosives, and the potions also. She is due any moment if her raven is to be believed."

"Start without her, you have demon blood in your veins, use that power! Fire and shadows will get you all through those walls without needing to rely on one insane lady's explosives. Your ancestors would be disappointed." The snarl released by the king shook the

244

ground, stones vibrating a little. Murmurs of fear spread through the ranks behind the king and his generals. Halki bowed down further, teeth gritted a little, trying to show no fear to him.

"If that is my Lord's wish then it shall be done." There were a few gasps and muttered words from behind them when Halki agreed to their king's request to charge.

"We will be shot with arrows."

"The casualties..."

"The explosives can be thrown."

"Our magic won't do much from this distance."

"Those who just spoke, step forward. You will lead the charge." Aphir's grin was sickening; it made even Culvat's skin crawl from where he stood in his place next to the man.

"Well?" Aphir raised an eyebrow, looking at Halki. "Begin the charge!"

Halki snapped into motion, pointing at those who had complained then at the battalions she knew were faster, had stronger magic. If they were attacking without the cover of Velka, then she would try her best to minimise their losses before the war even truly began.

"Move forward. Those with shadow manipulation create illusions – do your best to muddle their simple minds. Confuse where they should aim. Those with fire magic, aim for the archers. Light your own arrows if you are incapable of throwing your fire so far. Get to those walls. Sifth riders flank the sides, get your beasts over those walls."

Saren watched his daughter with a proud smirk on his face as the general moved to mount his sifth. The massive black-spotted feline towered over them and their army. The animal's teeth curled out its jaw, like that of a sabre

245

tooth, only far more deadly. The saliva of the beast could kill you in minutes if it got into a wound.

These were one of the things every nation knew. If you saw them, you feared them. These cats were something that even the angel-bloods had struggled to combat in the Blooded Wars.

"Come on, you rotten lot! Ride, or become a knave, a deserter and feel my blade!" With that Saren charged, and groups of twenty sifths raced off in two directions, covering ground fast to circle the sides of Revel.

The moment their riders of death took to the plains, the demon-blooded footmen charged. Eerie war cries constantly filled the air. Their blackened steel armour, catching the sun, lit them up. They moved like a wave of death, ready to swallow and kill, to turn the earth to ash below their feet. And Aphir, he couldn't have had a bigger smile on his face, teeth showing, eyes wide and flashing wild and crazy. The look only grew more disturbing with every one of his soldiers that raced forward.

"Come on, angel scum, come save your precious mortals," he cackled, rubbing his hands together, watching the scene before him, watching the sky, the walls. Waiting for those white angels of light to file in for their death. He was sure that the pompous king of theirs would send a few creatures of his realm to help.

He'd slaughter them all, cut them into tiny pieces and send them back to Eeaneuls. Prove to the prick that he would need to send all his forces to defeat his army. And when he did, Aphir would have his weapon back, and he could get the ultimate revenge. Have the angel-bloods wiped out by one of their own.

Culvat watched his king laughing darkly to himself with a wary look; each day he was sure his king dropped further and further into insanity, becoming far more unstable then Culvat had initially calculated for. He rested his hand on his chin, just thinking about what could be done to stabilise Aphir, at least for now.

~

Meanwhile within the safety of the Revel walls, everyone was racing around. Prince Beau stood at the gates that led into the pass, ushering the last few civilians through. Within was one continuous line of people, running as fast as they could. No longer were they fearful of those that could attack them in the pass. No. Now it was the only option they had to give these people a chance to live. As many soldiers, guards and horses that could be spared were sent with them. The once vibrant and lively city had become desolate in a matter of days.

"Keep going! Don't stop! The elves are waiting to evacuate you further!" Beau yelled, waving his hands in a motion to keep going. His gaze flashed toward the walls when he heard cries. Shouts of war had started. He gritted his teeth and yelled for his people to move, sending the guards he was stationed with into the pass at the rear of the line.

"Archers, fire!" Beau clenched his palm tightly around his sword. He could hear the whistling of the arrows, then the mighty swing and thump of their own siege weapons. But against demon-bloods he knew the likelihood of arrows, or even hunkering stones, killing more than a handful was an unlikely hope.

He had heard stories – their shadows could confuse even the most talented warrior, destroy even the hardest stone. The moment they reached their walls, they would be overrun in a matter of hours. If even that long.

"Beau! Go seal the gate! Leave now."

The young prince's eyes widened as he heard his father's voice, gaze moving around violently to find a glimpse of his face. Tears filled his eyes as he saw his old man, his uncles, his friends, all standing atop that wall. All their older generation knights lined the battlements, stood in the streets. Ready to fight, as they sent the young and strong to guard their people. As his father the king gave his title to his son, to ensure their people did not give up.

"Go now!" his father screamed over the ever-increasing cries of war. Beau could do nothing but look away, pulling these massive gates shut with his guards. Watching slowly as the image of his father grew smaller until finally the gates shut with a thud.

Beau rubbed his eyes hard with the underside of his arm, avoiding slicing his face on the metal bracers. He could not cry now. Not when he had people he had to protect.

The young prince pulled from his neck a circular amulet. It was nothing special in looks. It glowed a faint blue through lines that ran in spiral patterns through the metal. Instead of pulling it back on, Beau took a step back and threw it hard to the ground. It immediately exploded in dazzling light, a barrier rushing up into the air. Shimmering gold, as it sealed the entrance to the pass off completely.

The amulet had been of angel-blooded make, passed down through the generations, a gift given to their people during the Blooded Wars all those years ago. Now it had finally been used, to try and buy his people time to get to the elves. Because the angel-bloods themselves had not once answered their calls for aid, they had been left alone, all they could do was run. None of them had the power to combat against Aphir's wrath.

"My King, we must move now." A hand rested on Beau's shoulder. He took a deep breath, stealing his nerves. Yes, he was a king now, he could not focus on anything but his people.

Beau finally turned away from the gate and nodded.

"We do not stop unless necessary. We must get to the elves before they can break the barrier, our knights will hold them off as long as they can."

His guards nodded, and shouted to move out, the small contingent protecting their new king as they followed the refugees, the civilians, through the dark passageway of the Valyrine pass.

~

Culvat stepped forward fast, eyes wide when the ray of light shot up into the sky, the glittering gold barrier expanding to seal off the entire pass entrance. Who knew they had such an artefact in their grasp.

"Annoying angels. Not even here and still a hindrance," Culvat growled.

Aphir on the other hand doubled over in fits of laughter. The haunting sound seemed to drown out the cries of death. No longer was the region filled with the thunking of arrows in flesh, the shrill screams of men being burned alive, the howls of the sifths. No, just the echoing of maniacal laughter.

"My King?" Culvat took several steps backwards, worried Aphir would lash out, the laughter was that disturbing. That barrier would make getting to the elves far more difficult. Angel-bloods' magic was not a thing to be taken lightly after all.

"That prick thinks giving them a trinket is enough to stop me. We aren't worth sending any of your precious people." His lips curled sharply as he finally stopped laughing, lifting his head to show dark murderous eyes. "You will feel the wrath of the demons, you snivelling pig. I'll make sure your mortals are all slaughtered!" he screamed into the air.

Culvat stayed silent as he listened to his king curse the sky. If anything, Aphir laughing and screaming like this had spurred their people on. The battle had ramped up in every sense. The sifth teams were trying to scale up the rocky mountain face to leap in over the side of the wall. Their soldiers had started pressing themselves flat to the walls and those with darkness as their source of magic were ripping the ground open with shadows. Ripping at the stone walls like it was nothing, while their fire users burnt the arrows before they could hit. The humans seemed to have realised now that their last stand was upon them.

He could watch as they moved, like little ants upon the wall, all in their place. Culvat would give the mortals credit. They did not back down, they fought still even with the knowledge they would be overrun and had yet to even kill ten of their enemies.

"My Lord, Revel will soon be ours."

"Get me Velka now."

Culvat looked slightly perturbed when his comment was ignored, but Aphir seemed to have at least snapped back into his silent and stern nature again. A leader that could actually command an army, not just try to get as many killed as he possibly could.

"Yes, my Lord." Culvat bowed down before swiftly moving through the thousands of his kinsmen to try and locate where that lunatic Velka was. Her being late was not uncommon, but Culvat could not understand why the king had always let her get away with these infractions that others had been burned for. But then he supposed she was the only person capable of making the Draught of Zaro. So regretfully he knew that until that had been administered effectively to the weapon they couldn't risk being rid of Velka.

He hoped once they had administered it, that Aphir would finally lose patience with the loose cannon that was their potions "master". Although he did have to admit she certainly did entertain him, even if she pulled every nerve most of the time. Perhaps that was why she had lived so long within the castle.

"How can one woman be so disobedient?" Culvat ran a hand over his face, a heavy sigh leaving his lips as he kept looking for the still-missing Velka.

Culvat found himself about to try the west side of their forces when he heard a shrill laugh ring through their lines. He knew that laugh. With a groan he pivoted, heading back towards his king, listening as best he could to the conversation between Aphir and Velka.

"Oh Aphy, what an idea!" Velka squealed, kicking her feet away happily, hands clasped together as she listened to her lord, eyes filled with a dreamy look.

"Do not disappoint me, Velka. Take your team and leave. Enough time has been wasted." Aphir glared down hard at the woman before him, eyebrow twitched in irritation at her childlike nature.

"Don't ya worry, Aphy. Velka's got this, your little weapon will be back here before you can say 'Velka is the world's most awesome potion creator'." She jumped up, punching the air, a wickedly creepy grin on her face, eyes open so wide. "Come on, my lackeys, let's go find us a cave," she cackled away, rubbing her hands together before she started skipping back to her horse.

A small group of well-armed soldiers raced after her the second she called them, each with a terrified expression on their face. None of them wanted to piss her off – the last time one of them had, she had tested her new pain toxin on them. The poor man was still unable to move his arm from fear of the pain it had caused him.

"Where are you sending her, my King?" Culvat could not help but ask. He reached the plinth his king stood upon, watching Velka already racing away like an orc chasing its prey, her team close behind.

"To find a cave."

"A cave? My King... why a cave?"

"Goblins, trolls, even giants have lived in these mountains for thousands of years, Culvat. Use your head. Do you truly believe that the valley will be our only way through?"

"I was not aware there were any caves through the mountains that had not been blocked or guarded by the wood elves."

"Velka will deal with any elves stupid enough to try to attack a demon-blooded."

"Is it wise to trust... Velka with this task?" Culvat paused in his question, deciding after a moment it was worth risking incineration to get the answer.

"We shall see." Aphir's gaze stayed focused on the slowly disappearing Velka. Then his gaze went back to the rippling, shimmering barrier of light magic.

"I want that thing destroyed. I do not care how you do it. Just get it down." At that Aphir spun around, walking with his hands clasped behind his back to his tent, disappearing under the flap, not bothering to watch the rest of the battle.

"As you wish, my Lord." With that Culvat moved to start barking orders at Halki. He needed a scholar here immediately to work out how to destroy the barrier as quick as possible.

Chapter 24

Lord and Lady

Lulen walked in silence along the wooden bridges that connected the trees of their home. The wood was worn, creating a smooth white-blotched surface. Vines and all manner of different flowers – reds, blues, purples, pinks, greens – all twisted and wove beautifully over everything. From the inside their buildings looked organic, intricately crafted and planned. Whereas the outside had stayed wild, their structures housed by plant life. Their home was just as much the home of animals.

It was far different than any place Fayon had seen. Even the woods they had travelled through before this was completely different, devoid of life, of the beauty the elves had clearly nurtured here.

Lulen stopped every few minutes to talk to people he passed on the bridge. He was not particularly wanting to speak to any of them, but he did so in order to have Fayon catch up. He currently found himself engaged in conversation with one of the aid coordinators set up by his lord. It would seem an evacuation of the refugees and their own people would soon be in effect.

Of course, he had finally made it home after a hundred years only to have to evacuate it a few weeks later. But so was the nature of war. If it would keep their people safe, a place could be abandoned. Home would be where they were. Not the forest. No matter how much it meant to them.

"Thank you, I will let you carry on." Lulen bowed his head, putting an end to that conversation and allowing the other to hurry past him. With a sigh he ran his hand over his face, looking out to the forest. Getting Fen and the children back here would have to be his next stop after this. Angels knew where Luven had taken them exploring, but now was really not the time to be away from their patrolled borders.

Fayon let out a slightly confused sound that made Lulen turn around, snapping him out of his thoughts. He chuckled loudly, crossed his arms and smirked as he watched a dove nestle into Fayon's hair.

"Looks like you make a good nest."

"What do I do?" Fayon whispered, completely frozen, not making any kind of movement. The big bad demon-blooded, feared by nations, looked absolutely helpless, a startling image really. Frozen and tense as such a small creature tested his hair. That can't be good for his wounds, Lulen thought.

"Just walk, she will leave on her own. Come on." He waved his hand, turning to walk again.

This time, Fayon hurried to catch up, keeping his head incredibly straight and his neck and shoulders taut.

Lulen led them towards the centre of Fareen. The trees grew less dense, opening up to a fairly sizable clearing. In the middle of that clearing was a massive ancient grove tree. It towered over the forest, its leaves a beautiful blossom pink, white petals perpetually falling gracefully to the ground. The bridges that connected the rest of the forest all converged here, at all manner of different levels. Some so high up that Fayon could not even crane his neck to see, while some were so low down that they hit the ground at points.

The tree had hundreds of little openings; the bark had seemingly opened naturally for the elves in order to protect and house them when they first settled here all those years ago.

Soft warm light emitted from each and every one of the openings. The whole atmosphere was serene, comforting, calming, and peaceful, exactly as Lulen had described his home to him all those years ago.

"What is this place?"

"This is the heart of the forest, and the home of my Lord and Lady… and my angry wife." Lulen laughed nervously. God, he hoped she wasn't going to kill him in his sleep one day.

"Incredible… Has Fen seen this place?" Fayon couldn't help but ask that. This clearing was by far the most magical place he had ever seen. Fen would adore it.

"I imagine my brother will have shown him most of the forest by now. He talks a lot when he gets going." The look on Lulen's face told Fayon he was not so impressed with his brother's ability to speak, which caused a little chuckle to escape him, scaring the dove from his head.

"At least you can walk without breaking your neck now," Lulen said in an amused attempt to cheer the surprisingly pouty Fayon up.

Fayon moved his arm to try and punch his friend, only to realise the movement pulled horribly at his chest wound and he immediately lowered his arm again, grumbling under his breath as he finally followed Lulen inside of the giant tree.

The inside was much grander than that of the healing rooms he had awoken in. Although built of the same materials and just as interwoven with nature, the details were far more intricate as they were absolutely littered with amazing flowers, thick wooden branches acting as beams. A brown-laced marble provided a thickness to the walls, to help with warmth and comfort. He had not thought such a grand ancient tree could look even grander on the inside.

Fayon walked in stunned silence. His father was very wrong in his belief that their people were the most advanced. His homeland had nothing compared to Lulen's home, and he loved it. The atmosphere, the craftsmanship and the camaraderie – his homeland fell behind in all these aspects. His father was wrong. They were not advanced.

Then, distracted as he was, Fayon found himself walking straight into Lulen, who had stopped, dropped to one knee with one arm bent out in front of him, bowing to the two people who stood in an incredible library. All the shelves were carved into the tree itself. Fayon, who had started admiring the library from the marbled flood to the leather or cloth-bound books, turned a rather impressive shade of red when he noticed the three occupants in the room staring at him. Lulen looked as if he was trying admirably hard to keep his stoic face and not burst into fits of laughter.

One should keep their decorum in front of the Lord and Lady of Fareen.

The slender, blue-eyed, brown-haired beauty that had been standing beside the much taller blonde-haired, green-eyed male hurried to Fayon's side, a look of concern on her smooth silk like features. She completely ignored the embarrassed look, most definitely not acting as a Lady in Fayon's kingdom would.

"Are you alright?" Her voice was like a beautiful melody.

Fayon gave an awkward nod as he let who he thought

was a guard, judging by the leather armour and silver short sword at her waist, help him to stand again.

"Thank you, my Lady," Fayon said with a clear of his throat, avoiding bringing any more attention to the fact he had done something as embarrassing as walking into Lulen.

"Fayon, meet Lady Miana and Lord Aetris of Fareen."

To say Fayon went pale hearing that was an understatement. *Not a guard. The Lord and Lady. Oh, this could not have been more embarrassing if he had tried.*

"It is good to see you finally awake, young Prince." Aetris had a kind smile on his face as he set down the scroll in his hand, walking forward to join his wife.

"How does your wound fare?" Miana asked, the worried look still on her face. She would not have had him up and walking so soon.

Fayon stood there in silence, not knowing what to say. He had expected many things when they finally arrived in Lulen's homeland, but to be received with no fear, and instead with kindness was not one of them.

Lulen gently nudged his friend's arm, eyebrow raised, staring at him, telling him to not be rude. Standing in silence when a ruler of a people asks you something is not generally appreciated by anyone.

"It is healing, thank you for your concern." He spoke quickly after he realised he was in fact being rude, which just earned chuckles from both Lord and Lady.

"Lulen, go easy on him, I doubt he expected to be trusted." Aetris spoke with a gentle smile on his face, moving back to his desk again. "Come." He motioned the pair over, his wife following behind them, until they all stood at each corner of the oak desk, a large map weighted down at each corner with a polished crystal.

"Despite you having only just awoken, I'm afraid the rest you need will not be possible. With your people on the move, I was hoping you may give us some insight on your father's military strategies." Aetris smoothed his hand over the section of the map they were looking at as his wife spoke.

"Anything you can tell us will aid in our decisions."

Fayon had a small frown on his face as he stared at the map, eyes stuck on Revel, the human city that his father could destroy in moments if he chose to. He chewed on the inside of his lip. So many innocents had already been killed, and so many more would be. But giving information that could have his own people hurt? Most of which he knew were kind, and had been tricked into fighting this war. It was an impossible choice. Save thousands of innocents or protect his own.

This was a decision he had very little time to think about. In the end he knew the obvious choice. The lives of many outweigh the lives of the few. These people had done nothing to warrant the massacres his father had ordered. In the end, his people were the aggressors no matter if they had been tricked. One day maybe he could stop his father's plans, save his people from that madman's rule. But right now, all he could do was make sure those who housed and healed him could live to see the next sunrise.

"He won't send all his forces from one direction. He will always find ways to gain advantage," Fayon said after a moment, eyes locked on the map, remembering the lessons of war and attrition he had been taught since he was old enough to remember.

"The valley is the only way for him to get to us,"

Miana spoke up while Lulen shook his head.

"That is not true, my Lady. There are plenty of abandoned tunnels and cave systems... they could even sail if they had the time."

"Lulen is correct," Fayon said. "They are allies with the goblins within those mountains – we have no way to know what plans they have arranged over the years. My father would not send his strongest warriors through this valley. He will send anyone he deems expendable. He may send in the sifth riders with them or have them scale the mountains. They would be small units but they are deadly. If they got onto solid ground again, killing them without binding magic would be impossible. If there are caves, he would send teams in, and then the bulk of his army would come up behind once he thinks you are overrun. He will send as little of his forces as possible. My father wants his strong troops ready for when the angel-bloods arrive."

Aetris listened with his hand holding his chin, examining the map. His fair features definitely held a worried tone, no longer relaxed in expression.

"Your father will not be seeing any angel-blooded. All messenger birds sent requesting aid returned with the note untouched. They are not coming." Aetris spoke with a heavy voice, betrayal lacing his tone. Clearly no one had expected the angel-bloods to abandon their allies.

"They what?" Fayon was entirely shocked. Never in history had angels or their kin abandoned those they promised to protect. They always came to aid against demons and their kin.

"They have not given aid in any conflict for a long time now," Miana spoke softly, concerned rather than betrayal in her voice.

"Some have questioned whether any still exist, your Fen being the first one seen in over six hundred years".

"Is that why you looked so shocked to see Fen?" Fayon glanced at Lulen who gave a slight nod.

"We were all shocked to see him, which is why we have had Luven take him exploring. I believe the stares made him uncomfortable." Miana gave Fayon a small smile, seeing the thankful look on his face.

"Thank you for that." Fayon bowed a little to them for the first time, before going back to looking at the map, then the elves around him. "Your best chance, everyone's best chance... is to evacuate. Your people alone cannot defeat mine. Trust me, please."

Chapter 25

Evacuation Begins

The group stood in silence. The air was void of any sound, no swishing of clothing, no words spoken. Even breathing seemed to be withheld at this moment. The three elves stared at Fayon, judging him, trying to decide whether his words were to save them or to save his own people.

The demon-blooded in question just stared back, the sincerest look within his eyes. He genuinely spoke from the heart. He did not want anyone here to die, they would not win. Now he knew no help was coming from the angel-bloods, evacuation – staying ahead of his father's army – was the only logical choice. Maybe if they could build up an army of multiple races and kingdoms they could make a stand, but with just the human evacuees and the elves, victory was unattainable.

"Please," Fayon's word was softly spoken, pleading for them to believe he had stated what was the best for them.

"This is our home, never have we abandoned it, not even in the ancient wars. We have always held it," Miana's voice had grown harder, more strained, far from the musical voice Fayon first heard her speak with.

"Although that is the truth, my Lady, times have changed. Our people are already prepared to evacuate. I learned such on my way here. It is the people, not the forest, that is to be protected now."

"Lulen, do you take his side because he saved you from death? Do you have a sick sense of duty towards him or is it because you would rather flee than fight? Our people would rather die here than flee like cowards." The aggression in Miana's tone had Lulen's eyes narrowing.

He stepped forward, growling out, "Is my Lady truly questioning my judgement? Because if so, you have lost your mind!"

"Enough of this!" Aetris slammed his fist down upon the desk, his face dark as he glanced between his wife and Lulen.

"Childish arguments are not needed now. If you wish to fight then I will include neither of you in this decision." Aetris stared hard at the pair. Lulen crossed his arms, pursing his lips to keep silent, while Miana looked down, ashamed to make eye contact with her husband any longer.

"I apologise for my callousness to your Ladyship," Lulen spoke through gritted teeth, clearly not thinking he needed to apologise. Unfortunately, she was of a much higher status than himself. The fact Miana responded with a simple nod had his eyebrow twitching to no end, as well as making Aetris sigh.

"If I may?" Fayon waited for confirmation by way of Aetris giving a slight incline of his head, before he continued. "Although you have never abandoned your home in past wars, in the Elemental Wars you had angels as well as demons on your side. During the Annihilation Wars the angels were on your side. The Blooded Wars, the angel-bloods on your side. You have never fought a war with my people without the angel-bloods on the front lines."

"Are you saying we are incapable of defending ourselves without those no-good angel-bloods?" Miana lunged slightly only for Aetris to grab, twist her arm and force her down onto the stool behind him.

"Your short temper is not a trait you should give into, my wife." His voice was rather cold as he held firmly onto her arm. "You may not like to hear those words from him but heed mine. Fayon is correct. Never have we won battle or war against the demon-bloods without aid of the angel-bloods."

"That does not mean we are unable to win!"

"Are you willing to bet the lives of our kinsmen? The lives of the mortals who have come to use for aid?"

"My Lord, are you going to evacuate as he says? We are not a race of cowards, how dare you..."

"Do not call me a coward, Miana! This is not about cowardice or our people's pride. It is about ensuring we do not become another mark on the list of extinct peoples."

Miana gritted her teeth but said nothing further, seemingly understanding that she was not going to win this argument. Her husband was already in agreement with Fayon. He was choosing to abandon their ancestral homes rather than die defending it.

She yanked her arm free. Giving a final glare to all three males, she strode out of the room, disappearing down the halls, no longer choosing to be involved in this conversation. Honestly, Lulen understood where his wife got her temper from now, and he most certainly didn't envy Aetris when he had to deal with that anger later on. *Enlynn held grudges, like him forgetting to tell men and children he was married... Okay, she could have been mad because Rina was in the group. But still, it had not been a priority, okay? Yeah, he could be sure her sister was also a professional grudge holder. Likely even worse than Enlynn was.*

"My Lord?" Lulen asked after they watched Miana leave.

"Yes Lulen?"

"What do you wish for us to do? I will get preparations ready."

"Start moving all the mortals into carts, onto horses, whatever we have available. Begin migrating them south to Nisroc Point."

"That far?" Lulen looked shocked; it would take weeks even for an elf to make it that far. For mortals who required far more rest, it could take months.

"We cannot afford to stay on this land. After the mortals have all left, our people will follow, spread my order. Everyone is to pack only the essentials; the young are to leave with one parent beside the mortals as soon as possible. The moment we close the valley off, the rest of us follow." Aetris looked pained with every word he spoke. He clearly did not want to abandon his homeland, but Fayon was correct. This was not a war they could win alone.

Lulen bent an arm to his chest, dropping to one knee and bowed his head forward. "I will deliver the order straight away, my Lord." Lulen glanced at Fayon as he stood before he left the room. He headed to the base of the Great Tree, where their army barracks were located. Gathering a group of rangers would be his best way to get the news spread fast, and the required supplies collected in a matter of hours. The faster they could start the evacuation of the refugee camps as well as their people, the better.

Fayon remained beside the elven lord for a few moments as the pair stood in mutual silence just staring down at the map before them.

"What can I do to help?"

"Are you well enough to help?"

"Am I not up and moving as we speak? Although my movement is admittedly hindered, I will heal fast now I have awoken. So put me to work."

"Very well. If you wish to help, go aid my people in getting supplies loaded up, we have very little time to prepare for such a journey, and we must be as prepared as possible."

Fayon tried his best to bow the same way Lulen had. Getting down to one knee hadn't been the challenge, but getting back up without pulling on his still-healing wound was. Aetris moved to help him stand when he had noticed the young one's struggle, but Fayon had shaken his head, and got up himself.

"I will get started instantly." Fayon left the room, not knowing where he was going, but knowing he would find somewhere he could be useful.

This war was because of him after all. He had not succeeded in stopping his father's plan, and now thousands had already been displaced. Countless murdered, as well as a whole race now being forced to abandon their home. This was the least he could do to make up for his failings.

Aetris stayed in his library. The moment he was left alone the elven lord fell back into his chair, elbow resting on the armrest, hand covering his face.

"Forgive me, watch over us, Ilrune, protect our people." His words came out in a whisper as he sat there fearful for what the coming days would bring.

Chapter 26

The Time To Leave Has Come.

The following days passed by in a blur. There was never a quiet moment, and as a result Fayon had not seen Fen since he awoke. After Fen's last reaction to such noise and crowds, Lulen had deemed it necessary that Fen be kept away. The angel-blood had refused to leave without them, so Luven, Lulen's brother, had kept Fen and the children with him. The group had been collecting every herb, every forageable under the sun. Clanne, Myst and Nilee would often run back with Moon at their heels, their baskets full before leaving with empty ones.

Varys and Rina spent the days aiding at the valley entrance, herding through the steady flow of refugees, making sure each had water and some food before they were sent on their way again. The line of evacuees could be seen for miles, winding the entire length of the forest as well as the grassy green slopes beyond. Children, pregnant women, those with injuries were loaded onto wagons. The rest had to walk; they were prioritising use of space to ensure the growing caravan of people could move as fast as possible.

Dried goods, fresh foraged produce, medical herbs, skins of fresh water, whatever people could carry was being given. More than half the population of Fareen had joined the convoy now, leaving only those organising everything and the members of the guard in the forest, and yet it was still loud. Panic, tension, the stress of the situation was mounting with every passing day. The smoke that had started billowing in the sky above did nothing to ease the fear. Loud pulsating thuds shuddered the ground as Aphir had his men tried to take down the barrier of light.

What they had worried for had come to pass. Aphir and his army had attacked, likely decimating the human settlement. Which meant he could be on them any day now. Every second they remained in the forest was time they allowed for Aphir to close the distance between them. But no one was willing to abandon their station until every last refugee was out of that valley.

Lulen had spent the days patrolling the borders where the forest met the mountains. He and the men at his command looked into every crack, every hole that remotely looked like it could fit someone through, sealing them closed with plant magic. If demon-bloods did come through, the vines would not hold them off for long, but as long as they were a fire user it should alert them long before they could launch any attack.

Of course, they could only seal so many, and go so high. There were likely many areas they had missed, but at least for now they had limited lower ground level access from the more sinister inhabitants of the mountains.

Fayon had found himself spending the entire time making small bundles of food alongside Enlynn, who had made it her job to make sure he did nothing to risk hindering his healing. So, sitting down creating bundles was the only thing she had allowed him to do. Fayon was quite honestly far more terrified of her than anyone else.

But her persistence had meant in the few days he had been awake his wound had healed to where there was barely even a scab left over the once-gouged skin. His advanced healing had finally kicked in now he'd awoken, with food in his body.

Despite having been packing the supplies Fen and the children had collected, Fayon had been avoiding contact with them all. He made sure they never saw him, he would duck, turn. Blatantly ignore them. He just knew he couldn't face them. He was supposed to protect them, he was meant to stop the war that would put their lives at risk. Stop Fen from being needed for whatever his father's plan with him was. He felt useless, a disappointment again.

Only this time he had failed people who truly cared for him. He had failed his own people and the people of Aleria by not stopping his father. Fayon just couldn't face them, nor did he want to risk seeing looks of disappointment on their faces. So instead, he had ignored them. He couldn't find the words to apologise for not getting them somewhere safe as he had promised. Instead, he just hurt them further, and he knew it.

His heart had broken when he ignored Fen's calls asking him if he was there, asking if he was okay. Fayon had all but shunned him away. Fen had not tried returning after that night. The guilt was weighing heavily on his heart.

"Fayon... Fayon!" His name came with a rough shake of his shoulder, making the demon-blooded blink his eyes, focusing in on Lulen in front of him.

"Huh... Sorry Lulen, what did you say?" Fayon asked, not even remotely trying to cover for the fact he had not heard a single word that Lulen had said.

"We are sealing the valley. Prince... *King* Beau confirmed he was the last to enter the valley."

"That means it is time, correct?"

Lulen gave a short nod of his head, glancing at his

wife. "We are all to be ready to leave within the hour."

"An hour!?" Enlynn stood and was away in seconds, moving like a whirlwind to get home and gather the things she refused to leave. She had not had time in the past days to remotely think about packing her own things.

"You should go help her." Fayon pushed himself up, dusting his robe off before picking his sword up from where it rested between the roots of some trees.

"I would be more of a hindrance than aid in this situation. I do not know where anything is stored in that home anymore."

Fayon looked down when he said that. He truly seemed to be in a defeated state, thinking about how he hadn't been able to keep Lulen away from capture, which had resulted in him now feeling alien in his own home. With a wife who still had not forgiven him.

Fayon's eyes went wide when suddenly he felt a pang of pain to his forehead. Lulen had flicked him.

"I can see that brain of yours working. None of this is your fault. One day you will believe me when I tell you this. Just make sure it is before you lose all the people you hold dear. Ignoring everyone will end with you alone if you are not careful."

"Maybe I would be better alone, everyone might be better off if I was not around. Ow!" Fayon rubbed the back of his head having just been dealt a harsh strike. The young demon-blooded prince was now officially glaring at Lulen.

"That is for being mopey, and thinking we would ever let you go off alone." Lulen's expression was very stern. He meant business and he would hit the teen again if he said one more thing like that. Then if that did not work, he was sure he had some other methods that would work just fine. Such as torture, tickling, and if all else failed, sending Fen to hug him to death.

"You hit hard," Fayon muttered glaring at him.

"That was not hard, believe me. Now since we are all leaving, we need to go get the rest of our group."

"Go get them? Have they not already been told to come back?"

"I thought I would task us with that job. Step to it, Princeling, try to say no and I will hurt you. They have missed you and I am incapable of looking at Fen's disappointed face one more time. One can only take those eyes so many times before it causes bodily harm."

Fayon's mouth snapped shut, before he let out a faint chuckle at the idea of Lulen, of all people, being incapable of withstanding one person's sad face. That smile faded when he realised Fen was sad because of him. Before he could even think about it, his feet were moving on their own, following after Lulen to go and collect Fen and the children.

Chapter 27

Pursuit

Velka cackled to herself as she finally emerged into daylight, the sounds of life telling her she made it through the mountains before the elves had left. If she was lucky, the boy she wished to find would be here still. Then she could impress Aphir and become his favourite.

"Maybe he will make me his new queen." She cupped her hands in front of her face, swaying side to side, a dreamy expression gracing her features.

The soldiers behind her all shifted uncomfortably, covered in dust, spider webs and grime. None of them wished to comment on what had been said.

"I'd be the best queen there ever was, don't you all just agree?" She spun around at the cave entrance, her usual creepy cat-like grin upon her face, the cobwebs in her hair making for a terrifying image. The sudden movement had her on one leg, arms waving wildly as she nearly fell backwards.

To the disappointment of her followers the witch did not fall, causing them all to vicariously start nodding in response to her question, while the goblins that stood behind the group of demon-bloods all stood looking confused.

"Miss, are we not going to attack?" One goblin stepped forward, not wanting to wait any longer to draw blood. Its voice was all snarled and gruff, almost like it had lost most of its voice.

"Attack." Velka smirked, stretching her arms up in the air, before folding them behind her back. The demon-bloods instantly shrank to the side. Parting, pressing themselves against the cave's cold walls. Just as they had finished moving, she moved her hands again, flicking a needle from her hair straight through the left eye of the goblin who had spoken.

It fell backwards with a shrill scream, writhing in agony for mere moments before it went limp. The screams of its clanmates filling the cave, angry shouts, cries for revenge. All which died down when Velka stomped her foot down fast. Her shadows splintered the stone around them.

"Silence, you filthy creatures. Do not forget your place. Do not speak to us; we demon-bloods do not wish to befriend you. You are here to do as I say, when I say. Nothing else," she hissed, yellow eyes glowing in the darkness.

The goblins quickly shrunk back, their cries going silent in fear that she might bring the cave walls down around them.

Velka gave a pleased smile when everyone went silent again, turning slowly away to look out the entrance. She leaned out, wobbling occasionally as she inspected how high up they were, as well as judging how far they were from the main elven settlement.

"Hmmm, incompetent. This is not close at all to where I need to be. Very well, a walk in the woods will be good for you all." With that she stepped out, falling forward fast. She let herself freefall, not caring the height from which she fell, as she landed gracefully with the aid of her shadows catching her before she could hit the green forest floor.

The rest of the demon-bloods followed suit. Those with the same power over darkness and shadows fell the same way Velka had, while those who possessed the power of fire slid down the cliff face in silence, not even loosening a single rock.

The goblins descended last, on all fours, scrambling down the stone with practised ease, but without the silence of the demon-bloods. Their attempts to suppress their whoops of war and snarled chants were very much unsuccessful, causing Velka's eyebrows to twitch horribly in irritation.

"Fools." She pinched the bridge of her nose with her sharp nails, before clicking her fingers, sending her shadows wrapping around each and every one of the hundred goblins' mouths.

"If you are incapable of silencing yourselves I shall do it for you." Velka stood rolling her shoulders, enjoying the momentary silence.

That silence was quickly shattered by the snapping of a stick, causing her to spin around, her robes moving gracefully around her. Eyes locked onto the bush in front, the snarled cat-like smile gracing her face again as she stared at the two small girls in front of her.

"And you must be those two missing slaves everyone has been wondering so much about," Velka cackled. So, they had left with Fayon and the weapon. Which must mean one or both of them were very close. Perhaps these goblins were not so incompetent after all.

Myst slowly moved further in front of Nilee, holding tightly onto her arm, both girls breathing incredibly fast. They knew who Velka was, there was not a sane demon-blooded who didn't, and not one who wasn't terrified of her.

The young demon-bloods stared at the elder, who had raised her hand to stop anyone from moving in that moment. Myst however was slowly taking steps backwards, staying placed in front of Nilee, not letting any of them see her.

"Don't be afraid, little ones, I am not here to hurt you." Velka crouched down, cat eyes all wide as she reached out her other hand towards them. "On the contrary – you could be so very useful to me, yes you could." She cooed to them as if they were babies, about ready to try and snatch Myst by the collar.

"Run!" Nilee shrieked, gripping and pulling Myst with her, running as fast as her legs could carry her, only running faster when she heard Velka's laughs echoing behind them.

Myst stumbled along at first before she caught her footing and became the one pulling Nilee along, her grip ever so tight around her younger twin's wrist.

"Fen! Lulen! Fayon! Luven! Anyone!" Myst screamed as they ran, knowing at least Fen would hear them. He would come and rescue them... he *had* to come rescue them.

Nilee had tears running down her face as they ran, flashes of the future going through her mind. There was so much blood, she couldn't make sense of what she was seeing. She couldn't tell who was hurt. Her panicked mind made her vision cloudy and unfocused. Which meant in the end it was useless.

Velka smirked as she stayed crouched, watching the two girls run.

"Aww bless, they think they can be saved." She slowly stood, plucking vials from her belt, throwing them back to the goblins.

"Dip your arrows in that." She never took her eyes off those girls as they disappeared into the forest.

"What are your orders, Lady Velka?" one brave demon-blooded stepped forward hesitantly to ask, relaxing considerably when Velka stayed calm. She didn't laugh nor did she narrow those freaky eyes of hers.

"Follow them. Those we are hunting will come to save them, and when they do, kill everyone but our king's weapon. Make it a blood bath!" Her eyes lit up in excitement as she watched her men as well as the goblins rush past her in pursuit.

Velka herself just followed behind at a leisurely pace, thinking about all the different ingredients she could create from dissecting their eventual victims. She started skipping, whistling happily, getting more and more giddy at the thought of dried elf pancreas, or jars of brains, or even better: a string of elven ears. They were the best decoration, after all.

Soon she would have all the ingredients her heart desired. She would have Fayon dead, her king's master weapon back where it belonged, and she would definitely become the new queen for all her success.

"Queen Velka. No one else can be queen. I will be the queen of the world," she sang to herself happily as she continued following those imbeciles in front of her.

Chapter 28

You Said You Wouldn't Leave

Fen crouched down beside a currant bush, carefully loosening them from their branches without damaging them, letting the berries roll from his fingers into the basket he had with him.

Clanne was sat beside Luven helping him pick out strands of grass from their herb basket. Luven looked incredibly like Lulen, same blonde spiky hair, same facial structure. Although his resting face was calm and gentle rather than stern as Lulen's was. The male had mismatched eyes, one green one blue. He had told them it was as a result of using his magic so often.

Luven was the wood elf's high mage, which was why he was dressed in finer garments: a reddish-brown silk tunic, dark brown pants with soft leather boots, and adorned with all kinds of gold bracelets, necklaces, rings, and even a head circlet. It showed how valued he was in the community. His ability to control plant life was the best in their history.

This had resulted in him being the one to guard the two demon-blood children as well as the angel-blooded. He was the most qualified to combat any tricks they could pull.

Luven had however soon discovered, as his brother told people repeatedly, there was no reason to fear them, resulting in him making fast friends with the small group. It was also why they had been allowed to stay when others were evacuating, because Luven had told Aetris he would take care of them.

"What do these do exactly?" Clanne asked, looking expectantly at Luven, who smiled softly at the child.

"See the ones with the broad leaves? They have a purple vein system. We use these to help with inflammation."

"What about the blue flowers?"

"Nausea."

"Hmmm, these ones?"

"Those are used as part of a pain relief tea, but they are poisonous if ingested raw."

"Whoa." Clanne looked absolutely fascinated as he pulled out another herb to ask about.

Fen listened to the pair with a smile on his face. It was nice to see Clanne look happy. He paused his berry picking just to listen to them for a moment. Until then he had heard nothing out of the ordinary within the forest. But now he frowned slightly. Fen inclined his head in the direction of the mountain. His ears twitched a little, sliding his eyes closed, putting all his focus on just his ears. Something was moving on the mountain side, he could hear little rocks falling, cracking as if something was moving down it.

There were too many falling and tumbling for it to just be stones dislodged by the wind. He slowly raised himself to his feet, a frown on his face, trying to dissect what he was hearing. There were voices, that he was sure of. No animal made sounds at that octave, but for the life of him, he could not make out the few words he caught.

"Fen?" Clanne had his own head tilted, brown tufts of wavy hair falling in front of his eyes as he watched the angel-blooded curiously.

Luven himself had closed his eyes to listen. By Fen's demeanour he was certain he was hearing something, however Luven was getting nothing but the usual forest ambience, mixed with the commotion of his people in the distance. The falling rocks, the voices, were all drowned out by the forest to him. "What do you hear?"

Lulen had informed him, Aetris and Miana when he first arrived of Fen's unique abilities. Of course, even one as old as Aetris had no idea why Fen possessed the abilities he had, which had been of much disappointment to Lulen as well as Fen to hear. He had received no answers. However, it did mean that Luven knew Fen could hear something he couldn't, making the mage quickly become guarded, scanning around carefully.

"Fen?" Clanne asked again, now his voice wavering a bit as Luven slowly moved to stand. The child's body tensed as the two adults remained silent.

Fen kept his eyes closed, the frown lines on his forehead deepening. *Was that running?* He could make out the sounds of crunching leaves, snapping sticks, heading towards them. They were by no means close but they were definitely headed this way. That was when he heard the voice again. He picked up a few words such as *kill* and *all*, but those two words were overpowered by the screams of voices he knew by heart.

His eyes snapped open instantly, beautiful blue nearly overtaken completely by gold in that moment, fear filling them. He was running before he could even utter a word.

"Fen!?"

"Get Fayon! Get anyone!" Fen yelled from behind him. His robes swished fast as he raced over the uneven terrain of the forest, looking majestic as ever, even with hair moving wildly. His face was full of terror, pushing himself to run faster, always faster.

Luven knew instantly something was very wrong.

279

"Clanne, run back to the city, find the first guard you see and tell them we have a breach. This is important, tell them Luven needs aid immediately at the western mountain range. Go run!" Luven waited a split second for the boy to start running as told, before the elf raced fast after Fen, his heart pounding in his chest, their baskets left abandoned in their small clearing.

Clanne scrambled back as fast as he could along a practised path he'd come to learn off by heart over the past few days. The small boy was scared. So obviously scared. But he had determination in his eyes as he raced to get help, even though he had no idea what was actually happening.

The small boy arrived back in record speed; it was only a ten-minute walk from where they had been but for the running child it had seemed like an eternity. He was panting hard, sweat dripping from his forehead. Breaths came in big gasps as he pushed himself that last bit of distance, clenching his eyes closed as he did so. He ran face first into a bewildered looking Lulen.

"Clanne?" he asked as he steadied the heaving child, his gaze moving to Fayon who stood beside him.

Fayon instantly looked concerned, looking behind where Clanne had run from to see if Fen and the others were coming. The fact he could not see anyone had his heart in the pit of his stomach.

"Help... aid... Luven... west... help!" Clanne's words were broken apart by the heaving of air. The boy desperately tried to get out the information he was told to relay.

The child had to say no more before Fayon took off in the direction Clanne came from, the demon-blooded moving with incredible speed through the forest.

"Fayon, wait!" Lulen yelled after his friend, gritting his teeth. His brother needed aid, but he did not know how much. He couldn't give chase, he needed to get more backup.

With his teeth still gritted, he bent down, scooping Clanne into his arms and started running back to their main forces who were working on sealing the valley's entrance off.

"Get your weapons! We are under attack!" Lulen yelled as he ran. Clanne was passed off to Enlynn the second he saw her, before he was grabbing more arrows as other warriors hurried over. Varys and Rina were among them, Moon at their heels. The white wolf went straight to Clanne as the alarm horns started to blare. But not for Lulen's cries of attack.

No, over the mountain ridge the lookouts had caught sight of the sifth riders scrambling fast down the mountain side. At the same time sounds of explosions caught everyone's ears, smoke rising in the west. It was an attack from two fronts.

"Lulen, take your team and go! We will hold them off here!" Aetris yelled, the elven lord standing with his bow drawn.

"Go!" Miana snapped after Lulen did not move immediately.

"Stop their advance from the west, we can deal with these ones." Enlynn gently pushed her husband's shoulder. Moon lowered herself to the ground in a growl, as if telling him to go as well.

Lulen swallowed hard. This was not a choice he wished to make – save his brother and friends or save his people. With gritted teeth Lulen turned and with his group of twenty guards, Varys and Rina, he raced towards the growing smoke in the west.

Enlynn moved fast to hide Clanne in one of the carts.

"Do not come out until I come and get you." She spoke softly, brushing the hair from the mortal's face, before covering him with blankets. She looked down at Moon. "Stay beside him."

The white wolf immediately took up a guarding position in front of the cart as Enlynn moved to stand beside her elder sister.

"Don't die."

"That's funny, I was about to say the same thing to you." Miana spoke in a soothing tone and moved to take her sister's hand for a moment, squeezing it as they waited for the beasts and their riders to come into range of their arrow fire.

~

As help raced towards them, Myst and Nilee ran for their life, screaming in fear as arrows started to rain down towards them. Myst waved her fire around madly as they ran, trying to burn the arrows up before they got close. The moment her fire hit the tip of the arrows they exploded in the air. Those that hit the ground created massive craters on impact, dirt rocks and stones flying everywhere.

The powder given by Velka to the goblin had been an extremely volatile compound. It would explode after impacting with anything other than the metal of a weapon, making it an extremely effective item to lace your arrows with. It would also cause enough noise to draw out those she was here for.

Nilee screamed in terror with every explosion. The two small children desperately tried not to fall as they ran, continuously screaming for the people they trusted most to save them. To them it felt as if no one was coming. They had run so far, their small legs burned. Dirt covered them, faces, clothes all a mess of muddy brown from the spray of each explosion.

"Nilee! Myst!" Fen's voice rang out through the forest. The two girls' faces went from despair to hope within a second. Fen was coming. He would save them.

"Fennnnn," Nilee sobbed out as Myst started dragging her towards Fen's voice. The angel-blooded called out for them repeatedly, as if trying to reassure himself they were still unharmed.

Velka's smile grew exponentially when she heard Fen calling. He had come alone. She could discern no close footsteps behind him. He would be easy to grab. This voice must belong to the angel-blooded she was after. After all, Fen was not the name of the prince.

"Get ready, boys." She ran her tongue along her teeth with a cackle. "Take 'em all down." The laughter filled the air as more arrows started to rain down.

Fen barely paid any mind to where he ran or how far he went. The angel-blooded just knew he needed to get to the girls. They needed him. Panic was clouding his mind further and further with each scream, each explosion.

Then he finally caught sight of dust, and a flash of ash grey. His heart lifted; he was nearly there, he nearly had them. Fen vaulted over a fallen tree, arm outstretched, glowing bright blue as he went to create a dome of ice around the two girls as they fled towards him.

Nilee tripped, falling face first into the ground with a heavy thud. Her arm yanked free of Myst as a result. The older of the two twins instantly skidded to a stop, turning around, eyes wide. Her baby twin was scrambling to stand. Velka's creepy laugh of death echoed through the woods as her archers took deadly aim.

The world all at once slowed to a grinding halt for Fen. A scream he didn't hear left his lips, as a last attempt to stop what he saw coming. He threw out a blast of ice through the air, aiming to take the arrows out of the sky.

Air left his lungs, ice completely shattering. Fen stood rooted to the spot as he watched Myst fall backwards.

An arrow had sliced through the air with deadly speed and frightening accuracy. Even Fen with all his abilities could not send out his ice fast enough to stop it from striking its mark.

The moment Myst had turned around, the arrow sliced through her skull as if it were made of silk. The small wound at the front of her head turned into a gaping hole at the back as the arrow passed straight through.

Blood and brain matter went flying through the air. Nilee's left side was covered in her sister's blood, causing the young girl to scream in horror. Fen still stood there, in absolute shock, the gunk all on the front of his own robes. He couldn't move, he couldn't breathe. Everything was frozen until Myst finally hit the ground. Red eyes open but dull. Blood rolling down her features. The once spunky, sarcastic girl lay lifeless on the forest floor.

Nilee screamed, cried, clawed her way through the dirt to cling onto her sister's lifeless body, not caring at all about the explosions or rain of arrows still going on around her.

"Myst! Myst!" she screamed, breaths coming in panicked gasps, clawing, holding her close, as she sobbed and cried for her older sister. The young girl couldn't believe she was gone. Her sister wouldn't leave her...

"You promised you would never leave! Wake up!

Wake up... Myst, *please...*" she sobbed, pressing her face against her twin's blooded cooling forehead. "Please," she whimpered.

"Don't worry, slave, you will be joining your sister oh so soon," Velka sneered in a horrific taunting tone.

"Stop," Nilee sobbed as she threw her body over her sister's. She wouldn't let anyone hurt her sister again, she wasn't gone. She couldn't be dead.

"Stop? Stop!? If your dear Fen hadn't escaped, little slavey girl would still be alive." Velka gave Nilee a big old pout as she said that, before using her middle finger to motion Fen to come closer.

"Come on, Angel Boy, come back to me and I might just let the other girly live. Does that sound like a fair deal?" Velka laughed hard along with all her followers, until she felt the air grow cold and that laughter slowly died out.

Chapter 29

One by One

Velka's laughter slowly died down as the air around them turned chillingly cold. The pressure the air was creating around them was causing pain to shoot through their heads. Her ears felt like they were bleeding. Everything around her pulsed in an unnatural way. It felt like her vision blurred with every pulse. For a few moments no one knew what was happening. Or how it was happening. Then it became all too obvious.

Fen suddenly let loose a gut-wrenching scream, eyes going from pure grief as he stared at Nilee and Myst, to deep intense hatred. His gaze moved to Velka, teeth gritted in a hateful snarl. Rage filled those beautiful eyes. The wind picked up around him, steaming from the cold emitting from his body, pulses of magic matching to his heartbeat.

Velka took several steps backwards as Fen started moving forward. He walked like a zombie, gaze fixed on her, limbs stiff, moving until Nilee was safely behind him. The goblins and demon-bloods shifted back, fear in their eyes, unsure of what they were supposed to do now.

"W...what are you doing... don't just stand there – take him down!" Velka screamed, as she stumbled through her potions to try to find the Zaro draught, hands shaking in fear as everyone around her started moving.

Fen barely let them move before the magic pressure increased, the pulses coming faster and faster. He built up a suffocating amount of magic until he let it explode with a scream.

The ground instantly started cracking, trees shook and collapsed. Ice started frosting over everything. Of course, the demon-bloods countered with fire, destroying the ice before it could stick them in place, allowing for the goblins to charge forward over the cracking shaking ground.

Fen let out a dark laugh. Nilee looked back at him in fear. That laugh was cold, dark, unforgiving. It did not fit Fen at all. He was kind, not cruel.

Fen tilted his head, eyes narrowing when his ice melted.

"Alright, if ice won't stop you." Fen simply raised his eyebrows a fraction, clenched a fist out in front of him and the whole battle changed.

Luven arrived at the scene at this point, eyes widening as he took in what was unfolding in front of him. When he saw Myst and Nilee the forest elf immediately went to try to get to them, only to be pushed back hard by wind, sending him flying into a tree. He fell onto his hands and knees, coughing harshly as the air had been knocked out of him.

He held his ribs as he fought to stand, the wind constantly pushing him back to his knees. He didn't understand what was happening. No one here should have this magic, the only one that could would be Fen. If Lulen was correct he could do more than he had seen.

"Fen, let me up!" Luven yelled, trying to get his attention.

Fen ignored him. He just stood with a fist raised as he was being charged.

The elf's eyes widened in horror. "Don't stand there! Let me up! You will die!" Luven screamed at the angel-blooded. Nilee sobbed at those words.

"Fen!"

Fen just hardened his gaze and flicked open his fist. The magic went wild, out of the ground roots, ice... and shadows shot outwards, spearing goblins through the chest, legs, heads, blood spraying through the air as several creatures died in an instant.

Fen's robes and hair blew wildly as he built magic up again, a look of bloodlust on his face. Gone was the Fen who wished for peace, who never wished to kill anyone. In his place was the weapon Aphir had long wished to see unleashed upon the world.

He waved his hand in front of him, fingers stretched out as if he were holding something, slowly pulling them tighter and tighter. The shadows overtook the ice and plants, fire bubbling up between the cracks, almost as if he had drawn lava from deep within the earth, setting the forest alight.

"Go... Go... RUN YOU FOOLS." Velka forgot about her aspirations of capturing Fen and becoming queen. No, the power he possessed... The hated look that graced his fair face had her terrified to the core. She turned, pushing her way past others as she found herself racing for her life to get back to the mountains. Her own shadows no longer obeyed her command.

The Draught of Zaro was clenched in her hand but she found herself too afraid to stop to use it.

Fen did not stop. They fled; he attacked them from behind. He did not have to move an inch, the shadows followed his every whim, slithering across the ground like snakes until they were under a target, then they punched up, puncturing through flesh in an instant, filling the forest with shrill screams of pain and the stench of death.

Nilee sat there in fear. Holding Myst was all she could do, Luven unable to get to them because Fen had trapped him in place. His two friends watched a killer in action. This was not Fen. The longer he used the powers of the demon-blooded, the more deranged the look in his eyes became and the more the fire burned. They were soon surrounded by nothing but white-hot blazing heat, blocking anyone from escaping. Trapping every goblin, every demon-blooded, sealing their fate. They would all die here, Fen had long decided that.

"Fen!?" Fayon's voice penetrated the air – it felt like everything had gone silent just to let his voice ring through.

Fayon stood there, eyes wide with horror at the scene before him, gaze fixed on the angel-blooded at the centre of the massacre. He would have hardly recognised him as Fen to begin with if it wasn't for the robes he wore.

The usually fair sweet face was replaced with a snarl, with a heated glare. His eyes, a colour that usually had Fayon forgetting to breathe, were glowing a deep, bloody red. His hair, that white silk hair that Fayon often helped him style, just to feel it between his fingers, had become wild – it was turning black before his very eyes. The golden light emitted by his mark was slowly turning red.

Fayon couldn't breathe; this wasn't Fen. This wasn't the angel who had been too stubborn to even let him hurt wolves that attacked them. This wasn't the angel who had spared goblins despite them nearly killing him. Fen saw the good in everyone, everything. He wanted to save the world.

Fen could smile even when he had been tortured. He could see the beauty. Fen was light in the darkness.

He was *his* light.

He was not a weapon like his father wanted. This was not who he loved.

"Fen, stop this! Please, Fen!" Fayon pleaded, voice full of heartbreak as he raced forward, only to find himself forced down hard into the ground with an almighty cracking sound. Fayon cried out in pain, gritting his teeth.

"Fayon!"

"Fen stop!" he yelled again.

"Fen, you're hurting Fayon," Nilee whimpered.

"Snap out of it!" Luven yelled.

"Come on you, stubborn angel! Let me help you!"

Everything was just drowned out by the screams of Fen's enemies. He showed no sign of even hearing them. The only indication that he knew they were there was the fact that no fire or any other magic attacked them. Instead, it kept them firmly out the way.

That, however, all changed the moment Lulen arrived, with Varys, Rina, and several other elves all following behind him. Lulen didn't miss a beat as he fired an arrow straight towards Fen. This was his friend, yes, but right now he was out of control. If words couldn't get through to him maybe an arrow would.

"Lulen, NO!" Fayon screamed, trying to push himself off the ground, watching in desperation as the arrow flew through the air... only for it to stop inches before it could hit Fen. Burning up in mid-air.

Varys let out a small breath of relief, eyes going back to brown after a brief moment of glowing. That had been too close.

Fen had obviously also thought so too. The now blood red eyes turned from the enemies in front too Lulen behind him.

"Fen, NO!" Nilee screamed. She was clearly very aware of what was running through Fen's mind right now. She even let go of Myst's body to try and grab his legs, only to find herself shoved to the ground like Luven and Fayon.

Luven grunted, his eyes flashing green, arm outstretched in front of him as he watched Fen turn his attention to his younger brother. Tree roots erupted through the ground around Fen's feet, twisting up around him, locking his movements, tying his hands together to stop him from hurting anyone else.

Fen didn't seem to notice. He just cocked his head to the side, those bloody eyes shimmering red.

"Oh, by the demons," Varys cursed when he saw that flash. "You shouldn't be able to do that!" No one paid much heed to what the human said until he tackled Lulen hard to the side as fire exploded from beneath where he had once been standing.

"What the hell!?" Lulen looked bewildered, before looking at Varys. "Thanks…"

"You really had to go and piss him off more," Varys lifted the elf up by the arm.

"Watch out!" Rina's voice rang out, before Lulen and Varys went slamming backwards, splintering through a tree by a blast of light magic.

Lulen slumped down unconscious, blood pooling at his side, where a splinter of wood impaled him, while Varys clutched at his chest. The light burned through his veins.

"LULEN!" Luven was instantly fighting to stand, to crawl, to get to his little brother. Vines, roots, plants of all kinds were going crazy to protect the fallen elf.

Rina had abandoned her idea of figuring out how to

get Fayon up and instead had skidded on her knees to Varys' side. She ripped open his tunic to see the lattice of gold lines spiralling across his chest.

"Dracka," she whispered, a curse under her breath. Light poisoning. She had to deal with this fast.

Fayon lay there, eyes wide as he watched his friends hurt one by one. By Fen of all people. He gritted his teeth, fists clenching as he forced his arms under him, pushing up against the pressure keeping him down.

"Enough. That's enough, Fen!"

Chapter 30

Don't Leave Me

Fayon slowly stood, despite the pressure increasingly building on top of him. He got his fists locked under him, enabling him to use all his strength to lift his upper body up. Enough for him to inch by inch get his knees under him. Before getting on one knee, pushing himself up to both feet, even though gravity wanted to bring him back down. The weight of a hundred horses could be on top of him at that moment, but he wasn't letting it send him back to the floor.

Everyone, even Velka and her minions watched in stunned silence as Fayon, despite the torrent of magic around him, slowly walked step-by-step towards Fen. His whole body shook with the effort. Fen's eyes locked onto him and Fayon's locked onto his.

As Fayon got closer, he could see how swollen Fen's eyes were, he could see the tears still rolling down his face. Somewhere in that head he knew what he was doing, he just couldn't stop it. Fayon swallowed when he finally saw Myst. He hadn't noticed her before. Now he understood what had made Fen lose control. For the first time in a long time, Fayon felt tears flow down his own cheeks as he stood directly in front of Fen.

"Luven… take your vines away."

"Are you crazy! He will attack you the second I do."

"Please just remove them. He won't hurt me… you won't, will you Fen?" He gave a tiny smile as he watched the vines and roots disappear from around the younger's body.

293

Fayon let out a small breath when Fen did not move to attack him. Instead he just stood there, staring intensely into his eyes as if he was searching his memories for how he knew that face.

"It's Fay, it's me, you recognise me, right?"

The last time Fayon had stood like this in front of Fen, he had resisted his urge to hold him. Instead he had grasped his shoulders and shook him. Now this time, with his friends hurt, their enemies being slaughtered so cruelly they couldn't even retreat, Fayon chose to do what his heart told him.

Fayon wrapped his arms around Fen, pressing one hand to the small of Fen's back, the other cupped his head. His actions were gentle and tender as he held the smaller close, burying his face in the top of Fen's hair. A few tears rolled down his face.

"Come back to us, Fen... Come back to me," he whispered into his hair, tightening his grip around the younger. "You aren't a killer. This isn't you. Please wake up. See us, Fen, please..." A silent sob followed as Fen's body remained tense in his arms.

"Don't leave me, Fen. You can't leave me." His heart thundered in his chest, pain stabbing with every beat as Fen remained tense. The magic around them did not die down. He was truly losing hope. Had he really lost him?

"I'm sorry I failed you..." Fayon placed a small kiss on Fen's temple, eyes closed, hand reaching for his dagger. If he couldn't get Fen back, he wouldn't let him become what he never wanted to be. He was just about to wrap his hand around the hilt when his eyes snapped open.

Fen had slowly moved his arms around Fayon, holding onto him, fingers gripping into the dusty fabric of his robe. His body relaxed in Fayon's hold, a sob stifled by his face being pressed into the taller's chest. Fayon moved like lightning, hands going up to either side of Fen's head and gently pulling him so he could see his face.

Fayon let out a watery laugh as he gazed into those beautiful crystal-like eyes. The stunning mixture of gold and blue were back. He couldn't help but stroke those cheeks as he admired this angel, not the weapon his father had created.

"Fen," he breathed out.

"Fay... I...I didn't..." Fen hiccupped. He couldn't get his words out through his tears. Fayon just chuckled softly and shook his head.

"Shhh, it's okay, I have you. That wasn't you. I have you now. You're safe." He continued to stroke his face, Fen bringing his hands up to hold Fayon's, the magic around them finally settling. The wind returned to a gentle gust, the ground no longer rumbling. The lava cooled almost instantly, the shadows and roots that had been impaling everything they came in contact with disappeared. Bodies fell to the floor.

The exit for Velka and her team was no longer closed off.

The goblins took this chance to scramble away fast, not looking back. Whatever the demon-bloods wanted wasn't worth it to them any longer.

Velka, however, had taken the chance while everyone was distracted to pour the Draught of Zaro across her dagger and launched it straight towards the oblivious pair. The cat-like smirk was back as she watched it sail through the air.

"Come on, little angel. Notice or your princey dies,"

she whispered excitedly, unaware all the demon-bloods she was with had also taken the chance to flee.

Fen heard the slice of the blade against the wind, eyes darting over Fayon's shoulder. The angel-blooded instantly kicked the dirt pushing them down hard. Fayon hit the ground hard, the blade sailing over Fen's head, barely missing contact with skin, embedding itself uselessly in a tree behind them. He instantly shifted his gaze up to Velka.

She started laughing nervously, backing away, stumbling over twigs and rocks. "D...don't come any closer!" she shrieked as Fen and Fayon both stood. Velka looked around her to get her guards to protect her. Only then did she realise she was alone. "You snivelling cowards! Wait until our king hears! He will gut you like swine!" she seethed, hands pulling at her hair. What was she to do now? Her fingers tightened around the needles keeping the wild hair out the way. "If that's how it is..." Velka let out a cackle as she ripped the needles out fast, sending six flying through the air, taking that chance to run as fast as she could.

Fen reacted instantly, throwing out several light shields to protect Nilee, Lulen, Luven, Rina and Varys. But before he could protect himself, Fayon grabbed his arm, spinning him so he was safe inside his grasp. One of the needles grazed Fayon's own arm while the others thudded dully against the shields Fen had created.

"Your arm!"

"Fen, it is a scratch, do not worry." Fayon gave a small smile.

"I hate to break you up but I need help!" Luven snapped as he pressed his hands around his brother's wound. "Come on, Lulen, stay with me."

"Lulen!" Fayon let go of Fen to race to his friend's side, eyes wide as he helped Luven to put pressure around the splinter impaling him. Lulen let out a weak cough, blood trickling from the corner of his lip.

"I... I'm fine," he choked out. "They... under attack... need help..." Lulen barely got his sentence out before his head slumped forward, falling unconscious. Luven gritted his teeth as he caught his brother, glaring back towards Fen.

"You did this! Fix it! Come on, fix it!"

"Enough! It wasn't Fen's fault," Fayon snapped, defending Fen, who stood there staring at Lulen and Varys. His expression was awful.

"Then who's fault was it, huh!?"

"Take your pick. Anyone but Fen."

As the two males argued Fen looked off in the direction Velka and the others had run, then towards the elven settlement.

"He's not even listening; he doesn't give a crap about what he's done. We never should have trusted him! He's a weapon, an abomination!"

"Stop!" Nilee screamed, finally standing up on shaky legs, eyes red. She hovered close to Fen and her sister's body.

"Stop... everyone's in trouble... We have to help, or...or..." Her gaze went to Myst as she let out a sob. Or everyone will be like her, went unsaid.

The group went silent, Luven's anger simmering down, replaced with anxiety. Now that there was silence, the sounds of battle could be heard drifting through the forest. Cries, screams. No matter how distant, they were there. What was worse were the battle horns. Not the battle horns of the elves.

"How? The human... he said he sealed the pass with angel magic! They shouldn't be here yet." Luven looked panicked. If the demon-bloods' whole army was really attacking, there was no way they would survive.

"We need to go," Varys wheezed as Rina helped him to sit up. "Unless you all want to die."

"Filthy human! Are you suggesting we abandon my people!"

"If you want to survive, we have to!"

"Never! I would rather die with them than abandon everything I love."

"Please stop fighting, we have to help. Please!" Nilee ran over, desperate to get them to stop arguing.

Fen glanced at the arguing group, Luven and Varys' words growing more and more heated in the background as others tried to calm them.

"We can stop their attack, only for a time, but we can stop them, Fen."

Fen stood frozen, eyes darting around. No one else looked to have heard the strange voice.

"Do not fear, I am you, a part of you. Focus. You know what to do. You know how to stop death. Use our power, control it as you did when we escaped."

"Like when I escaped," he whispered quietly to himself, moving to stare at his hands. He clenched his fists, before holding them out in front of him.

"Feel your emotions, but don't let them control you."

Fen let out a slow breath as he closed his eyes, the air crystallising as he let his body temperature drop, the grass around his feet frosting over. He concentrated, connecting his fists together, channelling all his magic into them. The blue light illuminated his skin as he moved his hands apart forming a breathtaking sword of ice.

"Fen?" Fayon turned when he felt the chilling breeze. Worry instantly gripped him that Fen was losing control again and took a solitary step forward.

"Trust him." That voice… Fayon knew that voice… it sounded just like the demon from his dream. Although he knew it was a demon, and historically they could not be trusted, it told him to trust Fen. He realised he already did and halted his movements.

"What are you doing!?" Luven yelled as he pulled Lulen up into his arms.

"Just wait." Fayon held his arms out wide so no one could go towards Fen. They all stood there, everyone but Fayon filled with tension.

Fen only opened his eyes again once the sword was complete. They were such a stunning blue. Light almost smoked from them, his arms, hands. They were the same colour, pulsating and glowing this rich icy blue colour. Even the gold mark on his forehead had changed to match.

Fayon watched with bated breath, heart beating fast in his chest. Then Fen finally moved, grasping the hilt of the sword with two hands and thrusting it down into the earth. The angel-blood fell to his knees with it, grasping it with an unbreakable grip. The land around them instantly pulsed and rings of blue magic swirled rapidly around Fen.

Fen gritted his teeth as ice ran back through his veins, pain shooting through his body as he pulled in all the magic around him, thrusting it out into the ground through the sword. The ice rushed under everyone's feet in all directions. As soon as it hit the mountains it spread faster than the eye could see. Encasing everything Fen told it to.

Fayon's eyes widened as the floor beneath him changed to ice. He barely kept himself standing straight. But when he looked back to Fen, he lost all balance. His heart felt like it had stopped. He wasn't the only one frozen from shock. If anything, Varys and Rina, their expressions were far more emotional than anyone else. As if they had seen a ghost.

Behind Fen, created out of the beautiful blue light of his magic, was an angel. Its eyes were closed, its hands wrapped around Fen's. One wing spread out in the air, the other was missing. The expressions on the angel and Fen's faces were the same, matching features showing them calm. Their magic flowed into the earth through the sword at a magnificent rate. However, behind that calm exterior was pain. Blood steadily started to drip from Fen's nose, his eyes, his ears. The corner of his lip was stained, all masked by the blue light.

"The battle..." Nilee tugged on Fayon. "It's stopping."

The adults looked at her in confusion. But she was in fact correct. Just as the battle had been about to become a massacre Fen's magic had flooded through, stopping Sifth mid jump. Arrows dropped from the air. Swords froze mid swing, magic-encased. Fen had sent his ice through the ground and in one massive burst of energy had temporarily encased not only the mountain but every single demon-blood, each in a crystalline prison. They were unbreakable from the outside, but wouldn't last long enough to kill a demon-blooded before they broke free or the magic dissipated naturally.

"What happened?" Miana panted from where she stood, sword still drawn in front of her face. She had planted herself between a group of now frozen soldiers and her sister, who had Clanne protectively behind her.

"I don't know," Enlynn whispered.

As soon as the wave of ice magic came it was gone, the sword in Fen and the angel's hands crumbling away. The angel vanished along with the sword.

Fen's eyes fluttered open, the blue light finally fading and Fayon was finally able to see the blood.

"Fen!" he screamed as Fen hunched over, blood pouring from his mouth in a series of violent heaves. Before he collapsed sideways, Fayon slid to get to him, hand just catching his face from smacking the floor.

"Fen? No Fen, no no no... come on open your eyes. FEN!" Fayon screamed as he held the limp, lifeless teen in his arms.

Chapter 31

What Happens Now

Fayon stood watching the flames burn the pyres. The dead, including Myst, were all being laid to rest. The elves around him sobbed. This was not a traditional burial for them. But with them having abandoned their home, carried the dead so far, this was as good as they could give.

As soon as Fen had collapsed in his arms Fayon and the rest of the forest group had raced back to the settlement, where they found every single demon-blood had been encased in ice. Under some you could see the faint glow of fire. The decision was easy to make. The elves had gathered their dead and left. Rina carried Myst the entire time.

Aetris had easily made the choice to leave, rather than stay and risk his people against the unknown time until the demon-bloods escaped. So, for three days and three nights they travelled without rest, the wounded in carts being treated as best they could under the circumstances.

Lulen had woken up screaming when the chunk of bark lodged in his side had finally been pulled. But with the care of Enlynn as well as Luven he had recovered enough to be with his family as they said goodbye.

When Myst's pyre had been ignited he moved to stand with Fayon, a hand on the prince's shoulder as they said goodbye to the bright, spunky little girl. The one they both failed in protecting.

Fayon glanced behind him after a moment, eyes landing on Fen, who had only just regained consciousness two hours ago. His face was pale where he sat on the cart. Sorrow-filled eyes locked onto the silhouette of Myst's body within the flames. Clanne and Nilee were curled up on either side of the angel-blooded. Nilee had large bags under her red-rimmed eyes. The little girl had not stopped her silent sobs in days, breaking all their hearts. Clanne had not said a word since they had all come back.

Myst dead. Lulen, Varys and Fen all wounded. It had been too much for the already traumatised child. Fayon had thought it must have reminded him of losing his family all over again. At least with Fen finally awake he was letting someone close to him.

"How is Fen doing?" Lulen's question brought his thoughts back to the present. Tired eyes met with tired eyes.

"He is still weak. Will barely look at anyone or say a word."

"This is likely the first time he has lost someone he loves. He also lost a lot of energy... with whatever that was." Lulen glanced back at Fen himself. Varys and Rina had stayed suspiciously close to Fen ever since that angel had appeared behind him.

"We should not have lost her."

"No, we shouldn't have." Lulen nodded in agreement, eyes going back to watch the flames, which had now completely dissolved the silhouette of Myst. There was nothing but bright orange flames left.

"What happens now?"

Lulen stayed silent for a long time, not sure what the answer to that really was. Their goal had been to get to his people and live there safely. But that had long since become impossible. So, what did they do now? "Stay ahead of your father for one."

Fayon gave him a look, as if to tell him that was stating the obvious, was it not. Lulen gave a weak twitched smile. "Apart from that, Lulen."

"We survive."

Fayon gave a small nod. "Survive."

To be continued in book two.

Pronunciation Guide

Fen - F-e-n

Fayon - Fae-on

Lulen - Loo-len

Myst - M-i-st

Nilee - N-e-lee

Aphir- Ay-ph-ear

Clanne - C-la-n

Chasen - Ch-ay-s-en

Theliel - Th-e-lee-el

Saren - S-a-re-n

Irden - I-er-den

Phet - Pff-et

Cassian - Ca-ss-i-an

Zyrhou – Z-i-rh-ou

Zydrina - Zay-dre-na (Rina
- Ree-na)

Varys - V-air-ye-s

Tagas - Tay-g-as

Caru - Ca-ruu

Halki - Hal-key

Rexa - Rex-a

Culvat - Cul-v-at

Velka - Vell-kaa

Aetris - Aey-tr-is

Miana - Me-ana

Enlynn - En-l-i-nn

Elyon - Ee-ll-y-on

Beau - B-a-oo

Luven - Loo-v-en

Moon - M-oo-n

Locations:

Aleria - A-ler-i-a

Lior - Lee-or

Nisha - Nee-sh-a

Valsar Plains- Vall-s-ar

Fareen woodlands - F-are-een

Valyn Mountains - Val-yin

Nueay - Nou-ea

Celestia - S-le-s-t-ee-a

Prophet - P-ro-ph-et

Tong hill - T-o-n-g

Terret - T-er-rhet

Valyrine pass - Val-reen

Revel - Re-vel

Playlist

Whenever, Wherever – Shakira

Tattoo – Loreen

Don't deserve you – Plumb

Never Surrender – Liv Ash

Beautiful Mess – Kristian Kostov

Daylight – David Kushner

Royalty –Egzod& Maestro Chives. FT. Neoni

Unity – The Walkers & Alan Walker

Meet Me on the Battlefield – Svrcina

Wicked Game – Ursine Vulpine & Annaca

Land of Confusion – Hidden Citizens

Still Here – Forts, tiffany Aris, 2WEI

Broken Hero – 2WEI & Elena Westermann/ Onmyoji

Can You Hear Me – Unsecret. FT. Young Summer

Fight For You – Hidden Citizens. FT. Alaina Cross

One Last Breath – Emil Nilsson & Epic Music World

Acknowledgments

There are many people in my life who have helped me get to this point. Each of you have helped in so many ways.

First my parents. Dedicating this book to you is not enough to describe to you everything you have done for me. Your constant belief in me, despite at times I didn't know myself what I was doing, is the reason I am here today. You told me never to give up, encouraged me to do my best. That one day I would achieve my dream. Words will never describe how grateful I am to have you in my life.

Matty, you are the best little brother. Despite not liking fantasy books and never really getting my book, you have always been there when I was feeling downtrodden, when I had lost confidence in myself. You would tell me not to give up and sit there watching anime with me, making us both smile.

Lottie. You crazy amazing lady. So crazy I even made Velka based off you and you adored it. You are one of my best friends and have been my cheerleader, reading every draft, telling me when what I had written made no sense or was just plain weird. Don't stop being you, and I do hope you're looking forward to seeing what Velka gets up to in the future. You're always asking, after all.

Princess. Just thank you for everything you do. The best friend anyone could ever want in their lives. You are the reason some of these characters even exist! One day we were talking about what races I should add to the book and you go, "I love demons. A demon would be cool." From that second on I added a whole new dimension to this story. So many new characters and even a new book just from wanting to see actual demons. You cheered me on, read as much as you could with the rare free time you get. Thank you so much for just being you.

Sarah. You brought my characters to life, with a cover that blew my ideas out the water. You have been so excited every step of this journey and I cannot wait to create more dazzling cover designs with you as this journey continues.

Kerry. I am constantly bouncing ideas off you. Meeting just 9 months ago and already it's like you have been in my life forever. With DnD and Empire we always have so much to talk about and yet you always find time to help me when I am unsure in what I have written. Thank you for helping my confidence grow.

Finally, thank *you*. To each and every person who chooses to read this book. I may have written this, but it is you the readers who bring it to life. I hope you all love this world as I do and look forward to the books to come. I Love you all, Thank you for your support.

About The Author

Holly Lawton grew up in Northamptonshire, England. She was raised surrounded by books, enjoying getting lost in the pages of a new world. At a young age, Holly started writing. Her dream was to create her own fantasies and one day share them with the world. This has now been realised through her first novel, 'Threads of Fate.'

Holly works as a teaching assistant, witnessing how every day a book can spark someone's imagination. It was when she started this job that she began writing 'Threads of Fate.'

When Holly is not writing, she enjoys drawing or watching a good show, snuggling up with a book or playing DnD with her friends.

Holly is currently working on not only the next book in the 'Threads of Fate' series, but two other stories. She hopes that one day the world she has created will be filled with many stories bringing what she imagined to life!

Find out more by following Holly's social media:TikTok: @Holly.R.Lawton